THE
CREATION
Health
BREAKTHROUGH

**8 ESSENTIALS TO REVOLUTIONIZE YOUR HEALTH
PHYSICALLY, MENTALLY, AND SPIRITUALLY**

Monica Reed, MD
WITH
Donna K. Wallace

CENTER
STREET.

NEW YORK   BOSTON   NASHVILLE

CREDITS: General editor, Florida Hospital: Todd Chobotar
Florida Hospital review board: Ted Hamilton, MD; Des Cummings, PhD; Richard Duerksen
Photography by Spencer Freeman

PUBLISHER'S NOTE: This book is not intended to replace a one-on-one relationship with a qualified health care professional, but as a sharing of knowledge and information from the research and experience of the author. You are advised and encouraged to consult with your health care professional in all matters relating to your health and the health of your family. The publisher and author disclaim any liability arising directly or indirectly from the use of this book.

AUTHOR'S NOTE: This book contains numerous case histories and patient stories. In order to preserve the privacy of the people involved, we have disguised their appearances, names, and personal stories so that they are not identifiable. Case histories may also include composite characters.

Scriptures noted NKJV are taken from the New King James Version bible. Copyright © 1979, 1980, 1982, Thomas Nelson, Inc., Publishers.

Center Street
Hachette Book Group USA
1271 Avenue of the Americas
New York, NY 10020
Visit our Web site at www.centerstreet.com.

Center Street is a division of Hachette Book Group USA. The Center Street name and logo are trademarks of Hachette Book Group USA.

Printed in the United States of America

First Edition: January 2007
10 9 8 7 6 5 4 3 2 1

Library of Congress Cataloging-in-Publication Data

Reed, Monica, M.D.
    The creation health breakthrough : 8 essentials to revolutionize your health physically, mentally, and spiritually / Monica Reed, with Donna K. Wallace. — 1st ed.
        p. cm.
    ISBN-13: 978-0-446-57762-5

    1. Self-care, Health. I. Wallace, Donna K. II. Title.

    RA776.95.R44 2007
    613—dc22
                                                      2006011566

For my daughters,
Megan and Melanie,
and for you, Stan.

I love you.

Acknowledgments

I am so thankful for the people who have contributed to the success of this book. Its birth is the culmination of efforts by many people who have impacted my professional and personal journey. I remain profoundly grateful to each of you:

To Don Jernigan, PhD, President and CEO of Adventist Health Systems (AHS), for your unparalleled vision to blaze new trails in extending our mission. I remain eternally grateful to you for allowing me to write this book and choosing me to be an active participant in delivering preeminent faith-based health care.

Lars Houmann, President and CEO of Florida Hospital, thank you for creating tremendous flexibility in my responsibilities to take on this awesome project. Your confidence in my ability gave me the freedom to put my whole self into this book.

To all of my eleventh-floor colleagues—thank you for supporting me through this project and for standing in the gap for me during the hours, days, and sometimes weeks I spent writing. Without your flexibility and support this simply could not happen.

Louise Prairie; Janice Stephens; Lee Johnson; Harry Skidmore; Nicholas Avgeropoulos, MD; Karen Shimpf; Laura Orem; Fouad Hajjar, MD; Sandra Randolph; John Francis, PhD; and Debbie Francis—what a wonderful team of talented professionals you are! I never feared that anything would fall through the cracks in your capable hands. Thank you for your understanding and support during the year I worked on this book.

I'm especially thankful to the Florida Hospital Review Board—Ted Hamilton, MD; Dick Duerksen; and Des Cummings, PhD, my coauthor on the previous CREATION Health project—your collective willingness to critique this manuscript has been a godsend.

Thank you to each of you who so willingly gave of your time to perform peer reviews of individual chapters of this book. Your excellent comments helped make the final manuscript so much better: Mehul Dixit, MD; Pete Weber, BSN, MBA; Lenore Brantley, EdD; Kevin Edgerton, MA; Wayne Judd, MA, MDiv, MBA; Steve King, BS Economics, MA Religion; Karen Marcarelli, JD, MS, RN; Loretta Bacchiocchi, MSN, MPH, RN; Lee Johnson, MA, CCC-SLP; Kathy Ross, BED, MEP; Kris Gray, MD; Randy Haffner, BSBA, MBA, PhD; Connie Hamilton, MBA, BSN, RN; Joe Portoghese, MD; Loran Hauck, MD; Verbelee Neilson-Swanson; Clifford Goldstein; Robyn Edgerton; John Guarneri, MD, FACOG; Ed Noseworthy, MBA; Tom Werner, BSBA, MBA; Lenore Hodges, PhD, RD, LD; Shawn Noseworthy, MSA, RD; Sherri Flynt, MPH, RD, LD.

Sy Saliba, PhD, and the incredible marketing/PR team at Florida Hospital, including Samantha Olenick, M. K. Schlegel, Heather Allebaugh, and Melanie Travino—you guys are the best!

To my agent at Alive Communications, Lee Hough, you've been my "Lamaze coach"—the voice of calm, reason, and steadiness throughout my labor! I appreciate your talent, your skill, your knowledge, and your equanimity. When I was losing my focus you reminded me to breathe! Thank you. I look forward to a long, wonderful relationship.

Thanks to the whole team at Hachette—including Rolf Zettersten, publisher of Center Street; Chip MacGregor, associate publisher; my editor, Chris Park; Lori Quinn, director of marketing for Center Street; and Jana Burson, publicity director. You all have demonstrated great faith and enthusiasm in paving the way for millions to achieve their Breakthrough!

To Lillian Boyd, Sara Alsup, and Lorella Gilbert, three dedicated executive assistants who helped to keep this project on track, Sara for doing the challenging work of manipulating and remanipulating my schedule to accommodate my needs, Lillian for facilitating any and everything necessary for success, and Lorella for coming in and ably assisting at the eleventh hour—thank you.

Mason H. Grower III, "Trip," think it not odd to find your name here. You so willingly gave me your beautiful condo on the beach more than once, so that I could think and write "CREATION thoughts." Thank you. You are a wonderful colleague and friend!

Chris, people say only your hairdresser knows for sure, but personal trainers do too! You changed my life and my body. How can I not love you for that?! You are the embodiment of the "A" in CREATION. Thank you for challenging me to practice what I preach.

Cathy, I've always wanted a way to honor and thank you for the emotional training you consistently help me do. It's my delight to have it forever in print, everywhere: "Thank you for helping me live who I am." My Breakthrough doesn't happen without you.

Donna, Donna, Donna—my collaborator and friend. It cannot be easy to climb into this head of mine and make the thoughts, the ideas, and the passion come to life. Somehow, you did it! I value your talent *and* your heart. For your creativity, your guidance, and your attention to detail, I thank you. And to your family—James, Cierra, and Spencer—I'm grateful for your patience, understanding, and giving spirit through this journey.

Todd, I'm told physiologically men can't birth babies, but that can't be true, because I've watched you birth this one. From conception, through travail and delivery, you have been an integral part of this process. Without your creativity, your ideas, your dedication to CREATION Health and Florida Hospital, and most importantly, your passion and love for the written word, this book would not exist. You are as much a part of this book as Monica and

Donna. I'm blessed to have you as a professional colleague, cheer-leader, and friend. Jeannine, thank you for sharing Todd during the day, the night, and the weekends while we were finishing this labor of love. You have a wonderful union, and without your giving spirit this would have been a different story.

Ava, Cheri, Linda, Renee, Wendi, thank you for your words of encouragement, your shoulders, your ears, your Kleenex tissues—not just on this journey, but through life. Linda, specifically, thanks so much for always, always believing and encouraging me through the writing of this book, daily. Words cannot express what a blessing that has been to me. Thank you!

Negelle (David, Austin!)—my sister, friend, and fellow journey mate on the path to a deeper and broader calling. I appreciate you and remain inspired by who you are.

Mommy and Peter for having "no doubt" and being there for the kids on the days and nights when I needed you in so many ways. I appreciate you both.

Daddy and Linda, for having a story to tell, and doing what most of us don't even dare to dream. You make CREATION Health live!

Daryl and Stephan—for everything. It is because of you both that I write. Can you say "Jane Eyre"? Daryl, for extracting words out of me like a dentist goes after a bad tooth, and Stephan for forcing her to make me do it on my own. This book doesn't happen without you both. Thank you!

Megan, Melanie, you are such a support to Mommy. You guys took care of all kinds of stuff while I sat in the study working away on the book! And you even kept your voices down—most times. I couldn't want for better children. I love you!

Stan. What you have shouldered through this process (and *all* of my processes) is nothing short of amazing. Are you real? I love you and continue to love you with everything I can humanly muster.

God, through all the twists and turns, for all that you do, for who you are. I'm yours.

Contents

Before You Begin

HOW TO GET THE MOST OUT OF THIS BOOK

This book is packed with information that will dramatically improve your life. In fact, there are so many good things I want to share with you that it may feel a bit overwhelming at times. That's why I'd like to take a few moments before you begin to tell you how to get the most out of the book.

Mark this book up. I'm someone who loves books and believes in taking good care of them. In the past, this has led me (and others) to avoid making any marks in a book. Not so with this one. I encourage you to highlight it, dog-ear it, and write notes to yourself in the margins. Make this book your own. Personalize it. The books that impact my life the most are ones I interact with and not just read.

Get some friends and do this together. Making lifestyle changes may take a bit of adjustment, but when you do it with friends it becomes easier because you can support and encourage each other. So get your best friend to join you. Or find a group of friends who want to make a better life for themselves too. Go through the book and talk about the changes you want to make. Keep it fun. Stay in touch regularly. Together you can create great habits that will yield big rewards.

Consider doing the Rejuvenation Therapy first. If you want to read this book in its entirety but you're worried about finding the time, go to chapter 11 and follow the instructions for completing the CREATION Health Three-Day Rejuvenation Therapy. This therapy is a personal weekend retreat. As part of the retreat, you will be given the time to read the book and practice its suggestions. Doing the Rejuvenation Therapy is a great way to complete the book.

Put what you learn into action. This is the key to your success. When you translate your knowledge into action your life will change in powerful and lasting ways. This is such an important concept that I want to introduce you to something I call the Lifestyle Learning Continuum.[1] This continuum shows the four steps that you will take from knowing little (or nothing) about healthy living to consistently practicing a healthy lifestyle.

LIFESTYLE LEARNING CONTINUUM

STEP A	STEP B	STEP C	STEP D
Unconscious Incompetence	Conscious Incompetence	Conscious Competence	Unconscious Competence
I don't know that I don't know	*I know that I don't know*	*I consciously practice what I now know*	*I unconsciously practice what I know*

When it comes to knowledge of health, most of us start at Step A. We don't even realize that we are not living a healthy lifestyle. As long as we don't have some serious disease or illness we think we must be healthy. You may know some people like this. The fact that you have this book in your hands means that you're probably already to Step B. You sense that your life could or should be better. So you decided to read a book, take a seminar, or watch a program that will teach you about healthy living. Now you know how to be healthy. But knowing and doing are two different things.

Step C happens when we take this new knowledge and start practicing it. We make an action plan and live out the healthy behaviors we've learned. Now here's where the key component comes in. Step D is called Unconscious Competence. This simply means you have gotten so good at practicing healthy behaviors that they have become second nature. These behaviors become who you are. When this happens, your life is lived on a higher level. Your mind is sharper, your body stronger, your spirit more peaceful, your relationships better.

How does this relate to the CREATION Health Breakthrough? Just by reading this book you are moving from Step A to Step B. That is, you are learning what it means to live wholly healthy and where the gaps are in your life. This is important because you can't change your life unless you know that something should be different.

Next you need an action plan. I provide that for you in chapter 11. The CREATION Health Plan has three phases. In Phase 1 you will learn how to create a powerful, rejuvenating weekend experience that will set up your health breakthrough. In Phase 2 you will embark on an eight-week plan to help you integrate healthy behaviors into your lifestyle. Phase 3 gives you a strategy for staying healthy for the rest of your life.

By completing Phases 1 and 2 you will accomplish Step C of the Lifestyle Learning Continuum—you will put healthy behaviors into practice. This is a wonderful accomplishment. Then the greatest satisfaction and fulfillment comes once you achieve Step D in the continuum. That is what Phase 3 of the CREATION Health Plan is all about. Here you ingrain healthy behaviors into your life so they become what you do automatically.

Why am I taking time to explain the Lifestyle Learning Continuum to you? Because I want you to be a success. I want you to live a long, happy, healthy life. I want you to see that this book is about much more than providing a series of scientific facts and healthy tips. This book is about helping you live life to the *full*; a life where you feel whole mentally, physically, spiritually, and socially. I want to embark on that journey with you. Along the way there are some necessary steps and transformations you will go through. My ultimate goal is not to leave you with a simple set of do's and don'ts. My purpose is to help you live an abundant life in which healthy living becomes natural for you.

In this process it's vital to focus on progress, not perfection. Don't worry if you slip sometimes or take one step forward and two steps back. Realize that life is a series of small steps. You're not going to run a marathon just yet. But when you look back a year from now, you won't believe the change that you've experienced. I can guarantee you that even within a couple of months you'll see change. It's hard to see it when you're in it, but just keep moving forward and you will succeed.

Finding Your Breakthrough

1

THE PROBLEM, THE PROMISE, THE PRINCIPLE, THE PLAN

We live in a fast-paced, rapidly changing society where unhealthy habits easily become the norm. Lifestyle has become the number one "disease" threatening Americans today—and there are no drugs or surgeries to cure it.

IN THIS CHAPTER YOU WILL:

* Discover eight timeless, scientifically proven principles that will revolutionize your life.

* Learn what you need to know about the new number one killer in America today.

* Find out how to add ten more good years to your life.

Finding Your Breakthrough

As I see it, every day you do one of two things:
build health or produce disease in yourself.

ADELLE DAVIS

How many times have you read the "ideal" book about health and healing, only to discover its program is so far beyond the reach of your daily demands that you can never attain it? You love the exercise routine advertised on television that makes you buff and trim, but $500 later you realize that the new routine won't fit into your already packed schedule.

I've bought more than my fair share of those TV fitness products. In fact, at one time or another I feel like I've owned them all: ab-rollers, steppers, jump ropes, weights, bikes, books, and videos. One time I even bought something called a Gazelle, which is a modified rowing machine. My girlfriend and I went in on it together. It stayed in the box for over a month before we finally assembled it. After that we never used it. The only thing that became trimmer in that deal was my checkbook. The Gazelle became a standing joke because we knew neither of us would ever look like one.

We've all heard about fad diets, extreme makeovers, and get-slim-quick schemes. We've tried crash diets, liquid diets, low-calorie diets, high-protein diets, and everything in between. But in order to succeed we must know what it is we're searching for. Good health is more than simply dropping a few pounds. To offset the effects of how we live we can no longer entertain short-term fixes; we need a comprehensive and lasting breakthrough to health. That's why this book is about more than an exercise program or diet plan. It's about how to get the most out of life.

In this book I want to help you celebrate life fully, to discover your own tremendous power to make life-changing choices. I want to guide you through a powerful program to help increase your vitality, lengthen your life, and supercharge your health. I want to help you move from a health *breakdown* to a health *breakthrough*.

But before we talk solutions, let's understand the problem.

All too often we find ourselves anxious, stretched, and prone to neglect our most important asset—our health. We may think our current condition is only temporary and that things will change eventually, but for too many of us that time never comes. In some cases, neglecting a healthy lifestyle for years can lead to serious consequences.

That's exactly where Greg found himself.

After owning two businesses for more than twenty years, Greg rarely felt at rest or at peace. No matter the time of day or the day of the week, it seemed like there was always something that needed to be done. So he did it. Greg lived life under constant pressure. He was a hard worker, his employees gave him that. But his long hours and constant worries often left him irritable and short-tempered with his staff.

Due to the sustained level of stress in his life, Greg frequently had trouble sleeping. And even when he could sleep it was only for four to six hours at a time. Coffee and caffeinated soft drinks kept him going the rest of the day. Greg tried to get away from work from time to time to unwind, but while away he spent most of his time worrying about all the things he needed to do.

His family life suffered as well. After going through two divorces Greg started to think he wasn't cut out for relationships. He began holding people at a distance. His own children found him growing increasingly aloof. They couldn't even convince him to attend church with them at Christmas or Easter. Because he spent so much time at work, he had few friends, and, truth be told, he didn't worry much about it.

Greg never really got the hang of cooking. Most meals consisted of fast food or what came out of vending machines at work. His days were so long he never even considered exercise. In fact, he liked to joke that the most exercise he got was taking the trash to the curb twice a week. When extra pounds started gathering around his middle it bugged him. But he took solace in the fact that the same was true for many of his buddies. "A sign of maturity," he said. The extra weight made him feel sluggish during the day, especially in the afternoon. But the worst part of his weariness was how it affected his immune system. Greg started to pick up any sickness or virus that blew through town.

As a result of his lifestyle choices Greg was in poor health and was headed for a breakdown. It wasn't that he didn't want to make some changes in his life, it just seemed like he never had the time to consider them.

With his fiftieth birthday approaching, Greg convinced himself to start the year on the right foot. He scheduled an appointment with a physician at Florida Hospital for his "annual" physical exam (something he hadn't done in years), vowing that this year things were going to be different. After a series of tests the doctor came back with shocking news.

Before I tell you the rest of Greg's story I want to pause for just a moment. Do you know anyone like Greg? I don't mean exactly like Greg, but do you know people whose lives seems so busy or stressed that they have no time to care for their health? Maybe someone whose consistently poor lifestyle choices are contributing to low energy, an irritable attitude, and poor health? Are there some elements of Greg's story you can identify with yourself? Maybe you've wanted to make some lifestyle changes, but they just don't "stick," and before long you found yourself back in the same old unhealthy habits again. If so, you're not alone.

THE PROBLEM

We are living too short and dying too long.
Dr. Myron Wentz

As a nation, we face a significant problem. On the one hand, each of us is the beneficiary of never-before-imagined technological and medical advances, and yet, despite the scores of research, treatment, and explosive technology gains, we remain as unhealthy as ever. In fact, the top three causes of death in America today—heart disease, cancer, and stroke—remain unchanged. And all three are diseases largely related to how we live. But it hasn't always been this way, and for you it certainly doesn't *have* to be that way.

Living Inside Out

If you had been born 150 years ago, the thing most likely to kill you was an infectious disease. The four leading causes of death in the United States at that time were pneumonia, tuberculosis, diphtheria, and influenza—diseases that attacked the body from the *outside*.

With the advances in antibiotics, vaccines, and public health practices toward the end of the twentieth century, deaths due to infectious diseases declined dramatically. Today the diseases most likely to kill you are related to your lifestyle choices. The leading killers today are chronically debilitating diseases: coronary artery disease, cancer, stroke, diabetes, high blood pressure—diseases birthed from *within* our bodies. We are literally dying *from the inside out. We're dying because of how we live.*

Our lifestyles are the foundation of our most devastating and threatening illnesses. The number one cause of preventable death is cigarette smoking. Obesity runs a close second and will soon overtake smoking as the leading cause of preventable death.

Most cancers as well as heart disease are also related to lifestyle factors—primarily poor nutrition and lack of exercise. And yet the consequences of our choices go far beyond obesity, cancer, or heart disease. Illness starts deep on the inside where we can't see it, well before we ever see it evidenced on the outside. The pace of our living, the desire to achieve, the lack of satisfaction, technological advances that constantly bombard our senses, the perceived lack of time to rest and relax—all have created a different type of illness that affects not only our food choices and whether or not we exercise; it robs us of our vitality and our joy.

The Lifestyle Disease

Millions of people are suffering today from a condition I call the Lifestyle Disease. A simple definition:

> *The Lifestyle Disease is characterized by a group of harmful behaviors practiced over time, which result in a decreased quality of life and ultimately the onset of chronic illness leading to premature death.*

These behaviors may include:

* Poor eating habits
* Little or no physical exercise
* Lack of sufficient or fulfilling sleep
* Sustained exposure to unbuffered stress
* Participating in high-risk behaviors such as smoking or drug use
* Minimal or no personal playtime or time for solitude
* Limited family or meaningful relationship time
* Lack of spiritual connection

At the root of the lifestyle disease is a frenzied rhythm of overdrive. Even if you don't consider yourself "ambitious," whether or not you decide you "want it all," our modern society demands that you pick up the pace. We're constantly asked to do more in less time. And unless we choose to intentionally slow down and experience what's most important in our lives, turbo becomes our natural setting. It becomes our lifestyle, and we adopt compensating, harmful behaviors to survive. Our time is short so we don't exercise, get enough sleep, eat healthfully, or deepen our relationships. We get cranky and irritable, and make more poor choices.

The results of these poor lifestyle choices are twofold. First, the quality of life is decreased. Each day this group of harmful behaviors drains our vitality. Second, the effect of these behaviors practiced over time develops into chronic illness and often premature death. Medications and devices simply cannot correct all of the consequences of an unhealthy lifestyle.

Though I'm grateful for the medical community and its ability to step in during crisis moments to ease pain and prolong life, I want you to understand the other half of the story: in large part the *quantity* and the *quality* of living is up to you. How you live affects how long you live and how healthy you live. And starting now, you can begin applying the principles and plan in this book to change how you live and help you achieve your *breakthrough*.

THE PROMISE

He who enjoys good health is rich, though he knows it not.
ITALIAN PROVERB

Real Life

To better understand what I mean by a health breakthrough, let's take a closer look at the word "life" itself. From the Greek language we find two words, which translate into the English word "life." The first word, *bios*, means "physical life." This where we get our word "biology." It refers to all the cells and chemicals working together so our bodies don't die; in other words, "the physical state of being." Much of our attention and money is spent focusing on *bios*. Still, we know life encompasses much more than merely surviving or caring for this body. We are designed for much more. We must consider the element of life that reaches beyond survival.

"The answer we're looking for," writes Bill Ewing in his book *Rest Assured*, "is found in the other Greek word for life—*zöe*—a word which carries a much deeper and mystical meaning than *bios*. *Zöe* speaks of that life which reaches beyond the physical and is found at the core of who we are. It is the internal motivator that keeps us pushing forward each day. It is what we use to define who we are, why we do what we do, and why we have value. *Zöe* life is what makes our biological *bios* life worth living, giving us direction, vision, purpose,"[1] otherwise known as full, abundant health.

Now that we know the full definition of what it is we're looking for, we can ask the question, "Why do so many fitness and health plans fail?" Forgetting our internal motivator—our desire for *zöe* life—most other programs focus only on external *bios* needs. If you're confused about all the different health plans available, be encouraged. You are holding the guide to the health breakthrough you've been searching for.

I want to share a health plan with you as natural as breathing. If you follow it, your vitality will increase, your spirits will be lifted, your relationships will be more vibrant, and you'll reverse the course of the Lifestyle Disease.

ADD LIFE TO YOUR YEARS AND YEARS TO YOUR LIFE

Recently *National Geographic* published the results of a study conducted with three groups of people who live significantly longer lives. For the cover story, writer Dan Buettner interviewed more than fifty centenarians (men and women one hundred years of age or better). The article, entitled "The Secrets of Long Life," focused on longevity all-stars from three groups: mountain villagers in Sardinia, Italy; Seventh-day Adventists in Loma Linda, California; and island dwellers in Okinawa, Japan.

According to the article, all three of these groups "produce a high rate of centenarians who suffer a fraction of the diseases that commonly kill people in other parts of the developed world, and enjoy more healthy years of life. In sum, they offer three sets of 'best practices' to emulate." What are these best practices? The key habits practiced by all three groups include: putting family first, being active every day, no smoking, eating fruits, vegetables, and whole grains, and keeping socially engaged.* Buettner notes, "A long, healthy life is no accident. It begins with good genes, but it also depends on good habits. If you adopt the right lifestyle, experts say, chances are you may live up to a decade longer."[2]

------

*Practices for one or more groups also included: keeping lifelong friends, observing the Sabbath, having faith, finding purpose for their life, sharing the work burden with a spouse, eating small portions, drinking red wine (in moderation), and eating pecorino cheese (and other omega-3 foods), nuts, and beans.

THE PRINCIPLE

Safeguard the health of both body and soul.
CLEOBULUS

"As a scientist," says Dean Ornish, MD, "I live in a world of data, numbers, and randomized controlled clinical trials. Scientists believe what can be measured—blood pressures, cholesterol, blood flow . . . while anecdotal evidence—in other words, stories—is viewed with suspicion."[3] I would have to agree. Though this is true in the professional world, it is only half of the picture. Ornish continues, "As a physician and as a human being, I live in a world of stories. Our lives are unique, yet in the telling of stories we learn what makes us similar, what connects us all, what helps us transcend the isolation that separates us from each other and from ourselves."[4]

Principles from the Garden

I love Ornish's quote, because it lends truth as we turn to one of the best-known stories that connects us all . . . the Creation story. Found in the first three chapters of the book of Genesis—the Book of Beginnings—this story is valued by three of the world's largest faiths (Judaism, Islam, and Christianity) as revealing the origins of mankind. According to the story, the Creator formed the earth in six days and rested on the seventh. Part of his Creation plan included the planting of a garden where the first man and woman would live. This garden home was named Eden. Paradise.

The Garden of Eden story itself is quite brief, yet in its three short chapters we find powerful principles given by a Creator who fashioned an ideal setting for all living creatures. It's in this environment that the first human beings were meant not only to survive, but to thrive.

In this book, I'll tap into the wisdom found in the Garden. I'll draw on elements found within this story to derive eight timeless principles of health and well-being. I realize that for some readers this may seem rather odd. Why explore ways of achieving optimal health today based on wisdom found in an ancient spiritual text? One reason only: because *what we find at Creation, and specifically in the Garden of Eden story, continues to be validated by scientific research as being the key to living a long, healthy, disease-free, and joy-filled life.* Science will not be sacrificed. Medical research will validate each concept as we approach a model for health based on these timeless principles.

What Is CREATION Health?

CREATION Health is an exciting plan for changing your life. If you apply it rightly, you will achieve mental, physical, spiritual, and emotional well-being. Each letter of the word CREATION stands for one of the eight principles drawn from the Genesis story.

C—Choice. Choice is the first step toward improved health. Your destiny is empowered and determined in large part by your choices. Making healthy choices is the key to lifestyle improvement. People who believe they have more control over their lives tend to be healthier and live longer.

R—Rest. Rest comes with both a good night's sleep and taking time to relax during the day. It includes having a weekly day of rest and enjoying a regular vacation, which allows you to slow down. Deep rest and restoration are also found in the calm of spiritual peace.

E—Environment. Environment is the natural setting where you find peace and healing. Everything that affects the senses—sight, smell, sound, touch, and taste—in the natural environment as well as your personal environment influences your health.

A—Activity. Activity is the gift of movement. It includes regular exercise and play. The best kind of physical activity (like a walk in a park with friends) also enhances the mind, spirit, and relationships. Activity should be enjoyable and an integral part of your lifelong health.

T—Trust. Trust in Divine Power ensures that your life has a sense of purpose. It speaks to the important relationship between spirituality and your overall health and well-being. People who have an active trust in Divine Power experience a host of health benefits including a stronger immune system, less heart disease, lower blood pressure, and higher life satisfaction.

I—Interpersonal Relationships. Relational intimacy is found in those moments when you allow an aspect of your true self to be shared; when you open yourself up to the power of one heart touching another. Having confidence in the support of others who care contributes to improved health. Conversely, loneliness or toxic relationships can contribute to a downward spiral in overall health.

O—Outlook. Outlook is a gift you give to yourself. A positive mental attitude colors your life perspective and influences how you view your world and the people in it. Attitude is more than a state of mind. It influences health in powerful ways and can even impact the progression of disease.

N—*Nutrition.* Nutrition is the fuel that drives your body. A wholesome balanced diet produces energy and overall health. Of all the nutritional choices available, two are guaranteed to improve your health and enable you to live longer: eating less and eating higher-quality foods.

These eight essential components of health meld together to form the blueprint for the good health we yearn for and the life we are intended to live. Some of the concepts presented in the CRE-ATION Health acronym will seem like common sense—because they are exactly that. Other concepts you may not have been as familiar with but will learn about through the evidence of science. As the pieces of the picture come together like a jigsaw puzzle, you'll begin to see a simple yet profound unifying theme. We've tried to isolate the individual elements in the past, but they belong together for optimal living. You'll soon discover your own picture taking shape and with it the tremendous potential to live life to the full.

Remember, the CREATION Health Breakthrough begins the moment you can see the various parts of your life coming into balance and you catch a glimpse of your ultimate design. Once you've experienced a health breakthrough in your own life—and through these eight principles I'll show you how—you'll know when there's something in your life that needs a little tweaking. With this book you'll have the tools you need to make healthy changes for a lifetime.

THE PLAN

Happiness lies first of all in health.
GEORGE WILLIAM CURTIS

The CREATION Health Breakthrough is not a one-time occurrence in which you suddenly break beyond all the bad habits you've ever had in the past. The Breakthrough invites you to embrace new and exciting changes as you experience life as it was intended. Yes, there will be times when you will get off balance, times when you'll recognize that the Lifestyle Disease is rearing its ugly head. But that's what this health plan is about—helping you recognize the disease and giving you the tools you need to return to your best health.

If you feel there is a particular area or areas that need immediate attention, you can go immediately to that chapter, keeping in mind these three things:

* Good choices are the cornerstone of all lifestyle changes. There-fore, the Choice chapter (chapter 3) should be read first.
* Creating health is about complementary changes in the mind, body, and spirit. For the greatest results make sure you cover all eight principles.
* If you don't have time to read the book now, you may turn to the back immediately, plan the CREATION Health Three-Day Reju-venation Therapy, and follow the guided steps to reading the book during your getaway!

Special Features

The CREATION Health Breakthrough has been designed with a number of special features to help you get the most out of the ma-terial. These include:

* *My Personal Story.* I know the benefits of lifestyle change while living in the face of tremendous challenges. In fact, I will be sharing the intimate successes and failures of my own health jour-ney in chapter 2. Walk with me and let my story touch yours.
* *Life in the Garden.* Each chapter has an engaging look at life in the Garden of Eden and how it relates to the CREATION Health principles. Also included are timely medical facts and scientific re-search to support the principles of whole-person health.
* *The 3 M's.* Rather than embarking on too many changes at

once, I recommend focusing on an area you know is out of balance in your life. Then consider three simple steps featured at the end of each chapter to bring about immediate success. The 3 M's are: maximize, moderate, and minimize. Think of the 3 M's like a traffic light. Maximize is a green light. Move full speed ahead on these healthy habits. Moderate is your yellow light. Continue moving but proceed carefully on these behaviors. Minimize is your red light. Try to stop these unhealthy habits as soon as you can.

* *Breakthrough Stories.* At the end of each chapter I have included a case study that illustrates the personal struggles and triumphs of real people who have applied the CREATION Health principles in their own life and have been transformed by the experience. I call these Breakthrough Stories and I hope they encourage you.

* *CREATION Health Breakthrough Self-Assessment.* Once you understand the powerful principles behind CREATION Health you may wonder how to start implementing them in your life. This self-assessment tool helps you understand which areas of your life need the most attention and where you need to concentrate your efforts. For each letter of the CREATION acronym you will be asked five questions. Each question is rated on a scale of 1 to 5, then your CREATION Health score is tallied. A key is provided to help you understand your score and what areas you may want to work on (appendix A).

* *Three-Day Rejuvenation Therapy.* For many of us, our lives are so wildly out of balance that we can't even remember what it feels like to be calm, peaceful, and clearheaded. To help you gain this vital experience I have put together a Three-Day Rejuvenation Therapy that will slow you down enough to experience peace, rest, and a taste of balance. This plan is meant to completely structure a seventy-two-hour period so you can experience firsthand the benefits of CREATION Health. Some have called it a lifestyle detox weekend. I believe you will see immediate benefits from doing it. Detailed instructions for planning and experiencing this program can be found in chapter 11.

❋ *Eight-Week Lifestyle Transformation Plan.* This is a step-by-step approach to incorporating healthy behaviors into your life. It is a gradual approach that can be used after the Three-Day Rejuvenation Therapy to slowly integrate all the practices of whole-person health into your daily life (see chapter 11).

❋ *CREATION Health for Life.* Once you understand the concepts, behaviors, and habits behind the eight principles, you can use them independently to bring your life back into balance when necessary. This section of the book will show you how to use the CREATION Health Breakthrough whenever you need it most for the rest of your life.

Greg's Story

Remember Greg from the opening of the chapter? With his fiftieth birthday approaching, Greg scheduled an appointment with his doctor and received some shocking news. He had cancer. The news shook Greg to the core. He wasn't ready for it; he wasn't even fifty yet.

After the diagnosis, Greg decided it was time to make some serious lifestyle changes. He was willing to do all he could to live well—now. Greg sold one of his businesses and cut back on his hours at work. Though weakened by his chemotherapy treatments, he read all he could about healthy lifestyle habits. When the cancer went into remission Greg regained enough strength to start exercising. He stopped drinking coffee and avoided alcohol as much as possible. Next, he changed his diet by cutting out all red meat and eating mostly fish, fruits and vegetables, nuts and whole grains. He decided to take the weekends off completely and spend one of those days visiting with his four kids and two grandkids. He even agreed to attend church services every so often with his grandkids and started reading from scripture.

Two years into his remission Greg remarked that he had never felt better in his life. Despite the diagnosis of cancer, his stress level had decreased considerably. He could not believe the energy he now had and how much better he felt about himself, his family, and just about everyone he met. Though many of his relationships had suffered, he began reconnecting with the people who were important to him. Even his sense of humor returned. "If I'd known life could be this good I would have started living it years ago," he said. "I have more energy now than I did in my thirties."

Greg had three good years in remission. Sadly, his cancer returned when he was fifty-four and he died just before his fifty-fifth birthday. But even to the end Greg was not bitter. "I've had three great years that were the best of my life," he said. "I wouldn't wish cancer on my worst enemy, but it's taught me how to live. Life is precious. That's a lesson I might not have learned any other way."

PUTTING IT ALL TOGETHER

Optimal health is not based on the sculpture of your physique,
but on the sculpture of your lifestyle.
DR. MYRON WENTZ

Without question, Lifestyle is the number one "disease" threatening the lives of Americans today, and there's no drug, surgery, or procedure to cure it. The good news is there's a health plan that will. Achieving your health breakthrough will increase your vitality, lift your spirits, prolong your life, increase your fulfillment, and minimize the risk of life-threatening illness. In the pages ahead you will discover this plan and how it can help you achieve a health breakthrough so you too can fully experience life as it was intended.

But before we delve into the details of CREATION Health, I want to tell you the story of the most difficult patient I've ever had to work with—me. You may have heard the expression "physicians make the worst patients." It's true. Let me take you through some of my own struggles. Perhaps the story of how I achieved a CREATION Health Breakthrough will encourage you as you pursue your own.

Physician, Heal Thyself!

2

TREATING THE TOUGHEST PATIENT I EVER HAD

I was on the verge of a health breakdown. Not because I had developed a life-threatening disease, but because I was having a life-threatening experience. A crucial conversation and an unexpected event led me to reevaluate my choices, my priorities, and my life. It was then that I experienced my "breakthrough."

IN THIS CHAPTER YOU WILL:

* Find out why the good things in life are not always the best things in life.

* Learn how to harness the power of a defining moment to change your life.

* Discover how to move from a health breakdown to a health breakthrough.

Physician, Heal Thyself!

Don't let the good things of life
rob you of the best things.

Maltbie D. Babcock

I couldn't sleep. I tossed, turned, and repositioned myself in bed trying to find the spot that would bring unconsciousness. That's what I wanted. Not just sleep. I wanted to be unconscious. I was tired of the fight. I was tired of refiguring and juggling to make things work. I was frustrated and maybe even depressed. No comfort in my bed? No surprise. There was no comfort in my life.

I'd finished med school ten years prior and had established a successful ob-gyn practice. I loved my patients and my staff and they loved and respected me. Even while I was still in medical training I knew I wanted to teach. So I felt fortunate to be the associate director of the Family Practice Residency Program at Florida Hospital. It was a sacrifice, though. Teaching residents was often no different from being a resident. That meant regular twenty-four-hour workdays and equal stretches of time when I was away from home. On nights when it was crazy busy and my head never touched the pillow, I wondered if I should be doing something *less* with my time, but I enjoyed teaching, so I stuck with it. Opportunities continued to open up. I established a new practice at Florida Hospital's destination facility, Celebration Health, and was named medical director of the Women's Health Program. I'd also accepted the medical news reporter position for the ABC television affiliate in Orlando. How cool! Life was filled with good things; it all felt so appropriate and so right.

So why wasn't I happy?

There was too much time away from home. I missed my little one. The hours I spent away from my little girl were more than I wanted or intended. We had a wonderful nanny, and my husband, Stan, capably picked up the slack. But for how long? I wondered. The slack pile grew greater almost daily. Was his frustration growing too?

Deeper than that, I missed *me*. I didn't have time for me anymore. I tried to juggle my schedule to have more time with Megan, more time with Stan, and more time to save the female world from gynecological terror. It wasn't working. I was being squeezed out of my own life.

As I lay in bed that night, all that responsibility and guilt sat on my chest like an elephant. Then it came to me: *Maybe this is not a schedule problem, maybe this is a "me" problem.*

Is Being Tough the Answer?

My mind immediately flashed back to my residency days. I loved delivering babies, but on one particular day, instead of bringing in a life, I'd actually lost one. Despite my best efforts, this mother had delivered five months early and the baby didn't survive. Feeling terrible, I sought my attending physician to unload. As I sat there second-guessing myself, he said to me, "Monica, I appreciate that you feel bad. But these kinds of things happen from time to time. It's the way life is. You need to learn to accept it and toughen up."

Toughen up. It sounded sensible. I'd accepted it as the solution then and perhaps it was the answer now. *All right then, maybe I'm just not tough enough. Maybe I just need to buck up.*

A few days later I discovered that nothing could have been further from the truth. After a morning packed with surgery and an afternoon of back-to-back patients, I finally made it home. I was exhausted, but I took satisfaction in knowing that today, unlike other days this week, I'd made it through the door in enough time for Nanny to make it home during daylight. Ushering her out the door with a quick hug and a "thanks, see you tomorrow," I breathed a sigh of relief. With my little one fed, changed, and content I could relax for a few moments. Dropping my briefcase, I gathered Megan in my arms, and the two of us plopped down in a rocking chair.

She snuggled comfortably against me and we slowly rocked back and forth. I don't know how long we rocked, but the rare moment of solitude was a thing of beauty that relaxed and refreshed us both. In that treasured quiet time together, I began reflecting on my life again. The phone rang, breaking my revelry. I recognized my aunt's voice calling to check in. After chatting a while, I asked her the question plaguing my own mind. "Auntie," I said. "Are you happy with your life?"

She answered without hesitation. "Oh yes, I'm very happy with my life. In fact, I *love* my life."

My steady rocking came to a halt. Her emphatic answer stunned me. She specifically said she *loved* her life. Was that actually possible—to love your life? I knew I could deal with life; hang in there with it, yes. But love it? In that moment, I realized total fulfillment existed, but I didn't have it. Was it because I wasn't good enough to get my life into balance?

I was working hard and doing good, *but I didn't feel good.* In fact, health-wise, I felt terrible. I was overworked, overstressed, and couldn't sleep. But I couldn't figure out how to improve things. My life was a paradox—I was healing others, yet I was a mess. From the outside looking in, every aspect of my life seemed like the gold standard. I had a solid marriage, a healthy child, a great job . . . and yet I was on the verge of having a health breakdown. Something had to change, but I wasn't sure exactly what.

Neglecting to Take My Own Advice

You might think my profession would offer me some definite health advantages. No such luck. Medical school was a time to obsess on the structure and function of the human body, not the needs of the body, mind, and spirit. It was a time to learn the biochemistry of nutrition but not the practice of healthy eating. My personal application of anything that came close to health was constantly overshadowed by lectures from dawn to dusk followed by hours of studying from dusk till almost dawn. Healthy eating? A good night's sleep? Balance? Not quite. I figured I could save that for later, when I got my life back.

Almost imperceptibly, the abuse of my body and spirit became routine. Residency training was filled with hundred-hour work-weeks, interrupted rest, half the day passing without going to the bathroom (we used to joke about needing to attach catheters to our legs), gobbles of food between deliveries, and little social contact outside of the hospital. When I left residency training and entered private practice the hours improved somewhat, but they were still long. We only lived a mile away from the hospital, but there were times when I was so tired that I'd ask Stan to come pick me up so I wouldn't have to drive home. Okay, maybe that was a little extreme, but I needed that extra TLC!

When it came to ensuring the health and well-being of my patients, things were better. I addressed their obstetric and gynecologic needs and then went through the preventive medicine checklist. I made sure they had their Paps and mammograms, asked about their smoking and alcohol habits, asked overweight patients about diet and exercise. You know the drill. In our fifteen "managed care" minutes together, I did it all by rote, without ever questioning my own lagging health. I heard myself asking questions and offering solutions that I wasn't living. My life was out of whack.

Sitting in that rocking chair, in that simple yet profound moment, I realized I needed to find the missing elements in my life. It didn't take a tragic accident or a terminal diagnosis. It took only this: the lack of fulfillment in my life was significant enough and painful enough that I was ready to seek change. I was fortunate not to have yet developed a life-threatening disease, but I was having a life-threatening *experience*. My pace and personal neglect were robbing me of both my present and my future. I didn't want to do life like this anymore.

Medical training notwithstanding, when we get right down to it, my struggle to achieve a healthy lifestyle is just as challenging as yours. Every day, just like you, I have to decide (several times a day, in fact) what I'll eat, what I'll drink, if I'll be active or pass on anything physical; whether I'll forgive or be resentful, if I'll pray, play with my kids, make love to my husband or read a book.

I'm a physician, yes . . . I'm also a wife, a mother, a daughter, and a friend. Every week I sit down with my husband and we figure out who is going to shuttle the kids; who will drive Melanie to basketball and piano, who will pick up Megan from softball and clarinet; how we will fit in a decent evening meal around our activities. When it comes to private, daily living my story converges with yours.

Defining Moments

Life offers many defining moments like the one I had in the rocking chair, but those moments prove challenging to identify if you're constantly on the move. Can you imagine how difficult it would be for me to determine what ails you if I couldn't get you to lie still while performing an exam? It would be impossible! If you want change in your life, no matter who you are—cancer survivor, physician, or stay-at-home dad—you must be still and look at your present circumstances. How do they shape up? Are you your best self?

Your defining moment may be as simple as the realization that you're not able to climb a flight of stairs without being winded, or that you haven't climbed a flight in years. It may be alienation from family members, a lack of variety in your life, embarrassment about your size, or an inability to balance work and play. Maybe for you it's immobilizing anger or depression. Whatever it is, once you're confronted with your discontent, it can take remarkable courage and determination to break out of your safe routine and do something different.

Change is often uncomfortable and in some instances downright painful. Have you ever taken a brisk walk and experienced a cramp in your side or itching all over your legs? I have. It made me want to quit after the first day! But what's the alternative? To stay inactive, sluggish, and overweight? I'm not willing to live that way. Have you ever done the work of resolving a broken relationship? Now, that's painful stuff. I wanted to quit after the first conversation. But again, what's the alternative? Leave myself broken and depressed? I wasn't created to live that way, and you weren't either. There is an opportunity for greater living available for each of us. It's worth the bumps and scrapes. Once you break past the barriers, and in time you will, you won't want to live any other way. You'll discover greater freedom than you've ever experienced prior to making your change.

THE JOURNEY BEGINS

Do not wait for ideal circumstances,
nor the best opportunities;
they will never come.
JANET ERSKINE STUART

My life was terribly out of balance and I knew I needed some type of picture or model to help me. I didn't want to simply react with a knee-jerk solution; I wanted to define where I wanted to go and have a good idea of how to get there. I had plenty of medical theory and science, but not much understanding of health and happiness . . . and I didn't have a plan.

Society doesn't offer immediate assistance. The media's concept of health is locked tight on the body—airbrushed models, athletes with bulging muscles—the focus is overtly physical. But reducing my health to how my body appeared and what I had to do to achieve a certain look was shortsighted. Health definitely includes the shape I'm in physically, but I already knew through my own experience that it was much more than that. Health is about who I am mentally, emotionally, and spiritually.

Think about this: we tell pregnant women they're beautiful. You've probably said it yourself. You see the vibrant aura about them, but the reality is they've gained an extraordinary amount of weight, their ankles are swollen, their skin's discolored, and . . . they may even waddle! According to society's standards, a pregnant woman's features don't come close to how we define "beautiful," yet there's something happening to them *internally* that you see externally which makes you think, "Incredible!" The word you usually hear to describe this beautiful phenomenon is "glowing." Physiological changes occurring on the inside result in a radiance that is perceived on the outside. Just as life is bursting forth from a mother in waiting, similarly, beautiful internal changes—improved relationships, a spirit of well-being and gratitude, and a sense of security and purpose—will result in a physical glow of longevity and vitality as new life begins to spring forth from within.

A Picture of Healthy Living

I didn't have a clear picture of healthy living, so I started reading, listening, and looking at a broad range of topics on health and well-being. I started with the obvious—nutrition and exercise. I branched out into other areas as well. Breathing, intimacy, simplicity, peace: each definitely had its own unique health benefit, but I couldn't find a unifying theme or framework to bring them all together for holistic living. Finally, the answers started coming together—at my job.

I was asked to join a national team of well-respected health care administrators, medical professionals, and creative designers to envision and create the "hospital of the future"—a wellness facility that would combine the best practices of health and healing. Together we planned a facility that focused on prevention as well as diagnosis and treatment. These leaders agreed that overall health and improved healing experiences for patients were optimally achieved when considering the needs of the mind, body, and spirit simultaneously instead of separately. Florida Hospital–Celebration Health,* a full-service hospital and wellness center providing inpatient and outpatient care for the whole person, was established to meet that need. All of the eight principles making up the acronym of CREATION Health were first established at Celebration Health and now form the guiding principles for the health care delivery model of Florida Hospital.

Being a part of this team brought my beliefs about healthy living from out of the periphery. When we designed the program for the Women's Center we systematically incorporated the CREATION Health model as a foundation for wellness. My visit with each patient brought more intentional focus on all aspects of life that influence health. Office visits centered on resolving immediate medical problems as well as long-term strategies for living. I started writing prescriptions for nutrition as well as medication; for volunteer work as well as for yearly mammograms. I still had the same fifteen managed-care minutes to get my work done, but the visits were different because I was different.

The more I inquired about my patients' lifestyle habits, the more challenged I was to confront my own. The more I wanted for my patients, the more I wanted for me. It was time to adjust and bring balance to my own picture. I'd finally found the unifying theme for living long and living well, and I wanted to experience what I knew.

*Florida Hospital's Celebration Health campus opened its doors in 1997 in the Disney-owned town of Celebration. It is one of seven Florida Hospital campuses in central Florida and is one of the leading medical facilities in the country focusing on emerging technology, treatment, and prevention. For more on Celebration Health, visit www.CelebrationHealth.com.

My Body

I started with the most obvious area that needed change—my body. I was overweight and out of shape and that meant I needed to address my activity and nutrition. I wasn't looking for a thirty-day miracle; I wanted a lifestyle I could maintain. I started going to a gym, and for the sake of accountability—and encouragement—I worked with a trainer.

Even though I was doing this for my body, I was amazed at the almost immediate effect that exercising had on my mood. I woke up in the morning ready for my day—and for a person who absolutely despised mornings, this was nothing short of a miracle! With consistent exercise, I woke up feeling good and I felt excited about living.

I was sleeping better. I'd always struggled with the amount and quality of my sleep, yet with the addition of daily stretching, regular aerobic exercise, and resistance training, I was appropriately tired at the end of the day. I wasn't worn out; I was merely satisfied and ready for bed. I couldn't remember the last time I'd consistently slept like that, but I knew it had been at least a decade. What a gift it was to have a full night of contented rest!

These good vibrations weren't just because of exercise. I'd started eating a balanced breakfast each morning, something I hadn't done since high school, and I was cutting back on most processed foods. I drank more water and less juice. It wasn't easy, but I made a twelve-week commitment to pay attention to what I ate, when I ate, and how much I ate. Within three months, I'd dropped fifteen pounds and two sizes. As my kids would say, "Dude!" I was looking good!

My Mind and Emotions

A decent diet and exercise program made a huge difference in my life. I felt good; my outlook was positive; I was smiling more. The change in my diet removed the "afternoon sludge" and my thoughts soon became clearer, my disposition brighter. My staff noticed and commented politely, but I know behind closed doors they talked freely about the change in "Dr. Serious." We enjoyed one another more.

My relationship with my husband benefited as well. I'll never forget the day when he said to me in the tender way only a husband can, "Honey, I like the change. You're different. You don't . . . bark anymore!" Okay. I should have punched him for that, but it was sad, truthful commentary. I couldn't even get upset. Oh, I still let out an occasional bark—but when my tone is too sharp even for my ears, I know I need to stop and do a quick self-check. *Am I tired? How's my diet been? Did I get in my time at the gym this week?* More often than not, one of these questions will reveal the root cause of my frustration—it's usually not the husband, the kids, the job, or other external circumstances.

With these early successes I was encouraged to brave some heavier lifting. I had a personal trainer to help me with my *physical* challenges, and eventually I got over myself enough and sought the help of an *emotional* trainer. For me, seeing a counselor was much harder work than lifting weights in a gym. My professional life was dedicated to caring for other people and meeting their needs, and it was tough to admit that I needed help to take care of me. Talk about intense workouts! But the results were clear, and over the course of the year I started shedding emotional pounds. "Dude!"

With the beginnings of emotional healing, I was able to pay more attention to my relationships. How was I connecting? Who made me laugh? What experiences did I enjoy outside of work to give me a greater sense of fulfillment? What was I doing for fun? Believe it or not, these were challenging questions for me to answer. I was exercising, eating well, and now I was seeing a counselor who was helping me emotionally. Clearly, changes were taking place, but after a while I found myself reaching a plateau.

My Spirit

I was hitting another wall. My schedule was full of good things, but it was still getting the best of me. I was constantly challenged to get to the gym, to keep appointments with the counselor, and still take care of the responsibilities of mother, doctor, wife, medical news reporter. My journaling reflected my ongoing frustration:

> *It's becoming an increasing quandary for me to balance my time, to not be overwhelmed with the volume of things I have to do, all of the activity . . .*
>
> *And then (there are) the feelings of failure with my kids—no play time, no bath time, no worship time, no learning time. No time to even comb their hair.*
>
> *Feeling myself get tired . . .*
>
> *When I look at where I am investing my time:*
>
> *It's in things that will pass away—my career.*
>
> *The things that won't—my health, my husband, my children, my God—these are suffering.*

I read that now and I think, "Wow. No time to comb hair?! What did my kids look like every day?!" But that time was real. I know, and I keep knowing, that the greatest enemy of my peace and well-being is busyness. Despite my improvement in diet, exercise, and emotional fitness, being busy was robbing me of my joy. "Busy" was robbing me of being spiritually grounded. And when I'm not spiritually grounded I lose my sense of purpose. And once I lose my sense of purpose, I quickly lose my way.

Taking the time to listen with my spirit has never come easy for me, but I'm always so much better when I do. In this area I was an infant. I started at the very beginning of learning how to trust God more readily and deeply. Finding quiet was like finding a new and fascinating toy. I "experimented" with it and tried intentional pauses between activities. I began learning to listen to me and was discovering what it really meant to be healthy.

FROM BREAKDOWN TO BREAKTHROUGH

To travel is to take a journey into yourself.
DANNY KAYE

About a year and a half after I started at Celebration, my husband was offered a tremendous job opportunity, a great stepping-stone for his career. The catch? Leave Florida and move to Alabama. Well, that caused a moment of serious reflection and silence. If you haven't noticed already, I'm wired for high performance. I was solidly established in Orlando. And yet, I wanted to balance my dreams with my husband's. Stan had made huge sacrifices for me so I could successfully complete my residency and establish my early medical career. It was his turn.

And truth be told, I was tired.

I loved what I was doing, but all of the accomplishments and tasks required a sustained energy that was pushing me toward a health breakdown—not just body fatigue, but a deep soul tiredness. Despite my impressive strides toward holistic health, I still had several areas that needed addressing if I was to achieve the health that I desired. I knew I still needed to pull back, so that I could truly "live."

We would move to Alabama. And I would take a time-out.

Have you ever watched a little child in "time-out"? He pouts a little. He slumps and fusses. He might cry or call out for his parent asking if his time is up yet. My time-out was voluntary. Still, nothing about it came easy. I kicked and I slumped and I pouted a little (okay, a lot). I cried. Not just because I was leaving friends, home, community, and income (although that was seriously traumatic), but because I was leaving Dr. Reed—Physician, Administrator,

Television Star—Superhero! In our little Alabama home ("cabin," as my five-year-old daughter, Megan, called it), with rabbit ears for four-channel television reception, I faced some brand-new and extremely difficult questions: Who was I? What was my purpose? How do I live? My journaling reflected the quandary:

> *I have always been one to preach "being" over "doing," but I didn't see how very important my doing had become to me. Indeed, it is how I've come to determine my self-worth . . .*
>
> *And now it's time to balance. It's painful and scary.*
>
> *What will it be like to wake up without an external identity? Who is Monica?*

Have you ever had a time of cataclysmic reordering? This was it for me; not just in what I did, but in who I was.

At different points along the road we're given unique treasures and wisdom for life. In a way I would never have anticipated, my Alabama experience allowed me to step away from the fray and gave me the colors to fill in the sketch of my life that I'd started in Orlando. The pace was slow enough to explore how I felt, what I thought, and why I thought it. It gave me time to explore what really motivated me, what my priorities were, and what made me happy. It gave me time to clearly define and experience what it meant to be healthy.

For the first time in years, I slept without interruption. No more beepers in the middle of the night—no babies to deliver or emergency surgeries to perform. I got to know my children. We discovered we liked each other! Instead of going to the basketball arena to watch an NBA game, we went outside in the sunshine and fresh air to play the game ourselves. I was in the best shape of my life. I cooked. I was actually eating broccoli (a vegetable I previously loved to hate—and still don't really enjoy), I was juicing, and experimenting with foods. I even entered a national health and fitness competition and successfully made it all the way to the finals— and I've got the T-shirt to prove it!

In my own quiet moments, this stability seeker, this person who loved being in control, was learning how to survive change. My relationship with my husband deepened and became more real. In the crucible of "no distractions available," we learned to depend more on God and each other. We were either going to grow together or kill each other. We chose to grow.

I remember one of my patients calling to check on me and see how things were going. She asked me what I was doing and had a hearty chuckle when I told her I was doing laundry. She laughed and said, "I can't picture my doctor doing laundry." I looked around at my surroundings and thought, *If only you knew!* I had to laugh myself. Standing on the back porch over that old machine in rural Alabama, I told her, "I can barely picture it myself!" But there I was doing it.

I learned to live—by living. I was experiencing a breakthrough.

Over the course of two years I came to fully understand what it feels like to live the eight principles of CREATION Health—the book you hold in your hands. A solid picture of health began to take shape for me of living a life that revitalizes, rejuvenates, and revolutionizes one's being.

Understanding the Breakthrough

Okay, I hear you saying, "Not fair! You had two years off to experience your breakthrough. Give me two years and I'll achieve some real healthy living too!" I know. I used to say the same thing about Oprah. "Give me a personal chef and trainer to come to my house every day and I'll look great also." This may or may not be true, but it really isn't the point. Each of our circumstances is unique, but no matter where you are in life, you can always take responsibility for you.

A breakthrough to health will require various decisions, but one thing is certain: a breakthrough will *always* require a time for being still. The Three-Day Rejuvenation Therapy is specifically designed for just that. We want to give you a time of stillness to start your breakthrough—a holistic detox from the hustle and bustle and sludge of your world. It's designed for radical rest, creative choice, and delicious eating. All you need to do is set aside a three-day weekend away from your household chores and work-related duties and find the quiet place of your choice. The Three-Day Rejuvenation Therapy will help you redefine what health feels like. You will sketch your own picture of health. Then the Eight-Week Lifestyle Transformation Plan will help to solidify how each of these eight principles can change your life. This plan gives you a starting place to fully integrate these principles in your life. Finally, by following the guidelines of the CREATION Health Plan you can experience health for a lifetime.

I now had my picture of health. I knew how it felt to be well rested and well nourished; I knew what my body felt like when I was exercising regularly; I was comfortable with spending time alone and connecting with God. I had a deeper appreciation and knowledge of my family and the outdoors. My husband's career continued to evolve, and as a result of another opportunity for him, unbelievably we returned to Orlando. It was an opportunity for all of us.

Orlando was home. We moved back and our quiet rural life "ramped up" slowly. One year after our return, I was invited to return to Florida Hospital, this time in the role of senior medical officer over seven facilities in central Florida. Not to be taken lightly, the opportunity of being a full-time physician executive in a 2,000-bed hospital was a wonderful and challenging offer. Our family discussed it, and I took it.

In such a position, my picture of health painted with its bold strokes of color could have easily been tossed, but I determined I wouldn't let that happen. I pledged to keep my eight principles of CREATION Health prominently before me. And I did. I contemplated them as I raced to my meetings, munched on junk food, pounded out e-mails and obsessed over health care issues. I put on pounds. My patience waned and I started barking out orders again. But this time there was one profound difference. I knew why.

Prior to my breakthrough, I didn't know what it felt like to be well rested, so I didn't know when I was tired. Prior to the breakthrough, I didn't know that the body and brain sludge I felt was related to what I ate or my lack of activity. Prior to my breakthrough I didn't know the power of choice or the life-giving vitality of ten minutes of sunshine. Prior to the breakthrough, I didn't know to care.

But now I did. It took me a while and a few tries to readjust, but with a clear frame of reference and the eight guiding principles of CREATION, I allowed myself the flexibility and grace of figuring out how I would recapture that image and keep it real in the new set of circumstances I'd been given.

GRACE FOR THE JOURNEY

Freedom may come not from being in control of life,
but rather from a willingness to move with the events of life.
RACHEL NAOMI REMEN

Our world is fast-paced, highly stressed, and constantly changing. We will always have times in our lives where we'll get off course and have to recalibrate. It's okay; this is life. Expect it. What's most important is having a frame of reference that allows us to adapt, perform, and live life as it was intended. *This is the Breakthrough.*

Because of life's changes, so much of what we achieve depends on flexibility and hefty doses of grace. You may feel that you're in a decent place in your life right now, but if you get sick, if something happens to one of your children or your parents, if your job assignment changes—almost anything—it creates a new set of circumstances that will require an adjustment on your part. You may stress eat. You may not get the hours of sleep you need. You may not be able to talk to God. You may miss a couple of days of exercise (it may be more than a couple of days!). None of that means you've "lost it all."

Once you experience your own breakthrough, you will know *when* you're out of balance, you'll know *what's* out of balance, and you'll know *why*. The best part is this: you can use one or more of these eight principles to reestablish equilibrium. When life gets fuzzy around the edges and you lose focus and clarity, take a look at the eight CREATION Health principles (see the Self-Assessment in appendix A) and ask yourself which areas need attention.

You can't place a warranty on good health, but you can certainly maximize the possibilities of achieving it. CREATION Health will help you do just that. You will reduce your risk, extend your years, and open your arms to life as it was intended. With CREATION Health, you'll be able to embrace life as it is now and go through the difficult turns with confidence.

PUTTING IT ALL TOGETHER

Both the desire for health and the picture of health can reside firmly in you. It doesn't have to be a vague idea or vision; it can become a tangible part of who you are. Your years on this earth can and should be lived fully. There's always greater joy to discover, greater abundance, greater physical strength, greater emotional and spiritual understanding—and always so much more to share and give away. I choose to continue learning and growing.

Will you join me?

"C" is for Choice

3

Choice is your power and right to decide. It's the realization that you have more than one option. To choose is to know your future is greater than your past; it's an attitude that considers the best is yet to be. Choice is a conviction: you are worthy of the best life has to offer.

IN THIS CHAPTER YOU WILL:

* Discover the secret weapon for unleashing the power of change in your life.

* Find out how to break bad habits and banish them from your life.

* Learn the six steps to jump-start your personal journey to success.

"C" is for Choice

It's choice — not chance — that determines your destiny.

JEAN NIDETCH

In the 2005 romatic comedy *Hitch*, Will Smith plays a professional matchmaker who unprofessionally falls for a hardworking tabloid columnist. He reveals the secret of his success to her one day as she bemoans the fact that he's a morning person. Chuckling, he replies, "Well, like I always tell my clients, 'Begin each day as if it were on purpose.'"[1]

Living on purpose. What a profound adage! It is true that we don't always get to choose our circumstances, but we *can* certainly choose our destination. The key to your Health Breakthrough is seizing the power of choice.

When you make choices, you take responsibility and exert a degree of control. This is a major factor not only in your outlook and happiness in life, but in the progression or slowing of disease. Scientists have found that even laboratory animals respond differently depending on whether or not they are able to control their circumstances. When exposed to adversity, animals that are able to make a choice to stop the stress they are experiencing are far less likely to suffer from disease compared with animals that are not. The same is true for people. Your twenty-four-hour day should be spent living and experiencing all that life has to offer. *How* this happens for you and *what* happens to you in this life is largely dependent on how you choose.

So Many Choices, So Little Time

Think back to the days when we had plain ol' push-button telephones without any fancy features—no call-waiting, call forwarding, or caller ID. We talked to only one person at a time, and we completed a conversation with that same person. If someone else tried to call us, they got a busy signal.

Now we have headsets so we never have to break stride while "nurturing" our relationships. Some of our most treasured interactions are quick exchanges of information on the run while we thumb our Blackberries, balance our cell phones, and drive with our knees. Richard Swenson, in his book *Hurtling Toward Oblivion*, describes it well. "No matter where we look—it makes no difference—there is always more . . . There are more businesses offering more services and making more products . . . There are more buildings, more restaurants, more medications . . . more activities and commitments . . . There is, in short, more . . . of everything. Wherever we look, we are surrounded by more. Always."[2] *Life is doing us instead of us doing life.* And while progress has brought us "more," our advancements haven't seemed to make living an easy accomplishment.

When my family made the decision to move from Florida to Alabama, we had to get our house "market ready." We repaired closet doors, refinished our wood floors, painted the outside of our home, and spruced up the landscaping—our house looked fabulous. You'd think I'd be happy with all that was done, but I wasn't. Actually, I was furious! I couldn't believe I'd spent all that time (and money) getting my house ready for someone else to enjoy! Somehow, in the years that we'd been living there we were too busy to get those repairs done. We accepted the fact that we would get to it "eventually." We got it done eventually, all right, only now I was appreciating my beautiful home as I packed boxes to leave it. What a lesson! It became a turning point for me to choose to live differently, to choose to do things that I enjoy now, to choose to treat myself at least as well as I would treat a potential home buyer.

We seem to be resigned to accept our lifestyles as "just the way things are," when in reality we were designed to participate in creating our lives—to actively pursue planning our destiny. We weren't created to be beat up and run over by the events of our day. Our greatest asset for change is the power to choose.

Created to Choose

Since the beginning of time, humanity has been given the gift of choice. In fact, choice plays a pivotal role in the Creation story. It should come as no surprise then that choice is at the very heart of experiencing your breakthrough.

You were designed with the power to decide your own thoughts and behavior. You were fashioned to act according to your own free will. Depending on your choices you can reap tremendous benefits. God created you with the ability to choose so that you would participate with him in the ongoing creative process of life. Being made in his image means that you've been given immeasurable power to select your surroundings, your relationships, your vocations, what you'll eat, when you'll sleep, and what your attitude will be. You've been enabled with the incredible power to craft your own destiny.

CHARTING THE COURSE OF CHANGE

Though no one can go back and make a brand new start,
anyone can start from now and make a brand new ending.
CARL BARD

When I look at my life I see some triumphs and failures. I don't feel particularly great about all my decisions. I've learned, though, that while my past plays into my present, it doesn't have to immobilize me today. I hold the reins and can take ownership of my future. Realizing that I can take full possession of my life and that I have the power to choose means I can reshape my future.

I love hearing tales of events and adventures that have brought people to the place where they are today. I'm especially intrigued with lively centenarians, the elite few in this world who've celebrated their hundredth birthday. Some have stories with chapters of sadness and plenty of blunders, but the sheer number of their years speaks of a legacy of strength and vibrancy. One shared characteristic of people who are still fully alive into their eighties, nineties, and hundreds is a willingness to participate in choosing the direction their lives will take.

STILL CLIMBING

Mount Whitney, at 14,495 feet, has the distinction of being the highest mountain in the lower forty-eight United States. Writes Andress and Gohde in *Grandma Whitney: Queen of the Mountain,* "Whitney can be quite temperamental. She often unleashes her wrath with sudden fury . . . scorching sun, freezing cold, blustery thunderstorms. . . . Worst of all is the altitude sickness. Inflicted on those who are not used to vigorous climbing in (thin) air, its main symptoms are excruciating headaches and debilitating nausea."[3]

Hulda Crooks made that climb twenty-three times. She started at age sixty-six.

Jim Russell, in his article "The Backpacking Octogenarian," notes that "At age seventy-two she started running and jogging because it made her climbing easier. At age eighty-two she set a world record for her age group in the Senior Olympics. She ran the 1500 meters in 10 minutes and 58 seconds. In addition to her Whitney climbs, Hulda regularly took backpacking trips over other trails, such as the 212-mile John Muir Trail between Yosemite National Park and Mount Whitney . . . She also descended to the bottom of the Grand Canyon and crossed the High Sierras, eighty miles from west to east. Every month or so, she would climb one of the mountains of southern California."[4] Hulda's philosopy: "Human beings are allowed just one body per customer" . . . The length of our lease on life, and the quality of it, is largely up to each individual. It depends on how we take care of ourselves."[5]

Hulda's last climb was at age ninety-one—the oldest woman to ever climb Mount Whitney. "No mountain was ever too high for this gentle giant," wrote one journalist. "With a twinkle in her eye, and purpose in her step, 'Grandma Whitney' showed the world that mental, physical, and spiritual health is attainable at any age."[6] In 1991, Crooks Peak, located just south of Mount Whitney, was named in her honor.

Hulda Crooks died peacefully in her sleep on November 22, 1997. She was 101.

People like Hulda make active choices, but you also need to realize that not choosing is also a choice. It's a mistake to think that if you let things stay as they are, if you can just postpone choosing, then you can ride out the distressing circumstances and get through it. When you don't actively participate in making decisions, you are still choosing. You've chosen not to choose! And by not doing anything, you force change to be done to you. Choosing with thought and intention is your greatest power.

To Be Alive

Today, Josh is glad to be alive. Just a few short days ago it was uncertain. That was the day he had a head-on car collision. The moment of impact is seared into his memory. First came the instant of panic just before impact; then the wail of screeching tires and crunching metal. The explosion of air bags and shattering windshield filled his senses; he remembers vividly the violent shaking of his body and limbs. Then silence.

On the night of the crash, Josh had worked late at the office again. By the time he climbed into his car, the sun had long since set. His wife would likely be in bed, and he'd be arriving home to a quiet house. The talk radio host was droning in the background, giving advice to listeners about relationships. "Great," Josh said to himself. "Nothing like a little guilt." The host encouraged listeners to express love to their families every opportunity they had. She kept talking. Life was uncertain . . . Accidents happen, tragedies occur . . . None of us knows when we might meet an unexpected end.

Almost as if it were choreographed, Josh vaguely recalls a black pickup truck running a red light. The truck crossed into Josh's lane and smashed into his car head-on. In the split second before impact he had time for one thought:

I'm not ready to die.

Few of us feel ready to die at a moment's notice. Fortunately for Josh, the crash did not take his life. The car was mangled, but Josh was spared.

Take Responsibility

Josh was fortunate enough to get a "do-over," and he took advantage of it. We all know people who have made monumental changes in their lives as a result of some catastrophic experience, but wouldn't it be better to choose to take time off from work before the nervous breakdown? Why wait for a heart attack before choosing to spend more time with your family? Why wait to be diagnosed with lung cancer and *then* stop smoking?

It takes courage to change. We have to know where we're headed and we have to take responsibility to get there. Our response to hardship and challenging circumstances is choosing the ability to overcome.[7] Relationship guru Dr. Gary Smalley says, "I think the most exciting part of knowing I am made with the capacity to choose is that all my thoughts determine all of my actions and emotions. It doesn't matter what others do to me or what circumstances I face every day, I determine all of my feelings, by what I choose to think and how I choose to react to what happens to me. I love that freedom."[8] Choice opens up our future with possibility and hope.

(Un)Motivated to Change

Have you ever noticed how you can perform task after task throughout the day and feel "great," but if you sit down for five minutes, you realize you're actually exhausted? The fact is you were tired well before you realized it, but weren't able to determine how you really felt until you sat still. Many of us are amateurs when it comes to being still and taking time with ourselves, so we cannot necessarily rely on what we feel when measuring levels of discomfort or deciding what's best. This is important to realize because *it is only when our discomfort outweighs the pain of change that we are motivated to choose differently.* It's the way we're wired. In general, we won't change unless the pain of what we are thinking about doing is less than the discomfort of staying where we are.

Let's select an easy example like starting an exercise program. If you are only a few pounds over your ideal weight, and you can still fit in your clothes, the discomfort of snug waistlines may be more manageable than the pain of making a change such as going to the gym, paying for a membership, and driving twenty minutes before or after work three times a week. If, on the other hand, you've just received disturbing news from your physician regarding your high blood pressure and a shortened life expectancy as a result of your habits, then the pain of change (going to the gym) is now less than the discomfort created by your diagnosis.

With the way we live, rushing around and sublimating our feelings so we can survive the day, we can't always make choices based on how we feel. For most of us, some discomfort has become so routine that it's what is familiar. So to determine what's uncomfortable or unhealthy for your life, you can't just rely on what you feel. What you *know* must also make a difference.*

---

*Remember from your reading in the "Before You Begin" section that the first stage of the Lifestyle Learning Continuum is "not knowing that you don't know." What you gain from reading this book will help you realize where your change needs to occur, even if you don't "feel" you have a problem.

An important factor in making wise decisions is obtaining reliable information. Where do you get it? Not from Aunt Wilma who says, "We've always done it this way." Will Schutz, PhD, in his book *Profound Simplicity* says that to make decisions that last, we must first become more aware of our options and their consequences. This means we may have to break out of our culture a bit and try a new way of living. The more we read, study, and understand about health, the more likely we will discover our best options and benefits. We'll make more informed decisions about our health based on what we feel and on what we know.

Change Your Beliefs

I believe we often *act* our way into believing instead of believing our way into acting. Or, said in another way, our actions influence what we believe more often than our beliefs influence our actions.[9] Let's just admit it, we like to justify and make ourselves feel better about our behavior, whether that behavior is good for us or not. When we're looking to make positive changes in our lives, we must remember that action working with belief brings lasting change.

Take, for instance, my belief that I feel better with more sleep. In fact, I believe I bring harm to myself (and those around me!) when I don't get enough shuteye. As a practicing obstetrician, I had quite a history of poor sleep habits, even though I knew that more sleep was better for me both physically and mentally. I knew I needed to increase the hours of sleep I got per night. That was the belief part. The action? I had to close the book I was reading and go to bed!

Functioning on belief alone, I often rationalized why I needed to stay up just an hour longer. I finally had to get to the point where regardless of what justification I had as to why I needed just "ten more minutes" (I sounded like my kids) I had to turn off the light. When I performed the action and got more rest, I felt remarkably better in the morning, which reinforced my belief in the benefits of rest. The more often I go to bed at a decent hour, the better I feel. The better I feel, the more of a believer I become, and the more readily I take action. Each action-belief cycle positively perpetuates the next.

I don't want to oversimplify this or give the impression that change is as easy as 1-2-3. We both know it isn't. Making new choices and starting new actions is a challenge, but it is doable. Remember, when you choose to make changes, you are putting into action the belief that your future is greater than your past. With this knowledge, it becomes worthwhile to move from something in your lifestyle that you found comfortable (though unhealthy) to something that will be uncomfortable until it becomes habit. Choices *feel* comfortable once they become habit. Let's examine how habits are formed and can be harnessed to make positive choices.

Red Lights and Ice Cream—The Science of Change

"We are what we repeatedly do," wrote Aristotle. Habits are choices repeated so frequently that they can be considered automatic. They are learned patterns of behavior. In truth, most of what we do is by habit. This is a good thing when you automatically press on the brake at a red light, but not so good when you automatically go to the fridge for a bowl of ice cream every night before bed.

Our brains are amazingly complex and remarkably efficient. When we repeat patterns of behavior, a highway of nerve connections develops within our brains, which creates grooves of familiarity. These highways recognize not only the behavior (eating the bowl of ice cream) but also the patterns that trigger the behavior (changing out of your work clothes and turning on the television). This establishes a nerve pathway similar to a highway of activity.

The basal ganglia—the portion of your brain that appears to be intimately connected with habits—also responds powerfully to positive feedback. Thoughts and feelings like, "Mmm, that tastes good!" essentially help to seal the habit in place. Therefore, these pathways stay in place for the lifetime of the nerve cells, which pretty much means all of your life.[10]

By now you may be thinking, "How in the world can I ever change if the old pathway exists in my brain forever?" This is the challenge *and* the opportunity. The challenge? Changing the triggers that form the behaviors you want to change. For example, let's say you come home every night after work and take a shower, go to the kitchen, get two or three scoops of mint chocolate chip ice cream, and plop down in front of the television. You've developed a pattern. In your mind, television and a big bowl of ice cream go hand in hand at the end of the workday. If you want to change the pathway, you have to disrupt the pattern by picking a different activity with which to wind down other than ice cream or television.

Taking things away isn't fun. None of us likes feeling deprived. Studies show that our brains respond much better to positive reinforcement than to deprivation. In this case, maybe it's finding a healthier dessert or taking a walk around the block before you start your evening routine. Remember, new choices are an opportunity to develop new brain highways and will spark your breakthrough.

TRANSFORMING YOUR THOUGHTS

If you think you can, you can;
if you think you can't, you can't.
Either way, you're right.

HENRY FORD

Your brain is capable of major transformations. Habits once formed can be broken in the same way—by repeating actions of a different sort. It doesn't happen overnight, but it does happen. It's commonly accepted that it takes about twenty-one days to develop a new habit.*

---

* The plastic surgeon Dr. Richard W. Maltz noticed that it took twenty-one days for amputees to cease feeling phantom sensations in the amputated limb. From that somewhat obscure beginning, the "twenty-one-day phenomenon" has evolved into a staple of self-change literature.

Depending on the behavior you're trying to change, it may take longer.[11]

While lasting change can be challenging, it is possible! As you choose to take on new activities, you develop new highways that will also stay with you for the rest of your life. As these new highways are repeatedly used, they become the new accepted patterns of behavior and the way you automatically respond. The old highway is still present, but it is essentially an unused road, and will stay that way as long as you continue to reinforce your new behaviors.

Interestingly, when you choose to make a lifestyle change and repeatedly practice that change, your belief systems turn upside down. What seemed previously comfortable now becomes *un*comfortable, and what was previously uncomfortable now becomes comfortable!* For example, I never used to eat breakfast—not in college, not in medical school, and not in residency. There was no way you could have convinced me that breakfast was an important meal or that it was worth the twenty minutes to eat it. I was fine without it, wasn't I? Even when I started focusing on nutrition and exercise, breakfast wasn't a top priority. My trainer finally convinced me: "I know you don't believe it, but just do it, Monica. How can you start your day with an empty tank?"

It was a struggle at first. I wasn't hungry and it did add a few minutes to my morning. But I quickly found that I was more focused during the day and I actually ate less throughout the day. Now I love breakfast. It's the most consistent meal I eat!

Let's talk about exercise again. Many people come up with reasons why they should *not* exert themselves physically. I once had a colleague tell me he had only a set amount of hours on this earth, and he wasn't going to waste them exercising. For folks with this kind of mind-set, the comfort of not moving outweighs the discomfort of starting a new routine. But talk to anyone who has

---

*The CREATION Health Plan, specifically the Eight-Week Lifestyle Transformation Plan (see chapter 11), will help you with this change.

started a regular exercise program and they will tell you those good-feeling endorphins get them pumped up. Their body loves its newfound freedom, and it actually begins to feel miserable when they aren't actively moving. This same colleague chose to start exercising once he was diagnosed with high blood pressure, and now he wouldn't trade the hours he spends being active.

ENSURING SUCCESS

Success is never final.
Failure is never fatal.
Courage is all that counts.
Winston Churchill

Let's get to the bottom line. I know you want to embark on a journey in which you can succeed. There are many different ways to measure success, but the definition I like best comes from Paul J. Meyer: *Success is the progressive realization of worthwhile personal goals.* I like this definition for several reasons. First, achieving success is personal—what you need and want for your life, and how you achieve your breakthrough, will be different from someone else. If you want to make lasting change, your new choices can't be made for your spouse, your physician, your clergyperson, or anyone else. Lasting change comes because you want to do it for *you.*

My favorite word in the definition is "progressive." Success is a progressive realization. I get excited about this because it focuses on the journey and not just the destination. Pursuing a healthy lifestyle is a lifelong endeavor, and recognizing that it is an ongoing, ever-improving journey will give you hope. It took time to acquire your current state of discomfort and it will take time to develop a new way of living. Here are a few things you can do to jump-start your success:

1. *Banish the bad attitude.* A healthy lifestyle shouldn't be boring or annoying. Making new choices can be exciting and fun. For

some reason, when it comes to health, we obsess on what we need to take away from our lives instead of focusing on what we're *adding*—more rest, greater intimacy, healthier foods, more years, greater peace, and so on. These are wonderful things and should provide encouragement as you pursue a healthier lifestyle.

2. *Establish specific goals.* Decide what you want to do. Try to make your goals as specific as possible. Put them in writing if you can. When establishing goals it's important to spend time thinking about why you want to do it, how you want to do it, and when you will do it. Following a concrete plan helps seal your commitment to change. The three-phase CREATION Health Plan (see chapter 11) will help you do just that. Stay flexible, and review your goals periodically to make sure you're staying on track.

3. *Follow a realistic plan.* Good NBA teams don't push the panic button when they fall twenty points down early in the second half. Instead, they keep plugging away at the big lead, working their way back into the game. The same attitude works when following a realistic plan. If you haven't exercised in eons, why would you plan to go to the gym for two hours a day, five days a week at the start? A more realistic approach would be starting your day with a brisk walk around the neighborhood before heading off to work in the morning. Then you can build up your stamina to the point where you *want* to go to the gym several times a week.

4. *Seek the support of family and friends.* Talk about your new commitments with friends and family. Don't be bashful; solicit their encouragement. You'd be surprised at how many people are trying to do the same things you are. Sometimes you can convince family and friends to support and encourage you even when they are not doing the same things you are! Once I started focusing on my health I was excited to try new things. This time it was colon cleansing, but the thought of doing a program for seven days with little food was daunting. I approached my husband and two of our best friends with the idea, and amazingly they signed on. The husbands decided they would let the wives be the guinea pigs before

they got started. I'll spare you the details, but suffice it to say, I would never have made it through that experience without the support of a friend. And the men, not to be outdone, completed the challenge as well. We learned what we were made of during those seven days, and years later we still recall the experience and have a good laugh.

5. *Write your thoughts and struggles in a journal.* You may not think journaling is for you, but unexpected clarity takes place when you write down your hopes, dreams, setbacks, and moods on paper. Try listing your goals. Feel free to be brief. Write down the comforts and discomforts associated with your new choices. Allow this to help you determine what to do and how you should go about realizing your goals. Routine journaling also helps you keep a log of your progress. When you forget how far you've come, a written record will be a welcome reminder and encouragement.

6. *Begin developing your personal mission statement.* Unlike goals, which are specific and time-sensitive, a mission statement is a set of guidelines for life. Mission statements usually address five questions:

* What do I want from my life?
* What do I value?
* What are my talents?
* What do I believe in?
* By the end of my life, what do I want to have accomplished?

A mission statement is a way of discovering a sense of purpose by getting to know yourself on a deeper level. Your mission statement is a set of guiding principles for life. Hyrum W. Smith, author and motivational speaker, said, "Your governing values are the foundation of personal success and fulfillment." I believe this to be true.

My friend Todd has a personal mission statement that he goes over weekly. He uses it to bring focus to his daily tasks and activities. More than a single mission "statement," Todd has a set of statements that describe his ideals for the most important areas of his life, including marriage, family, spiritual life, work, community, character growth, and service. Rarely does he make a major decision without reviewing his mission statement first.

Arthur Gordon, British colonial governor, once said, "Nothing is easier than saying words. Nothing is harder than living them, day after day." Having a mission statement that you regularly review will help you add focus and direction to your life.

PUTTING IT ALL TOGETHER

Embracing your freedom to choose is the first preliminary motion leading you to all the other steps toward wholeness. In order to make new changes you must accept responsibility for the life you have now and your ability to choose for the better. Yes, it does take courage and honesty, but it is possible to change. Once you decide to change, you must act! Your repeated actions will not only establish new routines and habits, they will establish new beliefs.

When it's all said and done—the planning, seeking, reading, and writing—life is still a journey. Enjoy it! Celebrate the successes and appreciate the setbacks. You will have some of both, but don't lose sight of your big picture. Your success doesn't ride on perfection but rather on the "progressive realization" of your goals. Nothing is impossible if you have a willing heart, an open mind, and the 3 M's.

Maximize

Take ownership of your life by exercising your power of choice. Read each of the CREATION Health principles and make new choices that will revitalize your well-being.

Moderate

Don't bite off more than you can chew. It takes at least twenty-one days before new choices become habits. Remember that success is the *progressive* realization of your goals.

Minimize

Get rid of a deprivation mind-set. Make sure you focus on what you're adding to your life rather than what you're taking away.

Rob's Breakthrough Story
The Positive Power of Choice

An attorney at a multibillion-dollar corporation, Rob was confident he was actively climbing the ladder of success. He worked long hours, and that was okay initially.

"The harder I worked, the more responsibilities seemed to come my way. I enjoyed the satisfaction of a job well done and being an active player in a company with lofty goals. But to keep up with the growing list of projects and things to do, long hours became longer hours, and those hours started including my weekends.

"My balance was slipping away. My work time began bleeding into my evening family time, which meant later bedtimes. I started waking up later—just in enough time to get showered and go to work. I wasn't able to exercise like I used to. I was compromising my morning prayer time, which had been a mainstay in my life for many years. I started having migraines. My life was unraveling."

Rob and his wife were expecting a child. "After five years of working like this, I really had to do some soul-searching. Being successful was important to me and I wanted to avoid anything that hinted at failure, but I was paying a price in every aspect of my life. I wanted to be there for my wife and child," he said. Something had to change.

Rob had a series of heart-to-heart talks with his wife. He looked at what was ultimately most important to him—a sense of balance, time with his wife, being an active part of his child's life, keeping himself in shape, and maintaining his spiritual and social connections.

"It was clear that I couldn't have what I really wanted in life and keep working the way that I was. I had to make a choice. I had to make a change."

Rob made two major decisions: to leave his job and to leave the big city in search of a smaller community. "Scared? Sure I was scared. I was losing security financially, and possibly losing face with my corporate peers. It felt like I was stepping off of the ladder of success and out into thin air. But ultimately, my faith kept me holding on."

Two weeks after quitting his job, Rob took his family and moved to Kalispell, Montana, a small town of 14,000. "We now live in a quaint home with a great view of the mountains. Early on I wondered whether I had done something bright or quite stupid. But as we settled in, it was clear that I had chosen what was best for me and for my family."

His wife is a stay-at-home mom, and Rob serves as legal counsel to a Maryland-based Internet security firm. He works from home. "I have what I want. I have a flexible schedule. I'm more productive and not swamped with meetings and commutes. I'm exercising on a regular basis. I have a more meaningful spiritual connection and every morning I get to walk into my baby's room and see her smiling face.

"I've always wanted to have a reflective life and not a reflexive life. Being here allows me to do just that. Any doubts? Sure, sometimes. Any regrets? None."

"R" is for Rest

4

Rest is the refreshing ease of inactivity following a full day's work; it's the mental and emotional release from daily worries and concerns. Life-giving rest is found in the soothing calm and quiet of a good night's sleep and in the tranquillity of spiritual peace.

IN THIS CHAPTER YOU WILL:

* Learn how the most commonly used drug in the world could be sabotaging your health.

* Learn the seven steps for getting a great night's sleep.

* Discover why you *need* a weekly and yearly vacation—for the health of it!

"R" is for Rest

He that can take rest is greater than he that can take cities.

Benjamin Franklin

Melanie ran, laughed, and danced all day. Even by 8:00 p.m. my daughter was still going full speed. But as the night ticked on, instead of relaxing and getting snuggly, her energy level wound tighter and tighter. An hour later she was in a frenzied, half-crazed state. Throwing herself on the floor, screaming and fighting with all her strength, she was beyond reason. Melanie did not *want* to go to bed.

Anyone who's parented toddlers knows vivid scenes like this one firsthand. Children just don't want to stop. Going to bed means surrendering and accepting the possibility that they might miss out on something fun.

When my daughter finally collapsed and fell asleep, the little tyrant who'd been bringing the house down just minutes earlier now exuded that angelic essence we parents all know and love. Looking at her comfortably resting with a contented smile playing on her lips, I wanted to curl myself up right beside her. Not because she was so adorable but because I wanted to sleep like that!

I've known from the beginning where my daughter gets her determination to squeeze every last drop out of every day—her mother is the same way. Working, moving, doing. I often feel like I'm performing one task after another right up until I fall into bed. And even then I never seem to be fully asleep. I'm partly unconscious, but another part of me is still at the job.

We find our days are filled with activity, with little to no personal premium placed on rest. We push ourselves through life propped up with colas, lattes, energy supplements, and power drinks, fretful when things don't happen in an Internet second. When we finally survive the workday and get the kids down, we reward ourselves by staying up longer than we should watching TV or surfing the Net. Eventually we collapse in the bed, only to drag ourselves out a few hours later to start the cycle all over again.

The National Sleep Foundation estimates that 100 million Americans suffer from a lack of adequate sleep. While that number may seem staggering, millions more are suffering from a *lack of rest*. Rest involves your whole being, not just your body. Your mind and your spirit need rest too. With complete and regular rest, you will restore your health and achieve an amazing sense of well-being.

DESIGNED FOR REST

To everything there is a season,
and a time to every purpose under heaven.
KING SOLOMON

Nature is filled with rhythmic pauses. Day turns to night, winter gives birth to spring, and summer retires in the fall; mimosas extend their leaves in the daytime and fold them at night, morning glories slowly burst into bloom at dawn and fade at dusk; 162 different species of owls hunt at night and sleep soundly during the day. The list of nature's rhythm of activity and rest goes on and on. Rest is sacred. The Creator knows our nature as well as our immediate needs. He knows that we, just like little children, are prone to run and jump and strive until we too are spinning out of control, fearing that we might miss out on a marvelous opportunity or lose momentum by allowing someone else to gain unfair advantage over us while we sleep. But *we cannot possibly live fully without reprieve.* God did not breathe life into Adam's nostrils only to stand back and wait to see how long his creation could run until he dropped. He anticipated that we would dream, aspire, create, and rule. Knowing precisely each thread of the tapestry he had woven, the Creator fastened securely into place a time to rest, relax, and be rejuvenated—he gave us rhythmic pauses.

The Heart of the Matter

With each beat our heart teaches us the importance of respecting the natural rhythm of work and rest. Every day, without our conscious thought, the heart beats 100,000 times and pumps 2,000 gallons of blood throughout our bodies. Our heart will beat 2.5 billion times and pump 50 million gallons of blood during a life span.[1]

If you think your work is demanding, consider your heart's job! In fact, you may think that your heart never rests, but in fact, after each beat the heart must pause and rest. Following each contraction, there is a time of rest and recovery from the work that has been done. This resting period allows the heart to reload—to ready itself to do the work of the next beat. In medical terms, we call this the *absolute refractory period*, or the time in the cardiac cycle when the heart cannot beat. It must recover from its activity.

During this period of relaxation the heart not only *recovers* but also *refills*. Its relaxation phase is just long enough to allow the chambers to refill with the appropriate amount of blood necessary to do their work again in sustaining every organ and vital function of the body. Similar to our hearts, you and I need time to "refill." Our lifestyle, when properly balanced, must consist of work (pouring out), rest (cessation of all activity), and refilling (mental and spiritual nourishment). Most of us don't seem to have a problem getting the work part right, but the resting and refilling presents an ongoing challenge.

Proper rest and refilling is as important as the food you choose to eat and your daily need for exercise. Proper rest will revolutionize your health and establish a sense of peace and well-being physically, mentally, spiritually, and relationally.

THE HEART OF REST

1. If you were to have an EKG of your lifestyle what would it look like?
2. How many hours of sleep do you average each night?
3. What activities do you do on a daily/weekly basis to replenish your life?

A PERVASIVE LACK OF REST

It's hard for most of us to acknowledge that
we are the architects of our own sleep misery.
MICHAEL SMOLENSKY, PhD

Keeping in tune with our natural rhythms can be challenging. The world around us seeks to cram more and more into each twenty-four-hour day. Businesses run at an ever-quickening pace. People phone, fax, e-mail, page, and overnight-deliver to us a flood of demands wherever we are in the world. And we have to respond in kind—just to keep up.

At the core of our lives we find an interminable lack of rest. We were not created to perform, whether working or playing, for a ridiculous number of hours without rest. Our performance, mood, and ultimately our health decline with each excessive hour we tack on.

Constantly doing—even if your days are filled with doing good—is still bad for your health. I'll never forget the story of Dr. John Harvey Kellogg. Dr. Kellogg was the lead physician and administrator of the Battle Creek Sanitarium in the late 1800s. This phenomenal 1,300-bed facility, described as a combination "nineteenth century European health spa and a twentieth century Mayo clinic," was famed for its excellent medical treatments and emphasis on disease prevention. Dr. Kellogg became world-renowned for his emphasis on basic health principles that would promote life and prevent disease.

Still, he struggled in his own life to adhere to what he so passionately believed. For nine months straight, he worked eighteen to twenty hours per day. He wrote that the condition of his "brain and nerves were so worn out with anxiety that every day was a horror and a terror." At other times physical exhaustion set in until his eyes felt like "balls of fire." Kellogg's tendency to neglect his own health nearly cost him his life. Furthermore, he spoke of not having known once in ten years what it felt like to be fully rested.[2]

Dr. Kellogg's story is not unique. I see lives like his every single day. I see it in myself! Our world is not becoming any more "rest friendly." Multiple responsibilities and endless demands push us hard. And one of the first things to get pushed aside is sleep. If we're honest, most of us must admit we have to force our bodies out of bed when the alarm clock jars us awake each morning. We're worn out.

DID YOU KNOW? YOU CAN WORK YOURSELF TO DEATH

"Karoshi" (pronounced kah-roe-she) is a Japanese word that means "death from overwork." This syndrome of occupational sudden death is now so common in Japan that it claims approximately 30,000 lives each year due to stress-induced heart attacks and strokes.

Writes columnist Boyé Lafayette De Mente in the Asia Pacific Management Forum, "Japan's rise from the devastation of World War II to economic prominence was not without human cost. . . . It was not until the latter part of the 1980s, when several high-ranking business executives who were still in their prime years suddenly died without any previous sign of illness, that the news media began picking up on what appeared to be a new phenomenon."[3]

The symptoms now had a name, and news spread quickly of Japan's new epidemic. With "samurai-like pride," Japanese employees succumb to the psychological pressure and frenzied pace required to keep up with coworkers, outperform competing groups, and increase market shares.

Does any of this sound familiar? This phenomenon is not unique to Japan; Korea, with its Confucian-inspired work ethic, also has many adult

men and women working long hours six days a week. It is called *"gwarosa."*
Corporate America, too, is no stranger to burnout and exhaustion. We cannot
push ourselves twelve and fourteen hours a day, six or seven days a week,
without serious health implications.[4]

MUCH-NEEDED REST

Sleep is the golden chain that ties health and our bodies together.
THOMAS DEKKER

Your body was designed with an inborn refractory period—an
eight-hour period of time where it recovers in order to be prepared
for the work that you need to do the next day. It is called sleep.
Your most complete rest is attained when you sleep. Sleep gives
your nerve cells a chance to shut down and repair themselves.
Without it, these cells may become so depleted in energy that they
begin to malfunction, leaving you drowsy and unable to concentrate the next day. Your memory and physical performance are di-
minished.

When you close your eyes and drift into sleep, your heart beats
more slowly, your blood pressure is lowered, respiratory move-
ments are less frequent, and your muscles become more relaxed.
This prepares your body and brain to be alert and productive, and
readies you for a healthy tomorrow. Adequate sleep enhances
memory, on-the-job performance, and a sense of well-being. Most
importantly, *sleep will help prevent disease.*

At the University of Chicago, researchers restricted the sleep of
eleven young men to four hours a night for six days. The sleep-
deprived men began experiencing metabolic and hormonal changes
that doctors would usually see in patients older than sixty. Eve Van
Cauter, PhD, professor of medicine at the University of Chicago
School of Medicine, discussed these findings at the American Diabetes Association's annual meeting in June 2001. She reported that

people who regularly do not get enough sleep can become less sensitive to insulin, thus increasing their risk for diabetes and high blood pressure—both serious threats to the brain. Previous work by Dr. Van Cauter resulted in findings that prove "metabolic and endocrine changes resulting from a significant sleep debt mimic many of the hallmarks of aging." Says Van Cauter, "We suspect that chronic sleep loss may not only hasten the onset but could also increase the severity of age-related ailments such as diabetes, hypertension, obesity, and memory loss."[5] The conclusion is startling. Just like a poor diet or an inactive lifestyle, insufficient sleep is a significant risk factor for developing disease.

We all learned in elementary school that the human body needs eight hours of sleep *every night* to remain strong and healthy. Most of us *know* this truth, but what we *do* is quite a different story. Because we don't *get* eight hours of sleep a night, we convince ourselves that we don't *need* that many.* Having convinced ourselves that the "eight-hour rule" simply doesn't apply to us, we justify and rationalize and soon believe we can get by on less. While we sleep less, scientific evidence demonstrates that deep slumber, and enough of it, is critical for health and well-being.

DID YOU KNOW? THE INTERNAL CLOCK

Your body has an internal clock—a small group of cells located in your brain is known as the *suprachiasmatic nucleus*. This "clock" is set by the level of light your eye receives, and establishes the natural sleep-wake rhythm for your body. When the sun begins dipping below the horizon, your body naturally begins winding down for the day.

---

*This is a great example of actions creating belief, as discussed in the chapter on Choice.

Slumber and Our Children

Lack of sleep is not just a chronic problem for adults. The situation is equally bad (or worse) for children. While the setting of the internal clock may vary from child to child, children and teenagers generally need at least nine hours of sleep each night. Still, most behavioral studies show that on average, they are getting only seven hours. The result? Poor attention spans, subpar school performance, moodiness or depression. Our children are experiencing the fallout of our poor lifestyle choices. We must teach our children—by modeling—how to rest.

Numerous studies suggest that the longer children sit in front of the television during the day, the less likely they will be to sleep well at night. The evidence is even more alarming for young children with televisions in their bedrooms. These children are more apt to show bedtime resistance, have trouble falling asleep, experience anxiety, and undergo more overall sleep disturbances than children who don't have sets in their rooms.[6]

Teenagers, whose growing bodies need nine to nine and a half hours of nightly rest, are often sleeping less than their parents. They too have an internal rhythm, but during puberty the body's internal clock changes. Teenagers don't get the signal to get sleepy until close to 11 p.m. As a result, they naturally want to wake up about nine hours later at 8 a.m. Therein lies the problem. Many high schools around the country start class before eight o'clock. Some begin as early as seven o'clock. Teachers are being faced with classrooms full of sleepy, underperforming teens in the early-morning hours. Johnny's head is not down on his desk because he's lazy; it's that his body and mind are literally not awake yet.

The key to healthy sleep habits is *routine*. This means doing the same thing, in the same order, and at the same time before going to bed. This is true for both children and adults. I realize this is challenging, especially with the busy lifestyles we've established.

Remember, however, challenging doesn't mean impossible. The changes may not be immediate, but as you establish goals around bedtime and make a concerted effort to achieve them, you'll find a much happier, rested family.

Seven Steps to Better Snoozing

Like many people, I struggle when it comes to getting a good night's sleep. Maybe it's because of my residency training and having to stay awake for hours on end. At times I was so tired I could barely stand up. Yet even then, I couldn't go to sleep if there was a mother delivering a baby. Not only did I have to be awake, I had to be alert. Over time, and to my detriment, I learned to ignore my fatigue. And for years I felt that in order to go to sleep I had to be exhausted. If I'm not exhausted, I must not be ready to go to bed. I'm better now than I used to be. I know I don't have to feel completely worn out to go to bed. But I still struggle from time to time. If you're anything like me, your nightly rest can be improved by following a few steps for better snoozing:

1. *Keep a regular sleep-wake cycle.* You can condition your internal clock by having regular sleep times and wake-up times—even on weekends. By doing so, your body will learn to go to sleep at the appropriate time. Calming nighttime rituals such as taking warm baths, walking the dog, reading an enjoyable book, and sipping caffeine-free hot tea with honey help to reinforce sleep-wake cycles.

2. *Reduce the late-night stimulation coming your way.* It seems like there is always an endless list of tasks to do before going to bed—cleaning up the kitchen, doing homework with the kids, sorting through mail and e-mail, reading the newspaper, sifting through paperwork—and watching favorite TV shows. Try to complete your household tasks early enough in the evening so that you have a two-hour window of relaxation prior to going to bed. This may seem impossible (it certainly has at times in my life!), but

we must come to the point where we acknowledge there will always be things to do. Choose the most important ones and let the others go. We are never "finished." Despite the adage, in the big scheme of things what you don't get done today will not suffer terribly if it doesn't get done until tomorrow. Make your health a priority and let go of some of the "to-dos" around the house and at work. Determine a "cutoff" time and stick to it.

DID YOU KNOW? THE SCOOP ON CAFFEINE

If you need a cup of coffee in the morning just to get going or you find yourself reaching for a cola to make it through the day, chances are you're caffeine dependent. For some people, as little as 100 mg a day (the equivalent of one cup of brewed coffee) can cause a dependency. More than 200 mg and you may experience irritability, irregular heartbeat, and difficulty sleeping. Once you do fall asleep, you may not rest soundly.[7]

Yeah, yeah, I know. For me to even broach this subject is beyond bold on my part. After all, a morning cup of coffee is a part of who we are! But before you toss your empty cups and cans at me, I want you to remember that caffeine is a drug. After a while it'll take more than one cup to give you that same jolt. And once you're hooked, going without even one of those cups during the day can make you feel tired, cranky, headachy, and even depressed.[8]

Problems sleeping? Edgy? Check your caffeine intake. Then make a commitment to gradually cut back. Try decreasing the amount you drink by half a cup a day. The good news is that after the first few days of feeling crummy (maybe even up to a week), you'll actually experience a greater sense of well-being, and you'll be healthier for it.

3. *Take note of your bedroom environment.* In general, our bedroom should be a sanctuary for sleep and intimacy. Performing other activities in your bedroom may confuse your internal clock

into thinking there's more work to be done—not rest to be had. Make sure your bedroom helps you relax. Remember, your body clock responds to visual cues, so this is a good time to declutter your bedroom so you can escape into a soothing environment that invites sleep. Don't hesitate to use relaxing aromas. Your bedroom should be dark when the lights are off as well as the right temperature—somewhere between 65 and 70 degrees Fahrenheit. If you are too hot or too cold you will not sleep well. If possible, crack open the window so fresh air can circulate. Finally, make sure your bed is large enough. When my husband, Stan, and I first got married we slept in a full-size bed—which, despite its name, felt too small for two people. Stan's body is really hot! I got a bigger bed for comfort but kept the passion. Small beds can be wonderful for cuddling, but at some point we all need a little space for a good night's rest.

4. *Take a power nap.* Cornell psychologist Dr. James Maas, author of *Power Sleep*, writes that napping should be considered a part of one's daily exercise routine. That's right. Your body is programmed by your biological clock to experience two periods of sleepiness every twenty-four hours. The primary period for deep sleep is between midnight and 7:00 a.m. The second less intense period of sleepiness is midafternoon between 1:00 and 3:00 p.m. Unlike other more sleep-savvy nations, we in America blaze right through "siesta time." Our culture makes it nearly impossible for an hourlong nap. You can, however, put your head down on your desk, breathe deeply, and close your eyes for ten to fifteen minutes. These power naps will give you the boost you need to get through your afternoon.

5. *Be careful about using sleep aids.* When trying to address problems with poor sleep, it's tempting to go to the local drugstore or on the Internet and purchase a "little helper" to go to sleep. While sleep aids can be helpful during stressful times or for jet lag, prolonged use of them (longer than two weeks) can foster psychological dependence.

6. *Check for sleep apnea if your partner snores.* If your mate has a significant snoring problem, particularly if he or she periodically stops breathing or gasps for breath, an evaluation should be made for sleep apnea. Most common in men over age forty, sleep apnea affects over 12 million Americans and can be serious. It is characterized by excessive daytime sleepiness/fatigue or falling asleep when you don't intend to, and unrefreshing sleep with feelings of grogginess, dullness, and morning headaches. Sleep apnea requires an evaluation by a physician and can be successfully treated.

7. *If problems getting to sleep and staying asleep persist, see your doctor.* We can all experience a touch of insomnia from time to time. If sleep problems persist after you make the significant changes suggested above, it's time to see a doctor. Once lifestyle challenges are addressed, persistent problems with insomnia can be signals of a primary sleep disorder or an underlying medical condition.

BEYOND SLEEP— OTHER COMPONENTS OF REST

Take rest; a field that has rested gives a beautiful crop.
OVID

While sleep is absolutely essential, it is only a portion of our need for repose. Our mental, spiritual, and social lives also require *rest*. What sleep does for the body, reprieve and quiet reflection offer the spirit. Earlier I discussed how at the "heart of life" we find a steady rhythm bringing first an episode of work, followed by a period of reprieve and a time of refilling. Just like the heart, if we keep too rapid a pace, we cannot relax long enough to be refilled. While there are clearly benefits to the technological advancements we enjoy, they come with distinct tradeoffs, and increasingly we must seek time to refresh and renew our spirits.

Physical rest allows you to relate to your surroundings and your world, but refilling your spirit gives you the ability to connect with yourself and others in meaningful ways. The health of your spirit determines your outlook, passions, and thoughts. It's important to your health and well-being that you have both.

Daily Rest—Simplify

There is something to be said about slowing down and learning to do just one thing at a time. It takes conscious effort if you've grown accustomed to a life of multitasking. Try eating your food without doing anything else. You're more likely to appreciate the colors, smells, and taste of your food when you're not distracted by other things.

Great rewards can also come in relationships when you just focus on that one phone call and really choose to hear what's being said or what's being shared. Keeping your days as simple as possible is a choice you can make regardless of where you live and what your vocation might be.

Weekly Rest—Our Need for Sabbath

Science wasn't the first to discover the need for a cycle of rest. In fact, rest is part of a plan that goes back to the very beginning of human history. In the Genesis account of Creation, God formed the world and its inhabitants in six days, and on the seventh day—Sabbath—God rested.[9] I don't imagine the Creator of the Universe was in need of a nap. Rather, with great care, God was setting up a model for his creation—instituting a rhythm of spiritual rest into our weekly cycle. This cycle created for us from the very beginning of time is as much a part of our nature as the rhythm of our hearts: beat—rest, beat—rest. God was creating a sanctuary of rest at the end of each week for our whole-person restoration. Our Creator knew we would need it.

Remember that thing called "the weekend"? The week's end was meant to be a two-day period designed to enable us to release the mental load of the workweek and reconnect with those relationships we value most—our families, our friends, ourselves, our God. Unfortunately, this is not what weekends have evolved into for most households. In fact, they resemble almost any other day of the week when it comes to stress levels. Our busy, jam-packed weekdays flow right into the weekend like a creek into a swift river, and we find ourselves paddling just as hard on Saturday and Sunday as we did Monday through Friday.

We were not designed to live this way. Says Wayne Mueller, well-known author on the topic of Sabbath:

> [Celebrating] the Sabbath is more than the absence of work; it is not just a day off to catch up on television or errands. It is the presence of something that arises when we consecrate a period of time to listen to what is most deeply beautiful, nourishing or true. It is time consecrated with our attention, our mindfulness, honoring those quiet forces of grace or spirit that sustain and heal us. . . . During the Sabbath, we set aside a sanctuary in time, disconnect from the frenzy of consumption and accomplishment, and consecrate our day as an offering for healing all beings.[10]

I have come to appreciate Mueller's words in ways beyond description. I truly experienced Sabbath rest in med school. My weeks were filled with endless eighteen-hour days of classes and studying. But I committed to "keeping" Sabbath, and when it arrived at the end of each week, I breathed a full-body sigh of relief.

The Sabbath reminded me that I was still human, that my life and its purpose were bigger than anatomy lab, library, and my class rank. It was the day my prayers of desperation ("Dear God, if you would just guide my pencil to the right answer on this neuroanatomy test . . .") became prayers of dedication focused on the meaning and purpose of my chosen profession. During Sabbath hours I could be still and know that there was a purpose to my life and the way I was living it.

Medical school is decades behind me now, but in many respects my life feels no less challenging. My twelve- and sometimes fourteen-hour workdays are followed by homework with the kids, music, sports, bills, laundry, and grocery shopping. But on the Sabbath, with much gratitude, I put all that aside: no bills, no mall crawling, no homework, no television, no business. Sabbath is God and family time. We slow down to the natural speed of life, we worship, enjoy the outdoors, meet with friends, take naps, and commune with God. Sabbath is truly a time of refilling. Sabbath makes the other days of my week doable. Perhaps Wayne Mueller describes it best: "Like a path through the forest, Sabbath creates a marker for ourselves so, if we are lost, we can find our way back to our center. 'Remember the Sabbath' means remember that everything you received is a blessing. Remember to delight in your life, in the fruits of your labor. Remember to stop and offer thanks for the wonder of it."[11]

I can't encourage you strongly enough to be intentional about how you and your family will transform Sabbath into a day of spiritual rest and refilling. You have poured out all week long. Now it is time to be refilled. Gift yourself and those you love with the rhythm of rest your bodies so need. Visit a house of worship, go for a walk in the park, curl up with an inspirational book that you've been meaning to read far too long, invite a friend over for a good chat, or watch the sun set from a nearby hill. Make your rest day distinctly different from the other six days of the week. Make it a refuge of rest *and replenishment* for your spirit. Slow down and listen to your life. When you allow yourself to be refreshed on a weekly basis, only then does your picture of life come back into perspective, and you will discover how rich you are in the many graces given you.

Yearly Rest—The Beauty of Stress-free Vacations

Another overlooked area of rest is vacations. Trends show that families and couples are taking shorter and shorter vacations and calling them "long weekends." Our need for a break from the routine goes beyond three days of amusement parks and shopping. It is vitally important to have restful, not stressful, vacations to replenish our souls.

Vacations should be viewed as periods of *re-creation*—a time to recover from the stress of work. They need to be a time of reprieve, a time to laugh, play, lounge, consider new ideas, and dream a little. We need to vacation for our health.

SCIENCE SAYS: VACATIONS COUNT

One of the most notable long-term scientific studies in the medical world is the Framingham study, which has focused on a large group of men and women since 1965. At the beginning of the study, all of the women (ages 45–64) were free of coronary artery disease. The study followed this group of women for twenty years and discovered that among employed *and* homemaking women, *a lack of vacations was predictive of an increased incidence of heart disease.*[12]

In a different nine-year study performed at the University of Pittsburgh, 12,000 men at high risk for heart disease were asked about the vacations they had taken in the previous twelve months. Those with regular annual vacations demonstrated a lower risk of death than those who skipped vacations.[13]

We need to take extended time off. Our bodies not only demand it, our spirits do too. We will live longer, healthier lives if we do. This should come as welcome news. Don't feel guilty about taking time away from the job. Commit to taking a true vacation at least annually and schedule the time aside in advance. Resist the urge to plan activity-filled vacations, which have you on the go from sunup to long past sundown. Unfortunately, most people come home more tired from their vacations than they were before they left! Your vacations should be a time to "do" less and "be" more.

Beyond Vacation—Personal Retreats

While vacations offer much-needed time to play and reconnect with our families and friends, our spirits need times of quiet rest in solitude. Solitude offers the deepest, most fulfilling, life-enhancing, rejuvenating rest. When life starts feeling fragmented and strained, our body's dashboard lights up, signaling a need to center and re-align our priorities, hopes, and aspirations. This is a sure indicator that we need a time of personal refilling. These moments are central to a life of energy.

You can be sure that a night away for yourself will never happen without intentional planning. I realize many people wouldn't know what to do on a personal retreat. If you have never indulged in a personal retreat, don't feel remiss. I had you in mind while crafting just the getaway you need. Together we will explore the possibilities and help you to plan a deeply gratifying time away with the Three-Day Rejuvenation Therapy (see chapter 11).

PUTTING IT ALL TOGETHER

Science confirms what our Maker modeled for us in the Creation story: sleep and rest are imperative for our physical, mental, and spiritual well-being. Night hours and weekends are not merely extra hours to make up for time lost during the day. If the sun was set in its path to religiously dip below the horizon every twelve hours as well as giving our bodies a built-in signal to begin slowing and readying for rest at day's end, we were meant to rest. If the earth was cloaked in darkness, fitting our sleep patterns to be most deeply gratifying before the break of day, should we not heed this blueprint for our lives?

Choose now to be more fully rested. Start by focusing on the 3 M's.

Maximize

Snooze more! Make weekly increases in the amount of sleep you get each night until you're regularly sleeping eight hours a night. Enjoy the luxury of weekend naps.

Moderate

Watch your multitasking. Focus on doing one thing at a time and enjoy the time you spend doing it! Decrease your weekend to-do lists and keep your Sabbath time sacred.

Minimize

Be careful of excessive work hours. Determine the time you'll go home at the beginning of the day and stick to it! Don't short-change yourself—make sure you take at least one weeklong vacation annually.

Heather's Breakthrough Story
The Many Forms of Rest

As a busy wife and full-time physical therapist, Heather needed plenty of energy. What she felt instead was the almost constant drain of fatigue. It wasn't just that she was a newlywed; the real problem was that she felt completely exhausted after arriving home from work every day. Though her job was physically demanding, she felt a prevailing sense of tiredness that seemed to go beyond just physical exertion.

After trying everything from iron pills to jogging drills she discovered the root cause of the problem. "When my husband and I got married we started going to bed pretty late, usually about 11:00 or 11:30 p.m. Then I'd roll out of bed at six o'clock in the morning and still feel tired. I always thought I could get by on only six or seven hours of sleep. But now I know better; I need to get a full eight hours. If I don't, I simply can't perform at my best. Plus I'm not as much fun to be around."

To ensure she was getting enough sleep, Heather gradually began going to bed earlier and earlier. After about six months she was going to bed by 9:30 every night. As her husband saw the changes taking place in her disposition, he started to ask questions.

"My husband began to notice how different I was when I got a full eight hours of sleep. I told him my body needed that much rest and when I got it I felt so much better. He agreed and decided to do the same. So now we go to bed together at nine o'clock every night. Eight hours later I'm up at five o'clock ready to start the day with some exercise. For me it's just easier to exercise in the morning than at the end of the day when I come home from work feeling unmotivated."

But Heather's adventure in finding rest goes far beyond sleep. After she and her husband realized that the hectic pace of their life was causing frustrations at home, they made the decision for Heather to cut one day a week from her job to create more space for her to focus on other activities.

She believes the change in focus from job to home provides her with a new set of benefits. "I relax but I spend a lot of time doing things that I enjoy—working on home projects that bring me satisfaction. I put on some fun music and go to work around the house. And the best part is taking this day off to work around the house has helped my husband and me to grow closer. Now we have more time together in the evenings when we don't have to worry about doing all the household chores after coming back from work."

Heather's greatest time for rest and refreshment comes every weekend. "My husband and I have a day of rest that I couldn't live without. We go to church, spend time with friends, go out for a picnic or ride bikes around our lake. Having a day of rest is very important to me because it takes me away from all the worries of the week and all the responsibilities that I tend to fret about endlessly."

Does Heather see herself and her needs as unique? "Not really. I think everyone can benefit from getting more rest. Once you plan it into your life on a regular basis, it becomes addicting. I think it's one of the best miracle cures there is."

"E" is for Environment

5

Whether it's the majestic backdrop of the Rocky Mountains, beach sand squishing between your toes, or the heady fragrance of candles around your bathtub, environment sets the stage for healing of the human soul. Tailor-made for life-giving reprieve, a healthy environment brings refreshment and rejuvenation.

IN THIS CHAPTER YOU WILL:

* Discover how to beat stress by tapping into the healing power of nature.

* Find out which wonder vitamin can't be purchased but is essential to your good health.

* Learn six things you can do to reenergize your environment at home or work.

"E" is for Environment

How glorious a greeting the sun gives to the mountains!

JOHN MUIR

Let your mind wander to your favorite natural getaway. What images come to mind? Perhaps you love watching the dawn come up over the horizon or taking in the vibrant hues of a summer sunset. How about the reds, yellows, and oranges of the autumn trees? Maybe your favorite getaway is to escape to an open meadow bursting with lavender or to walk through the forest letting its pungent aromas or sights and sounds quicken your senses. For me it's going to the ocean, tasting the salty air and letting the sun warm my skin as I listen to the waves roll in.

Whether we are drawn to mountains, valleys, or the beach there is a calm and sense of awe we experience in nature that can't be found anywhere else. When we feel life spiraling out of control or moving too fast, most of us crave a quiet place in nature because we know when we get there we'll feel a sense of relief. Nature affords us a place of reprieve—but more than that, nature brings *rejuvenation*. We come away rested.

Have you ever wondered what it is about a landscape or most any natural setting that is so healing to the human soul? While lying out on the cool grass and watching the stars fill the night sky, has it ever crossed your mind that this is the very environment in which you were intended to regroup and find health?

A CLOSER LOOK AT GARDEN LIVING

Nature is the art of God.
SIR THOMAS BROWNE

When God created the first human family, he could have built them a luxurious condo, or made them a sprawling mansion. He didn't. God purposefully placed them in a garden. The Creator chose nature as the ideal environment for man and woman to reside. Why?

As the beauty of nature fills our senses daily, just imagine the surroundings of the first man and woman: pristine beauty, flora and fauna of every different species, a full spectrum of colors, textures, oceans, and magnificent skyscapes. The Garden of Eden was alive with the music of birdsong and trumpeting of beasts underpinned with music of wind and waterfalls.

Imagine the rich array of natural fragrances riding on the afternoon breezes of Paradise . . . fresh, unpolluted air infused with the scent of apple blossoms, honeysuckle, lemon zest, herbs, spices, and the earthy smell of soil. The Garden of Eden must have offered rich, exotic aromatherapy.

And the food! Eden's culinary delights featured classic dishes made of local organic ingredients: fresh veggies and fruits served on crusts of whole grains, seeds, or nuts, seasoned with delectable herb-infused oils and spices. The drink list must have included fresh-squeezed cocktails made with the choicest fruit and sparkling mountain spring water.

Sunlight warmed the first man and woman as they awakened on beds of velvet moss in the intimate embrace of one another. Each new day promised tactile discoveries in their natural spa-like environment as they fingered vegetation and stroked the fur and feathers of exotic animals and birds. After a day's work, Adam and Eve may have soaked in natural hot springs, showered under waterfalls, or bodysurfed in the waves on a beach nearby. Theirs was a reality ripe with stimulating touch.

A quiet hush settled over all creation as night fell, bringing the first couple's days to a close. Entwined in each other's embrace they slept soundly under the moon and stars to the sounds of bubbling brooks and whispering pines.

In Contrast: Our World

Contrast Eden with our more urban world and one word comes immediately to mind—concrete, and tons of it. Many of us live in cities that are full of congestion, traffic, crowding, and noise; our senses are constantly being bombarded by artificial sights and sounds. With the advance of society, we have increasingly surrounded ourselves with nonliving things. Over time, we've traded the sights and sounds of the Garden for the sights and sounds of industry and technology. By advancing, we've traded green for gray.

The environment we've created has been compromised by all the things we have come to associate with progress and prosperity. As a result, we live the majority of our lives with unnatural sights and sounds that drive out the beauty and natural wonders of a world that was designed for healing.

"I don't even notice it," you may say. It's true; we've learned to acclimate to our environments. Much like a newborn who falls asleep in a loud room, we have defense mechanisms to help protect us from sensory overload. But this doesn't mean it's healthy for us. This "disconnect mechanism" may help us to survive, but unless we consciously choose to reconnect with what is healthy and good, our health and well-being will suffer.

THE HEALING POWER OF NATURE

Flowers seem intended for the solace
of ordinary humanity.
JOHN RUSKIN

Biophilia, "the love of all living things," is an emerging area of scientific research established by Harvard biology professor Edward O. Wilson. Dr. Wilson believes that people have an innate need to connect with nature, which he views as an integral element of our genetic makeup.[1] While the connection between man and nature may not yet be proven scientifically, plenty of evidence abounds supporting nature as good medicine.

Roger S. Ulrich, PhD, has conducted extensive research on the effects of natural environments on human well-being. In his landmark study he found that patients recovering from gallbladder surgery who looked out at a view of trees had significantly shorter hospital stays, fewer complaints, and required less pain medication than those who only had a view of a brick wall.[2] More recent studies also show significant reduction in blood pressure, pulse rate, and respiration, in addition to enhanced well-being.[3] The health benefits of nature are so compelling that many hospitals are now restructuring their landscapes to incorporate "healing gardens" or are initiating horticultural therapy for patients who are recovering from stroke or trauma. Florida Hospital, where I have worked and practiced medicine for many years, has done considerable work on creating healing environments for patients and staff. Many other hospitals are following suit.

One of the reasons nature may be so effective in reducing stress is that it puts the mind in a state similar to meditation, according to Clare Cooper Marcus, MA, MCP, professor emerita at the University of California at Berkeley. "When you are looking intently at something, or you bend down to smell it, you bypass the [analytical] function of the mind. You naturally stop thinking, obsessing, and worrying. Your senses are awakened, which brings you into the present moment, and this has been shown to be very effective at reducing stress."[4]

CREATING YOUR OWN EDEN

I give to you forever this land. I give you the woods, the fruits, the rivers.
I give you the stars . . . I give you Myself.
C. S. Lewis, THE MAGICIAN'S NEPHEW

Life's Essentials: The Great Outdoors

Nature has a wonderful effect on our psyche, but what we receive from spending time outdoors is far greater than feelings of well-being. We frequently take our need for fresh air, sunlight, and water for granted. Much like the houseplants that receive our care, we need to make sure that our quantity and quality of these elements is adequate to nourish and sustain our lives. Let's take a closer look at some of these elements.

Fresh Air

Air is the most essential element to life. Our bodies need oxygen for nourishment and energy, and obviously, not all air is created equal (especially when you can see it!) and too few of us are getting the good stuff. Do you ever take time to consider your air? There is simply no substitute for pure air, which creates a serious conundrum for many of us. The air we breathe today may actually contain thousands of chemical and biological substances, otherwise known as pollutants and toxins.

Fresh air is chemically different than the recirculated indoor air that most people breathe in airports, offices, and in closed, poorly ventilated areas. Where do you find your best air? The air found around lakes, in forests, near rivers and waterfalls, at the seashore, and after a rainstorm is typically the cleanest and most refreshing.

We are most familiar with the dangers of air pollutants primarily associated with *outdoor activities*, especially when our eyes burn, or we cough or experience chest tightness. The effects of air pollution can go beyond minor to significant. Prolonged exposure to toxic air pollutants can damage our immune system, and can cause neurological, developmental, respiratory, and other health problems. It's important to be mindful of the quality of outside air and to consciously protect yourself from toxic areas.

But don't just focus on outdoor air. You also need to take inventory of the air quality *indoors*, where you spend more than 90 percent of your time. Research from the National Aeronautics and Space Administration (NASA) found measurable data supporting the fact that the air we breathe inside our homes, offices, and malls is filled with pollutants that may cause many unpleasant symptoms including headaches, dizziness, fatigue, and respiratory irritation.[5] The good news is that we can purify this polluted indoor air inexpensively and with attractive natural methods!

Plants, Our Natural Purifiers

Did you know that common indoor plants can cleanse the air dramatically by reducing toxic chemical levels? Living plants and trees recycle the bad air with fresh oxygenated air. Simply placing live plants throughout your home and office can significantly reduce toxic chemical levels in the air you breathe.

The best news is that some of the most efficient plants for fighting air pollution are easy to grow: weeping figs, bamboo palms, dracaenas, and corn plants are good choices for large treelike plants. Peace lilies, philodendrons, pothos, bromeliads, spider plants, and aglaonemas are ideal smaller plants for purifying your air.[6] Most of these are available at your local plant nursery, garden center, or on the Internet for delivery.

In addition to purifying air, plants also increase our sense of well-being. They relax our bodies, calm our senses, and revive our spirits. Studies show that people surrounded by plants demonstrate more positive emotions such as happiness, friendliness, and assertiveness and display less sadness, fear, and stress.[7]

Clean air is an essential we cannot afford to ignore. By focusing on minimizing pollutants in your environment and increasing your fresh air intake, you'll be amazed at how your body responds. Remember that cracking a window at bedtime is an easy way to increase fresh air in your life and improve your sleep. Fresh air will bring lasting health and daily rejuvenation to every cell in your body.

Sunlight

Not only are we coming up short on fresh air, we don't do well with sunlight either. Americans on average spend at least twenty-three out of twenty-four hours in the absence of sunlight. These statistics are not hard to believe when we take a closer look at our workweek. Many of us get up in the dark to prepare for work. We step from the kitchen to the garage, get inside our car or walk to a public transit station at the break of day. Upon driving to work and arriving at our job, we park our cars in a parking garage. We then enter the building and spend at least eight to ten hours there (for many it's becoming twelve hours). We go back into that garage at night to get our car, drive home after the sun has set, put our car in the garage, and step back into the house.

SCIENCE SAYS

Recent studies indicate that the U.S. workweek is now the longest in the world.[8] How many hours per week do you work on average? _____

Regardless of whether this example describes your typical workday, the fact remains that most of us spend too much time indoors. If you don't take advantage of one hour of sunlight at lunchtime, you may be out of luck! But as is the case for many of us, we're "too busy" even to treat our bodies to the outdoors at lunch. We either scarf down a packaged lunch at our desks or we don't eat at all. If they don't make an intentional effort, thousands of Americans can go days with little or no contact with natural air or sunlight.

With all the attention given to sun protection, we may have gone overboard with our fear of the sun. While it is true that you should never lie out in the sun to "bake," you do need its life-giving nutrients. By naturally spending twenty to thirty minutes in the sun each day you can reap distinct health benefits as well as decrease your risk for certain diseases.

On the flip side, the damage caused by staying too long in intense sunlight is associated with an increased risk of skin cancer. However, *safe* sun exposure has been shown to help alleviate a host of problems ranging from chronic skin conditions such as acne, eczema, and psoriasis to helping build strong bones and teeth—even lowering cholesterol levels, helping to prevent heart disease, and warding off depression.

Better yet, according to some health experts, sunshine may *prevent* cancer. Although the implications are still somewhat unclear, *Preventive Medicine* states that modest sun exposure has been associated with a decreased risk for colon and breast cancer in the United States.[9] This protective effect, which is believed to be linked to vitamin D, has been shown in laboratory tests to inhibit cancer cell growth. One of the distinct health benefits of sunlight—mainly through UVB exposure—is directly linked to its role in increasing production of vitamin D.[10]

THE WONDER VITAMIN[11]

Vitamin D can't be purchased and only a fraction of the vitamin D we need can be supplied by our diet. Where do we get the majority of our vitamin D? The sun. Adequate levels of vitamin D are maintained with adequate levels of sunlight.

Bones/teeth: Vitamin D is important in maintaining an adequate supply of calcium, on which our body depends to maintain healthy bones and teeth.

Immune system: Vitamin D is important for keeping a healthy immune system. Studies show that when the body is exposed to sunlight, the number of white blood cells increases. These cells are important in fighting infection and disease.

Mental health: Vitamin D also plays a role in increasing the amount of oxygen your blood can transport around the body, which in turn will boost your energy levels, sharpen your mental faculties, and give you an improved feeling of well-being.

Water

Whether it be as grand as the Atlantic or as trivial as a puddle after the rain, we can't stay out of water. Nothing is so beautiful as pure, crystal-like droplets of moisture. In fact, water appeals to each of our five senses. Visually we are drawn to its serene and mesmerizing beauty. What is more soothing than hearing raindrops splashing on a windowpane, the pulse of fountains in a city park, or waves crashing against the sand? To the touch, water not only cleanses and brings hours of recreation, it soothes and heals when we bathe, and invigorates us when we shower. We sleep better, work better, and feel better after spending time in the water. And nothing is more refreshing than a cool drink of fresh water or the scent of a rainstorm.

The use of water as therapy to maintain and promote health as well as to treat disease is centuries old. Today, hydrotherapy is used to relieve patients who have suffered extensive burns, whirlpools are used to relieve painful muscle and joint conditions, and underwater exercise has proved a useful physical therapy in cases of paralysis and stiffness of the extremities. And of course we cannot forget Grandma's remedy of reducing fever with the effective use of a cold sponge bath.

Water is pleasurable, healing, and essential for life. Over 50 percent of the body is composed of water (about half of your body weight), therefore keeping it hydrated is vital for optimal functioning. In general, eight glasses of water a day will result in improved energy and overall performance. Appropriate water intake can also help keep your skin healthy and assist in weight loss. For more on your body's need for hydration and tips for drinking water, read chapter 10, "'N' is for Nutrition."

Attaining your life essentials—air, sunlight, and water (in the highest quality you can)—is the first step to take toward creating your own Garden of Eden experience. Even slight improvements across a lifetime will bring significant results. However, it doesn't stop there.

BENEFITS OF GARDEN LIVING

The greatest gift of the garden is the
restoration of the five senses.
HANNA RION

As a physician I can't help but notice how patients' peace and well-being are heavily influenced by their surroundings. Fortunately, there are many ways you can create your own personal paradise. Focusing on each of your five senses, you can begin to craft a more healthful, Eden-like environment.

What Do You See?

Studies show that viewing certain scenes of nature or gardens can reduce stress within five minutes and increase your overall well-being. What can you do to bring soothing objects or scenes into your sight? If you can't bring nature in, you can certainly allow images of nature to inspire you. Screen savers, or pictures of the outdoors and wildlife that hold particular appeal to you, can be placed in your line of sight. Enjoy open spaces and skyscapes whenever possible. And of course, keep as many plants near you as you possibly can.

The use of color is a wonderful way to either reflect or change your mood. Did you know that the association of mood with color is a distinctly human phenomenon? It's been said that we don't see color, we *feel* it. Take the time to see how different colors affect you. In general, reds, yellows, and oranges are active colors that make us feel warm and energetic. Cool, neutral colors—blues, greens, and taupes—pacify us and elicit tranquillity and minimize stress. Take a look around you and see how you can use color to enhance your environment.

What Do You Hear?

Machines, beepers, buzzers, cell phones, televisions, automobiles—*noises*—often fill our day. The almost constant drone of these manmade sounds stands in sharp contrast to the serenity of nature's music. After considering which sounds would have been most dominant in the Garden of Eden, you can pick and choose some of your favorites and bring these calming sounds into your day. For a noisy area, you can start with a white noise generator and add other gentle sounds such as rainfall, birds singing, or ocean waves on CD. Soft, peaceful music with natural sounds is also available. Be creative.

The soft gurgle of an aquarium has a noticeable calming effect and is often chosen for doctor's offices as a highly effective means of alleviating stress and lowering blood pressure even in difficult situations such as dental surgery. Research indicates that aquariums lower blood pressure in both hypertensive and normal people. Sounds of nature are especially important when you feel stressed. Tabletop water fountains are also readily available today in a variety of sizes, shapes, and price ranges. Take advantage of the calming sound of flowing water in a place where you spend a good deal of time.

What Do You Smell?

One of the most overlooked pleasures in your day may be your olfactory sense. Smell is your most powerful sense—ten thousand times more sensitive than any of your other senses—and is said to be the longest-lasting sense for memory recall. Did you know that a room's scent can impact your work, learning speed, and productivity? "In 1995, a study at the Smell and Taste Treatment and Research Foundation showed that aromatic essences—especially floral scents—increased learning speed by 17 percent. Similarly, office workers worked more efficiently in offices filled with fragrant flowers than in odorless environments."[12]

Smell is a powerful trigger to the human nervous system, producing almost immediate results. Scientific studies have shown that chamomile can put people in a better mood and lavender can help with temporary insomnia by encouraging relaxation. Jasmine heightens alertness. Rosemary is known to be stimulating, and the fragrant ylang-ylang provides a noteworthy soothing effect. Aromatherapy can be introduced as an integral aspect of your healthy lifestyle, allowing for pleasure and relaxation. How can you incorporate aromatherapy into your day? Refer to the boxes on pages 87–88 for a list of natural fragrances and aromatherapy ideas to bring sensory pleasure into your environment.

RELAXING FRAGRANCES

Chamomile—The world's best-loved herb, with its fine leathery leaves and daisylike flowers, produces a subtle apple fragrance.

Lavender—One of the most famous of all herbs for the fragrance of its dried flowers, it is used often in sachets and perfumes.

Cedarwood—The red cedarwood gets its name from the beautiful, fragrant heartwood. It is used to make aromatic chests, cabinets, and other great-smelling products.

Rose—Perhaps no flower is more recognizable and no aroma more evocative than that of the rose. Its rich fragrance has perfumed human history for generations.

Basil—Its leaves produce a warm, sweet, mildly pungent essence, mildly reminiscent of anise.

Bay—An evergreen tree that produces leaves with a spicy scent. The fragrance is released by rubbing its leaves.

Cinnamon—A spice with a distinctive hot, peppery aroma. Its warm, spicy essence is often used in perfumery.

Jasmine—Its delicate white flowers produce a honey-sweet floral bouquet with fruity undertones. It is one of the most important and expensive extracts in use.

Patchouli—A tropical herb with a distinctive woody, sweet-spicy balsamic fragrance.

Sandalwood—An evergreen with a rich, warm, woody essence, often used in expensive perfumes.

STIMULATING FRAGRANCES

Eucalyptus—The silvery, blue-green leaves produce a cool, camphorous, highly potent essence. One of the most versatile scents in aromatherapy.

Lemongrass—A tall-stemmed, grasslike tropical plant with a refreshing, lemony scent.

Sage—A shrublike herb with wrinkled leaves and a strong, spicy fragrance with a hint of camphor.

Orange—A common citrus with an energizing yet soothingly familiar aroma.

Rosemary—A hardy evergreen shrub with narrow leaves that have a leather-like feel and a spicy, resinous fragrance.

Pine—Prized for its beautiful bluish-green needles and known for its sweet, refreshing aroma.

Peppermint—An herb with short, broad leaves and a distinctive sweet menthol aroma.

Tea Tree—A native tree of Australia with aromatic, essential-oil-containing leaves. It has an underlying intensely warm, nutmeglike scent.

Thyme—A low-growing, wiry-stemmed perennial with lilac flowers and very aromatic leaves. Produces an enjoyably stimulating aroma.

Adapted from Carol McGilvery, Jimi Reed, and Mira Mehta, *The Encyclopedia of Aromatherapy Massage and Yoga,* © Anness Publishing Limited (London: Hermes House, 2001).

What Do You Taste?

The flavor of a food is distinguished not only by its smell but also by its taste and texture. Have you ever tried holding your nose while eating a piece of chocolate? You aren't readily able to identify the chocolate flavor. That being said, the interplay between our sense of smell, texture, and whether a food is salty, bitter, sweet, or sour is important to our overall satisfaction when we eat.

Natural foods, particularly fruits and vegetables, have distinct and (mostly) enjoyable flavors. Before you dip, batter, butter, deep fry, sauce, and salt your food, take the time to really taste it! Experiment with various herbs and spices (buy fresh when you can) and see how you enjoy it.

For more on taste and nutrition see chapter 10.

What Do You Touch?

Is your sense of touch in a rut? One of the best places to start is with your clothing. The first inhabitants of Eden had the liberty of being naked . . . and we don't so much, but you can certainly make your clothing more comfortable. Is your wardrobe filled with constrictive, synthetic fabrics? When you undress, do you find creases or red imprints on your skin from tight elastic bands? We often turn to synthetic fabrics for their low cost and ease of care, but as your budget allows, make time for comfortable clothing of cotton and natural fibers. Clothing is where your environment touches you directly—all day long.

Awaken to all the lovely things to feel in your world: the sun, air, water, the bark of a tree, fallen leaves. Pet your cat, stroke a flower petal or your grandmother's face; splash in a puddle, skip barefoot in the grass, let mud squish between your toes. Get naked and rediscover your skin's keen sensory abilities. Doctor's orders!

Learn more about the importance of human touch in chapter 8, " 'I' is for Interpersonal Relationships."

CARETAKER OF YOUR
ENVIRONMENT

We get so caught up in the everyday things,
that we forget the simple beauties God has given us.
CATHY JARRELL

You may not be able to change the physical landscape, the conditions of your employment, or the city in which you live, but most of us have three personal spaces where we can create a breakthrough and bring rest and rejuvenation. These are the personal spaces where we spend the biggest chunks of our day: our work space, our traveling space (vehicle or public transit), and our home space.

Eden at Work

Though you may have little or no control of your workplace, you can take ownership of your personal space. I recently heard a story about a tollbooth clerk who was constantly singing and dancing while collecting fares from commuters. Though working in a constrictive box no larger than a few square feet in area, the young man never forgot who he was, a gifted performer . . . who just happened to work in a tollbooth. The number one thing you can always do to improve your environment is to improve your attitude. (See chapter 9, " 'O' is for Outlook," for more information.)

Along with attitude, there are some other simple things you can do. Think of your five senses and then set out to give yourself an environmental gift for each:

* a plant
* screen saver with restful images
* pictures of nature or your family
* music
* a comfortable chair or shoes
* a pleasant aroma

If your workplace is mobile or you labor out on a job site, you may need to consider other options such as putting a photo in your pocket or lunchbox. No matter where you work, taking short breaks to find a moment of calm or peace amid the fast pace is essential. Be sure to get outside for at least some portion of the sunlit day. If it's not practical at lunchtime; take a five- to ten-minute break outside. If you work in a loud or toxic environment, protecting your personal space is even more important. Make your break a time of calm, restful reprieve.

Eden in Transit

We spend a remarkable percentage of our time in transit. Looking at people on a subway or sitting on the freeways, we can see that many are not capitalizing on their commute time. (You do see a lot of cell phones attached to people's heads. Hopefully this means relationships are being built.) Business leaders encourage us to learn a language or take a course during commute time. These are wonderful recommendations, unless you are not taking any downtime for rest. Since there was no technology that we know of in the Garden of Eden, I want to challenge you to free yourself from cramming more into your day and take the opportunity to consider the beauty of your surroundings or favorite getaways during your commute.

Being intentional is the key to creating a Garden-like atmosphere in your personal commute space. Experiencing your natural environment as you travel to and from your home and during weekend activities becomes increasingly important in your ability to maintain a sense of well-being. Take inventory of your five senses as well as your posture. If you are not driving in a smog-laden atmosphere and the weather is pleasant, open a window. Look for the glory in the sunset and the beauty of the landscape and in the passing trees. Consider changing your route to include a lake or park if there is one nearby.

If you must listen to something, make it soothing. Build in variety. Give yourself one day of silent reflection while en route. Another day, choose relaxing instrumental music. On an alternate day choose something lively to listen to that puts you in a great mood. Slow the pace and be intentional about building in margins of time. While rewarding yourself with the gift of a peaceful commute, go the extra mile and enjoy a clean, clutter-free car!

Eden at Home

"A home filled with warmth, companionship, and serene comforts feeds the senses and nourishes the soul," writes Tracey McBride in her book *Frugal Luxuries.*[13] Whether you own your residence or live in a portion of a room temporarily, there is much you can do to create Eden at home. So often we forget that our dwelling place is to be a refuge of rest and safety, not merely our second or third workplace. Have you ever asked yourself why so many people like hanging out at coffee shops? Pay attention to the elements of their decorating style and atmosphere and duplicate it in your home—especially if you find the style inviting. See what you can do to capture the restful ambience. How about soft lighting or a set of wind chimes? Open some curtains for more natural light or create a cozy corner with a comfortable chair and a table that doesn't need a coaster. Other ideas include:

* Display books and heirlooms you cherish.
* Research which moods certain colors create.
* Decorate with colors and fabrics you enjoy.
* Be mindful of the seasons and lighting.

Adopt a Pet

Companion animals have been shown in many research studies to reduce stress and improve health. Besides the companionship and affection pets bring, they are also a reminder of nature. If it's possible for you to have a pet, you will find many benefits from finding the right companion for you.

Research at the State University of New York and at Purdue shows that pets can help lower blood pressure. Alan Beck, ScD, professor at Purdue University, has shown "that the simple act of petting your dog slows your heart rate and causes your blood pressure to drop."[14]

Adopting a pet may or may not be an option, but in any case, notice the outdoor animal world. Watching animals outdoors is a soothing distraction. If possible, consider placing bird feeders in sight of your windows. Otherwise, start to notice animal activity in the early morning and around dusk. You'll be surprised at how entertaining squirrels, rabbits, and other creatures can be. And if you live in a city, check out the local zoo or parks.

Try Gardening

Talk to anyone who gardens and they'll tell you that time spent digging, planting, and watering brings a whole new level of refreshment from the earth that is only found while crouched down on one knee with a handful of soil. It's an opportunity to pause and reflect, to organize the thoughts and wisdom we have gathered throughout the day, or to just interact with "earth."

No time or interest for gardening on a large scale? Try cultivating a little herb garden on your windowsill. Herbs make beautiful, fragrant gifts, and add delicious flavors to your menu. Many garden shops and flower shops have easy-to-grow herb boxes and starter kits you can purchase and enjoy.

A Sense of Order

The intricate workings of nature's intelligent design aren't, at first, obvious to the unlearned eye, so God intentionally prepared a mini-ecosystem for the first man and woman wherein they could learn about the earth as a whole and how to be good stewards of all creation. The Creator's choice of a garden atmosphere rather than an expansive wilderness for earth's first inhabitants hints at a subtle yet profound message—God intended a sense of order for us too. In our personal spaces, he meant for us to live free of chaos.

What does this mean for us?

Perhaps the most obvious lesson is that living in an environment with disorganization and clutter is not in keeping with the original design for a life of peace and tranquillity. In each of our personal spaces, this rule certainly applies. It is important to do what you can to bring more order into your life and simplify. Only surround yourself with those few items you enjoy and find useful. We feel marvelous when we declutter and share our excess with others who may be in need.

Your Private Eden

"If you don't get to a beautiful place every couple of years, you get to thinking everything is urban, as though when God made creation he just made some medium-size buildings, a bowling alley, and a burger place," writes Don Miller in *In Search of God Knows What*.[15] I agree. In addition to making healthy changes to our three most lived-in spaces, I don't want you to overlook the importance of finding a place of sanctuary to which you can retreat on a regular basis.

If you don't already have a favorite spot to call your own, it's time to get out and explore. Despite the concrete and the noise, most of us have access to areas or places of beauty within our community and certainly beyond. Even within the concrete jungles where many of us live, projects are being undertaken to beautify certain areas. Consider joining community efforts in improving natural sanctuaries.

Discover a park, nearby pond, or stream where you love to be. Most cities have beautiful walking trails. Choose a location (or several) you can visit regularly, anything from a few minutes to an hour away, where you can go for quiet contemplation. Your private Eden can be a quiet time of meditation before leaving for work in the early dawn, at break time, or a stop at a park on the way home. Recognize your need to go there and enjoy it.

Also find a location away from your nearby surroundings where you can escape to every year or so. This might be a favorite vacation spot in the mountains or an island paradise that's not so crowded that you have to trip over people while trying to enjoy the experience. For more about the importance of regular vacations and times of rest see chapter 4 on Rest.

DID YOU KNOW? TREES ENHANCE LONGEVITY

A Japanese study found that people living around trees had longer life spans than those living in treeless areas. This was true even for urban dwellers. When factors such as age, sex, and socioeconomic status were considered, the added longevity associated with living around trees had a real and lasting effect.[16]

REAWAKEN TO WONDER

A longing pure and not to be described
drove me to wander over woods and fields,
and in a mist of hot abundant tears
I felt a world arise and live for me.
GOETHE

In the midst of our metropolis, we are surrounded by the luxury of living things. We hear the sounds of birds chirping and feel the wind blowing, but in our rush to get to work, arrive back home, and hurry off to the next appointment it is far too easy for us to miss the beauty and the healing our own environment has to offer.

It's not even that we don't see them—we see them, but we are not mindful of experiencing them. Annie Dillard once said, "Beauty and grace are performed whether or not we will sense them. The least we can do is try to be there."

We need to allow ourselves to absorb the natural splendor of our environment. I live on a street lined with giant oak trees, which form a natural canopy for at least a mile. Just around the corner at the end of that mile is a shimmering little lake. But while those incredible trees and our lovely lake are always there, I am often so pressed for time and focused on the tasks awaiting me that I don't even notice my surroundings. I can easily miss all the natural wonders created for me that day.

It is only when I slow down enough to open my eyes in awe that I not only register with my eyes, but interact with my soul and am touched by the rhythm of nature all around me. Only then do I actually engage and am changed by the grandeur of my surroundings and allow it to have a soothing and rejuvenating effect on my spirit.

When I first arrived in Orlando, I was immediately struck by the city's charm. I reveled in its many natural treasures. It was lush and green and I delighted in the many unexpected lakes just waiting to be discovered. We had moved to an area of town where there were still a few cow pastures alongside the road. Gradually over the years, the area began to change. The mall came, apartment buildings went up, and the cow pastures disappeared. I suppose I had adapted to the developments without realizing how much I was missing until I spent a year in Huntsville, Alabama.

You have to understand the marked contrast between developing Orlando, Florida, and Huntsville, Alabama. In Orlando, we have huge colorful signs indicating which exits to take for Disney World. In Huntsville, there are road signs telling you to "Beware of Low-Flying Geese." What a thing of beauty it was to watch those geese as they came in flying low to land on the local pond, or the sight of fields bursting with cotton as far as the eye could see. We'd stop the car, giving right-of-way to a family of ducks waddling unhurriedly across the narrow country roads with their ducklings all in a row! But even then I had to make a personal choice to take in my surroundings each day. When I allowed myself to fully experience those moments—to see and to *feel*—I found that they brought me a sense of peace and wonder.

Ask yourself, "Has the miraculous become mundane?" Awe is

that sense of appreciation for life, the heart for discovery so necessary for embracing our environment. We don't seem to struggle with this when we take vacations. The difference is that we have been far enough removed from our daily distractions to see, hear, smell, and touch the short-term experience. When was the last time you saw a natural wonder, such as low-flying geese, and paused long enough to fully enjoy it? Nature was designed specifically with you and me in mind. When we become fully aware of our surroundings we can awaken to the soul-nourishing and healing benefits of our environment.

PUTTING IT ALL TOGETHER

Horticulturists know that with any landscape or garden three things are necessary: planting new life (maximizing), cultivating and caring for what is already growing (moderating), and hoeing out undesired elements (minimizing). The same is true while creating your own Eden living. Be mindful of the moment and regularly remove sensory pollution from your personal space. Implement some life-giving pleasures and be mindful as to what you are listening to and seeing by practicing the 3 M's.

Maximize

Get outside! Plan times to regularly get away to experience and interact with nature. Go to the park, visit the zoo, get away to the beach or the mountains. Find a new favorite spot to call your own.

Moderate

Protect your air. When you can, avoid secondhand smoke. Incorporate the sights and sounds into your living space. Add plants as natural air fresheners.

Minimize

Remove unwanted sights and sounds from your environment. If you're feeling overwhelmed with clutter, it's definitely time to simplify.

Lisa's Breakthrough Story
Finding Your Lifeline

Looking back, it seems Lisa had always been sensitive to her environment. As a child living in St. Croix, all she knew was beach, sun, and mountains. She and her brothers would spend all day outside swimming, canoeing, tying vines and swinging from trees. For Lisa, it was heaven!

When she left the islands, she always chose to live in locations that allowed outdoor activity. Living in Nigeria, she spent time hiking and horseback riding. In Miami, she waterskied, biked, and snorkeled. No matter where she resided, she always connected with the environment. It nurtured her. Too much time indoors and she felt off kilter and ineffective.

Then came a huge turning point. Her husband's mother was aging and they were too far away from where she lived, so Lisa and her husband decided to move. Her husband, Roger, had grown up in New York City and the love of the city remained in his blood (as only a true New Yorker can understand). Although she wasn't looking to move, it made sense in terms of their family's needs.

The couple moved to an apartment near the heart of the city. The constancy of the stimulation, the cars, the noise, the activity, the masses of sheer humanity, were at first overwhelming. Lisa wasn't prepared for such a monumental shift.

It takes a lot to survive a big city on a daily basis, and for Lisa her new lifestyle in the Big Apple held a rhythm that felt entirely unnatural—like everything was in fast forward. When she walked out her front door she was immediately swept into hyper-accelerated mode. For her, this life took a ton of energy.

Lisa didn't lose sight of why they had moved, but those first two years almost killed her. She became depressed as a result of living in an environment that drained her. She knew she had to figure out a way to stop focusing on the negatives of her surroundings. Even though she felt trapped in a concrete maze, she had to find a place that would allow her spirit to breathe and find rejuvenation.

She found it in Central Park. The park literally became her lifeline. The effect was almost immediate—as if she'd taken medication. She went to the park every day, even in the dead of winter or the pouring rain. She never missed a day. She started to feel alive again, happy to be surrounded by trees and birds and people. The park was the one place in the city where people didn't look stressed out and anxious.

Things weren't perfect, but they were better. Then, about a year later, Lisa and Roger purchased a getaway home in the Catskill Mountains. Originally a business venture, it quickly became her own personal wellness retreat. It was isolated, woodsy, and gorgeous. Now instead of just an hour in the park, she could get two to three full days of the outdoors.

She was there every weekend. She would hike, run, or sometimes just lie in the grass. Never having thought of herself as the Audubon type, she was now outside with her bird book, binoculars, and a cup of tea watching the birds and loving it! Those two or three days on the weekend made her other five days manageable.

We can easily forget how many more choices we have than what might at first appear to be. Certainly New York City would never have been Lisa's first choice, but you can't always predict life's circumstances. She found within that choice an unexpected outdoor sanctuary of peace and rejuvenation.

"A" is for Activity

6

Activity is the Fountain of Youth. It will prolong your life regardless of your genetics. It's your best medicine and fights almost any disease. It's a sleep aid, a cosmetic, and an antidepressant. Activity keeps you trim and limber. Whether you're lifting groceries or barbells, staying fit depends on staying active.

IN THIS CHAPTER YOU WILL:

* Learn the three essentials to increase energy, reduce injury, and improve your looks.

* Find out the easy way to motivate yourself to get more exercise.

* Discover the greatest hidden benefit of a stronger body and greater endurance.

"A" is for Activity

*Physical fitness is the basis
for all other forms of excellence.*

John F. Kennedy

We were designed to move. Every bone, muscle, and joint was set in place for our mobility. Yet, according to U.S. statistics, many of us haven't moved in years. Some of us haven't truly been active—ever! The thought of being physical after all those years of sitting can be downright scary. You used to jump rope as a kid, but now? Uh-uh. No way. Something might . . . jiggle loose or . . . break.

But there's something about activity that makes us feel *dynamic, energetic, lively*. Think about those words for a moment. What images do you see? I see a vibrant, fun-loving person. I see *happiness*. Movement does that, you know. Cast your mind as far as you have to in order to see yourself moving. Remember what it was like to be outside playing football or hopscotch or tag with your friends? Do you remember how you'd come racing through the front door to get a drink of water all sweaty and full of excitement? Remember leaving the dance floor feeling exhausted and exhilarated? What about the times you chased little ones around the house or went out with family or friends to go bowling? It really does feel great to move, doesn't it? There's a reason: you were designed that way.

DESIGNED FOR ACTIVITY

A body in motion tends to stay in motion,
And a body at rest tends to stay at rest.
SIR ISAAC NEWTON

Your body is an incredible machine *and* a magnificent work of art with parts designed to work synchronously and flawlessly. Scientists will never exhaust the body's intricacies. The human body is more than just cogs and wheels; there is grace, beauty, and symmetry about your body that truly makes it a work of art. But it's up to you to discover it.

Did you know you have more than two hundred bones and six hundred muscles in your body to support movement? Even your tiniest blood vessels have muscles that control their activity. If that wasn't enough, you have hinge joints, gliding joints, and ball-and-socket joints all held together by ligaments and tendons that are lubricated with tiny sacs of fluid to facilitate your every move. But in order to keep them functioning well, you need activity. You were created to run, skip, and dance. You were intended for outstanding physical performance, not to sit for hours on end.

Man and woman were the apex of Creation, God's final flourish. Though theories abound regarding the specifics on their shape and size, we can be certain Adam and Eve were the picture of perfectly honed bodies, flawless in frame and symmetry, faultless in grace and movement. As overseers of the earth, they were asked to tend and care for the Garden of Eden. We don't know specifically what this entailed, but we do know there was plenty for them to do. They were landscape architects in charge of propagating and tending the garden God put in their care. They worked and gathered, moved and played, swam and hiked, and they walked with their Maker in the cool of the day.

We don't see the first couple being instructed to "exercise." Why? Their entire lifestyle was built around being physically active.

We can be sure that Adam and Eve were in perpetual motion. Aerobic conditioning, resistance training, and stretching were always part of their everyday experience. Living in the rhythm God established, they "worked out" for six days and rested on the seventh.

Chances are, your grandparents didn't have to think much about their levels of physical activity either. I can remember standing at the washing board with my grandmother when I was a little girl. Her arms and hands worked as vigorously as any Maytag machine. I don't think she ever went to the cleaner's a day in her life. She ironed everything, and she certainly didn't have the luxury of the wrinkle-free fabrics we're blessed with today. She didn't own a car, either. We walked everywhere. She "owned" the streets of New York. Today, with our modern conveniences, critical changes have taken place.

The Thief: A Sedentary Lifestyle

Prior to the Industrial Revolution, people maintained their physical activity by doing their own farmwork and domestic chores, much like my grandmother. They had to rely on sheer muscle strength for their livelihood and transportation. But with the invention of machines and cars, we started moving less and less. For the first time in human history, physical activity became optional for both survival and recreation. Today the term "work" can mean any number of different things; for many of us, it defines the mental activity we perform while sitting in an office chair in front of a computer for eight to ten hours per day. For an increasing number of people, work has little to do with physical labor.

Our lives may feel more "on the go" than ever before, but it's not because we're moving. After tallying the miles traveled in a day, we may be surprised at the distance we've covered, but it's not by foot or bicycle, which means we're spending a large majority of our lives sitting in a vehicle or on some other form of public transportation. For the first time in our history, "busy" and "active" are not synonymous.

Not only is much of our "work" motionless, so is our leisure. Television remains a primary form of entertainment for many of us. As a matter of fact, "we spend nine times as many minutes watching TV or movies as we do on sports, exercise and all other leisure-time physical activities combined."[1] And with the reign of the remote control, it's a rare day that we'll get up to change the channel—at least not without tearing up the couch cushions first in an effort to find it! With our "lifestyle conveniences" our muscles have shrunk and our waistlines expanded. We're sedentary.

SCIENCE SAYS

Obesity, the result of poor nutrition and a lack of physical activity, is not just a cosmetic problem. According to a March 2005 *New England Journal of Medicine* report, studies suggest that two-thirds of American adults are overweight*—an increase of over 50 percent per decade—resulting in over 300,000 deaths annually.[2]

———

* Overweight is defined as having a body mass index (BMI) of 25 or more; obese as having a BMI of 30 or more; severely obese, as a BMI greater than 45. See appendix B to figure out your own BMI.

Children as young as three engage in less physical activity now than they did just ten years ago. The same is true for our teenagers. In many schools physical education is optional. This, coupled with television, video games, and computers has resulted in an epidemic of childhood obesity of sobering scale.[3]

I'm certainly not the dynamo my grandmother was, but while I was growing up, I played outside. I walked two miles to middle school (and no, it wasn't in the snow!), and I rode my bike to high school every day. My kids, on the other hand, get "dropped off" and "picked up" every day. I didn't think much of this until recently. We were driving home, and they asked me if I would take them to the store. I was tired and didn't have the energy to make another stop. I said the unthinkable.

"If you want to go to the store, you'll have to walk."

The silence was deafening. "Walk?" they said in unison. And then it started.

"Listen. When I was your age . . ."

They walked to the store. They probably would have walked anywhere to escape listening to me! When their father came home, they couldn't wait to "tell." "Dad! Something's wrong with Mom! She made us walk to the store . . . *and* walk home!" Something was wrong, all right. Those little chipmunks needed to get out and move!

Our lack of physical activity has become a problem of global proportions—both literally and figuratively. According to a recent study conducted at the University of Hong Kong, 20 percent of all deaths of people thirty-five and older were attributed to a lack of physical activity. The risk of dying from heart disease, cancer, and even certain respiratory ailments has more than doubled worldwide in people who do not exercise.[4]

AM I SEDENTARY?

A sedentary life is defined as being physically inactive at work and at home and failing to participate in at least twenty continuous minutes of exercise at least three times a week. For the next week, monitor your activities and the amount of time you were involved in each of them and determine if you need to get moving!

The statistics are sobering, but instead of letting the numbers immobilize you, take action! Once you make the choice to begin moving—even if you've never exercised in your life—you will never be the same.

Felicia's Story

"I was never really physically active and wasn't inclined toward sports. I didn't find athletics exciting; I never felt I was good at any of them. I just assumed that went for basic exercise as well. It simply wasn't for me. Exercise was something other people did."

Felicia will never forget her turning point. She was pregnant with her second child, and at her last doctor's visit before she delivered, Felicia climbed on the scale and couldn't believe the number she saw. Two hundred pounds.

In the past all she'd ever done to lose weight was change her diet. It had worked before, so three months after she delivered her baby, she began restricting her diet to lose weight. The dieting helped, but not enough. "A good friend who was also struggling with her weight asked me to join her in an exercise and strength training program. We made a commitment to each other that we would get together regularly for at least three months. The accountability really helped."

The first time they met was humbling. "I can still see it now," she says. "I couldn't even lift my body off the ground to do a push-up! But in three months I started seeing results. I was slimmer and stronger. I could even do push-ups! My confidence reached an all-time high."

Having reached that goal, Felicia was motivated to do something more for herself. Her older brother, an avid marathoner, suggested a marathon. She wasn't impressed with the suggestion. "I didn't like running—I still wasn't even sure I liked exercise. I was doing it for the weight loss, but I decided to test myself one day and see if I could run at a pace that was comfortable for me."

She ran four miles.

Encouraged, Felicia went to the leukemia society and signed up to train for their next marathon. She ran her first 26.2-mile race when she turned forty. It was nothing less than exhilarating. She loved it! Over time, things changed. Exercise became more than accomplishing goals—it became a way of life. She's still challenged to maintain her consistency with the kids, her job, and everything else, but she remains committed. Once she's able to get out there she feels great. "It's like I connect with a part of me that I can't find any other way. My body was made for this. I wouldn't trade it for the world."

DID YOU KNOW?

According to the American Heart Association, a woman who doesn't exercise is *twice as likely* to develop heart problems as a woman who gets thirty minutes of regular exercise three times a week.[5]

FINDING THE FOUNTAIN OF YOUTH

Life would be infinitely happier if we could only be born at the age of eighty and gradually approach eighteen.
MARK TWAIN

In the early 1500s, the Spanish explorer Don Ponce de Leon and his followers spent years exploring islands off the coast of Florida, searching for the Fountain of Youth. Tradition held that there was a fountain of such wonderful virtue that it would renew the youth and vitality of anyone who bathed in its waters. Five hundred years later, that particular fountain still hasn't been found, but scientists have discovered something else that restores health and vitality. You guessed it: exercise.

Staying physically fit *is* the Fountain of Youth. Scientific research has shown that exercise will markedly slow the effects of aging. Regular physical activity strengthens your immune system, reduces your risk for heart disease, lowers your risk for high blood pressure and cholesterol, and may even reduce your risk for colon and breast cancers. Your exercise capacity is a more powerful predictor of mortality than all other risk factors, including your family medical history or diet. According to Jonathan Myers, PhD, "Regardless of any other risk factors you may have, if you're physically fit, you can cut your risk of premature death in half."[6]

Exercise, Mood, and Self-Esteem

I usually exercise early in the morning before I go to work. Sometimes when the alarm goes off at 5 a.m., I'm not feeling especially motivated to get out there. And once I do get out, it takes me about fifteen minutes before I stop hating it. But after that I feel good. It's the endorphins. When you exercise, your brain releases these hormones, which suppress sensations of pain and produce a sense of well-being. Usually it takes about twenty minutes into an exercise session before endorphin production begins, and it peaks after forty-five minutes. In one fairly remarkable study at Duke University Medical Center, regular exercise programs were found to be equal in benefit to routine doses of Zoloft, a common antidepressant.[7]

Increased self-esteem is one of my favorite by-products of a stronger body and greater endurance as a result of regular exercise. There's nothing better to boost your spirits than to reach your ideal body weight and watch your physique change. Every woman feels a sense of accomplishment when she can fit into that favorite outfit she's been holding on to, and men feel great when they can comfortably cinch their belt buckle one more notch. It is wonderful when you're doing something that makes you feel good, look good, and benefits your health. While the physiological link between exercise and self-esteem may not be well understood, little question remains that exercise boosts self-esteem, and the better you feel and look, the more your commitment to physical activity is reinforced.

For lifelong health and vitality, we need to practice three components of activity: endurance (aerobic conditioning), resistance (strength training), and flexibility (stretching routine). These three combine to make us vibrant and ready for life's opportunities at any age.

ENDURANCE FOR A LIFETIME

Sweat cleanses from the inside.
It comes from places a shower will never reach.
GEORGE SHEEHAN, MD

Endurance exercise is also known as aerobic or cardiovascular exercise because it conditions two of the most important organs of your body: your heart and lungs. To endure is to be able to stick with something till the activity is completed. Your body needs to be challenged in order to consistently perform without getting tired out. Endurance training helps your heart, lungs, and muscles perform more efficiently. *Every day* a conditioned heart will beat about 30,000 times less than one that is not conditioned.[8] This means increased energy (or less feelings of fatigue) and greater productivity. No caffeine necessary. Exercise will power you through your day!

Endurance exercises aren't just limited to walking, running, or cycling. They can also include vigorous team sports like basketball, football, and soccer. Make it fun and exercise with the kids or family. You might play a game of tag or kickball with your children, jump rope, ice skate, even play table tennis. The list of fun activities is endless. They might not provide as potent a workout as running, cycling, or swimming, but over time the benefits add up. My aunt regularly jumps "double dutch" with her junior high school students. The kids think it's a hoot that "Mrs. Sherman" can jump rope as well as they do; she's sixty.

Benefits of Endurance

It's endurance or cardiovascular activity that's linked to the reduction in heart disease, blood pressure, cholesterol, diabetes, and cancer. A recent Harvard alumni study indicated that people who engage in moderately vigorous physical activity have a 41 percent lower risk of coronary heart disease compared to non-exercisers. Also, the higher the level of physical activity, the lower the risk of developing non-insulin-dependent diabetes in both men and women.[9]

What to Do

It doesn't take an enormous amount of physical exercise to achieve health-enhancing results. A mere thirty minutes a day of walking, swimming, jogging, cycling, or other cardiovascular exercise can have astounding positive health effects. Your aerobic exercise shouldn't be so intense that your muscle cells run short of oxygen. If you find yourself gasping for air, slow down until your breathing is steady again. A good gauge for appropriate intensity would be exercising at a level where you can still talk, but you would probably rather not, at least not for a sustained period of time.[10] Your cardiovascular fitness program should have three components: warm-up, conditioning aerobic exercise, and cool-down. This is the model I follow for endurance, resistance, and stretching activity. It is recommended by most fitness experts and has been reviewed by Harvard Medical School faculty.[11]

* The warm-up phase should be five to ten minutes and include low-intensity exercises to gradually increase your heart rate and blood flow to your muscles.
* Follow this with at least twenty minutes of moderate-intensity aerobic workout.
* End with five to ten minutes of low-intensity exercises, similar to your warm-up. Do some stretching at the end of your cool-down. A cool-down may take longer for some than it does for others. Essentially, cool-down is complete when you achieve your resting heart rate.

Your workout should be intense enough and long enough to achieve a cardiovascular training effect. Shoot for about thirty minutes, at least three times a week. If you haven't exercised recently, don't risk injury; start out with smaller blocks of time. I remember the first time I got on a stationary bike. I pedaled for five minutes and was exhausted. You must do what feels comfortable and then gradually challenge yourself by increasing your time. At thirty minutes, three days a week, you'll reap amazing health benefits and reduce the risk of disease.

If you are trying to lose weight, try to work your way up to sixty minutes most days of the week. Again, start slowly and gradually work your way up. The intensity of your exercise should be strenuous enough so that you feel you are working, but it doesn't need to be exhausting. If it is, you are less likely to stick with it. Get a doctor's approval before starting an exercise program if you are severely overweight, over age fifty, suffer from a chronic disease like heart disease or diabetes, or have immediate family members with a history of heart disease before the age of fifty-five.

STRENGTH FOR A LIFETIME

There is strength in numbers,
and those numbers come in pounds.
MIKE BERRY

What endurance training is to the heart and lungs, resistance training is to your skeletal muscles. While aerobic exercise has many excellent health benefits, lifting weights two or three times a week increases strength by building both muscle mass and bone density (which is especially important for those concerned with osteoporosis).

Strength training is important for weight control. The greater your muscle mass in proportion to your body fat, the higher your metabolic rate. The higher your metabolic rate, the more calories you'll naturally burn. Why? Your muscle is active tissue that consumes calories, while stored fat utilizes very little energy. Strength training can provide up to a 15 percent increase in metabolic rate, which is enormously helpful for long-term weight maintenance and overall health.

Benefits of Strength Training

Strength training is not just for young people or bodybuilders. Particularly as we grow older, strength training actually helps to reduce symptoms associated with conditions such as diabetes, arthritis, osteoporosis, and even depression. It can decrease back and joint pain and provide more strength to carry groceries, open jars, and lift heavy objects. According to Ray Strand, MD, in his book *Healthy for Life*, "It is a known fact that we begin losing muscle mass after age thirty-five unless we are involved in strength training. It was once believed that the loss of muscle mass, especially in the upper body, was a normal part of the aging process. This is far from the truth. Strength training not only helps prevent the loss of muscle but can actually increase it for people in their eighties and nineties."[12]

What to Do

Before starting your strength training exercises do some reading, watching, and listening. To get the most from your routine, good form is important to prevent injury and maximize benefit. There are many inexpensive resources you can use to help you—books, videos, DVDs, and the Web are readily available. It's not difficult to learn. Push-ups, crunches, and leg lifts are examples of strength training exercises. Today there are balls, rubber bands, and other tools that make these activities fun and more creative. Challenge yourself to try!

Try to perform twenty minutes of resistance training at least twice a week. A basic program would include exercises using the major muscle groups of the arms, legs, and your body's "core": the shoulders, chest, abdomen, hips, pelvis, and the upper to lower back muscles. A strong core enhances your posture, will help you tire less easily as you go about daily activities, and will improve your cardiovascular fitness.

Just like your endurance program, there are three parts to your resistance routine: a warm-up, strength training exercises, and then a cool-down (stretching).

* The warm-up phase should include five to ten minutes of low-intensity exercises, such as walking or climbing stairs, to gradually increase your heart rate and the blood flow to your muscles. If you're at home and don't want to go outside, marching in place can do the trick. (If you're working the upper body muscles, be sure to include some warm-up activity for these muscles.)
* Follow this with your twenty-minute workout.
* End with five minutes of low-intensity exercising such as walking and then some stretching of the muscles you've just worked out.

If you feel hesitant about strength training on your own, make sure you check out local gyms or YMCAs for instruction.

Work your way to ten to twelve repetitions of the same exercise, take a brief rest, then repeat another set. Typically two sets are sufficient. Some strength-building exercises require dumbbells or weights. If you're new to strength training start out with a weight that is comfortable for you and gradually increase the weight as your strength increases. No time or money to go out and buy weights? Use cans of food for starters and graduate to (half) gallons of water. Be creative! Tip: work opposing muscles on the same day for proper muscle balance. Some examples of opposing muscles are: chest and back; triceps and biceps; quadriceps and hamstrings.

Remember that the benefits of resistance training are tremendous. Muscle strengthening not only makes performing daily tasks easier it boosts your metabolism and reshapes your body to its optimal form. Women, contrary to popular belief, resistance training won't make you look masculine—your natural hormonal composition won't allow that to happen. You'll be stronger and look great!

FLEXIBILITY FOR A LIFETIME

I hope you dance.
SAUNDERS AND SILLERS

Stretching is very important to your physical health, as it helps relieve muscle tension and stiffness and helps you maintain your natural range of motion. Though flexibility received little attention in the past, we're seeing a resurgence of interest due to a better understanding of how flexibility helps prevent injury, especially as we age.

My father is an avid stretcher. He's practiced tae kwon do for years, and is quite proud of his maintained flexibility. He was able to show off for Megan and Melanie recently when they tenderly asked if he needed help getting up from the floor after sitting and playing a game. He thought the question was hilarious and theatrically popped up from the floor. He questioned their concern, and their answer was telling: "Grandpa Roger, old people don't usually get up that easily. We didn't want you to hurt yourself."

Stretching is not only for athletes. Cedric Bryant, chief exercise physiologist for the American Council on Exercise (ACE), says, "Stretching is important in maintaining our range of motion as we get older. It's something you don't think about until reaching up to put away the groceries and suddenly you can't reach above your shoulders," or you're sitting on the floor and can't get up.[13]

Benefits of Flexibility

While stretching gets mixed reviews in terms of its ability to prevent sports injuries, there are benefits everyone agrees on. Like strength training, increased flexibility will improve your daily performance of all activities. It will improve your posture and keep aches and pains to a minimum. Stretching ensures better balance and will enhance your coordination, keeping you mobile as you age.[14]

What to Do

Just as we suggested with other forms of exercise, it's important to warm up before stretching. Warming up will decrease stiffness and increase your range of motion while you stretch. Stretching "cold" muscles increases your risk for injury. Do a five-minute warm-up of your favorite exercise before you stretch. If you need to save time, stretch after you do your endurance/cardio workout. Engage in low-intensity, relaxed stretching, making sure that your stretch doesn't hurt. Stretching should feel good. Make sure you're stretching through the muscle's full range of movement until you feel a gentle resistance (not pain), then hold the maximum position for thirty to sixty seconds and relax. Don't bounce. Breathe freely through your range of motion. Make sure you're stretching all of your major muscle groups and areas of tension.

Stretching exercises should include your:

* upper and lower back
* quadriceps
* buttocks
* chest
* calves
* shoulders
* hamstrings
* neck

Stretching is a wonderful stress reliever, and with the lives most of us lead, we can certainly benefit from it on a daily basis. To reap its maximum benefits you should stretch at least three times a week. Stretching may also help reduce soreness after a workout, which is in part due to the increase in lactic acid in the muscles while exercising. Stretching will help break up this lactic acid, thus reducing potential soreness.

HURDLING THE BARRIER

My idea of exercise is a good brisk sit.
PHYLLIS DILLER

Before you read this chapter you knew you could benefit from increased activity and exercise. You may not have known all of the statistics, and you may have even been surprised at all of the benefits, but in general you knew! So what's the problem? What's the number one reason we give for not exercising? You got it—time.

I know the dilemma. But I also know that while half of America is *not* exercising regularly, the flip side of the coin is that the other half—those who function within the same twenty-four-hour time challenge—*are* exercising! Somehow, they've figured it out. And you can figure it out too. I'll never forget the good talking-to my trainer, Chris, gave me early on as I waxed and waned with my ability to get to the gym on a regular basis. "Monica," he said, "your problem is not time constraints, it's that each morning you're making a decision about *whether* you'll exercise or not. Each day you weigh what's most important for that day and determine what your priorities are. Obviously, exercise is coming up short."

With that way of thinking, there would be a significant number of days where exercise wouldn't make the cut in my day. People who exercise regularly don't decide every day whether they will or won't. It is a part of their *routine.** Think about it. When you get up in the morning and go through your priority list of what you can

---

*Remember what you read in the Choice chapter. Habits are just routines that we perform over and over again.

or cannot do, brushing your teeth is never a part of that mental conversation. You brush your teeth. It's not a priority-list decision. It's a given. It happens no matter how jam-packed your day is.

Obviously, regular exercise takes more time than brushing teeth; the point is that to start exercising you have to be consistent and do it regularly until it becomes routine. It may be bumpy at first and you may have to try several different methods and time slots before you find what works. Stick with it for one month and I guarantee it will start to take hold. The beautiful thing about exercise is that your body benefits immediately, and after you've done it you will feel and notice a significant difference. I've never met a person who gave up exercise because they didn't like the results.

Ready? Get Set. Go!

Becoming physically active is not expensive. It's an investment in time for the most part and a change in lifestyle. You can get started with a good pair of tennis shoes, some cans of food, and a floor! You can always walk, and most resistance and flexibility training can be done right at home. If you live in an area where it gets cold, you will need to invest a little more over time, but not much—it could be as simple as buying a jump rope or a stationary mount for the bike you already have. Take advantage of the cable stations, DVDs, or videos that you or your friend may have and find some good exercise programs. Start slowly and don't bite off more than you can chew.

If you have room in your budget, find a trainer. If you don't have the dollars now, save for a few months. This is one of the best ways you can invest in yourself. A good trainer will evaluate your fitness, ensure proper workout form, and show you how to properly challenge your body. You'll be amazed at your newfound ability. Coupled with appropriate nutrition (see chapter 10), you'll definitely see results. If a trainer is not an option, find a friend. Exercise always seems easier when we have an accountability partner, although it's not a necessity. The key to a good partner is finding someone who will motivate you, not drag you down or enable you to make excuses about why it's not a good idea to exercise today!

The great thing about activity is that you can get started at any age and still reap remarkable benefits. In a recent University of Texas Southwestern Medical Center study, Dr. Benjamin Levine and his colleagues found conclusive evidence that starting and sticking with an endurance training program plays a major role in reversing the damage done to the heart, even if that program is initiated later in life.[15]

LEAVE TIME TO PLAY

Each day, and the living of it, has to be a conscious
creation in which discipline and order
are relieved with some play.
MAY SARTON

It would be a shame to know all we do about the profound beauty and diversity of our world and then restrict our activity to working out in a gym. If you're a "gym rat," break out of those four walls and get outside. You will reap the benefits of a natural environment and improve your interpersonal relationships at the same time. Walking or running on the beach, at the park, or around your neighborhood can be a welcome change of pace from a treadmill. Are there any nature trails close by? Hiking can be something for the family or a group of friends to enjoy. Find out what's available in your neighborhood, your city, or your surrounding suburbs and take advantage of it. You don't have to be an expert or have all "the gear" to begin enjoying the outdoors. Comfortable shoes, plenty of water, a healthy snack, and appropriate sun and weather protection are all you need.

Try something different. What about canoeing or kayaking? You'll exercise virtually every muscle in your upper body by paddling a kayak. Thought about snow skiing? What activity have you always wanted to try? Be bold and train for a marathon or do a cycling tour. Your life will forever be changed.

Do you only have a couple hours, a day, a weekend? Plan a wonderful getaway. Guides are available if you don't know where to go or how to get started. Helping to keep you from getting stuck in a tourist trap, a guide can show you the area's hidden gems appropriate to your level of fitness. Go to a local outdoors store, the AAA, or a visitors' Web site. Be all you can be, and have a wonderful time doing it.

PUTTING IT ALL TOGETHER

People rarely make a distinction between activity and exercise. Perhaps fifty years ago, there was no perceivable difference, but today there is. Activity is the prize, the great reward of freedom we must work to keep through exercise. Release your body to do what it wants to do—move! It's an absolute necessity for those of us living in a world of technology and motorized transportation. If you have a sedentary occupation or lifestyle, choose to exercise. Nowhere else is the cliché "move it or lose it" more applicable. If you need to go to a gym to get active, do it. Stay fit by challenging your body to do different things. Your mind doesn't want to do the same things all the time; neither does your body. Even if you've never exercised a day in your life it's not too late. You can still reduce your risk for disease, enter deeper sleep, and think more clearly if you start being active—now. Start today with one of the 3 M's.

Maximize
Establish your "movement mind-set." Take the stairs, walk the parking lot, hand-wash your car. If you haven't already, get started with an endurance program. Start slowly and gradually pick up the pace. Add flexibility and strength training to round out your activities. If you already have an exercise program that incorpo-

rates all three, kudos! Keep up the good work by challenging your body to set new fitness goals.

Moderate

Don't get stuck in the gym. Keep in mind, this is about activity and not just exercise. On a weekly basis, spend some of your active time outdoors. Resist getting stuck in the same routine. Try different types of activities to spice up the routine. Experiment!

Minimize

Avoid reasons for delay. Too tired at the end of the day? Dare yourself to devote at least ten minutes to your chosen exercise, and if you are not feeling better by then, stop and try again the next day or call a friend to do it with you. Chances are that once you begin you will feel reenergized.

Steven's Breakthrough Story
At the Top of His Game

In his younger days Steven was always physically active. He was involved in all of his college's intramural sports. He played basketball, football, softball, he ran—he was in excellent shape. After he left college Steven got involved in community basketball and softball leagues, played volleyball, and even refereed at a local college. He messed around a bit with weights in the gym, but he didn't really know what to do and he never really saw much of the benefit. A few of the guys looked pretty serious, but most were just goofing off and having fun. In his mind, as long as he could still run up and down the basketball court, he was okay.

In time, his life changed. He had a family and a busy job, and his involvement in team sports fell completely by the wayside. He didn't do anything physically active for about seven years. Though his wife was consistent with her exercise program, he just "didn't have the time." The kids made jokes about Mommy exercising and Daddy not doing a thing. He had to admit he was developing quite a gut.

As a Christmas gift his family gave him a certificate to a local gym. He knew they meant it as a bit of a joke, but it was the jump-start he needed, and he started working out two to three times a week. He started walking three times a week as well.

"I had to admit, I felt great," Steven said. "I was sleeping better. I had more energy, a more positive outlook, and it was a great stress relief after a full day's work. Within two months I'd dropped ten pounds and my pants were fitting better." A few more months passed and Steven saw more significant changes in his body—his chest broadened, his legs were more muscular, his waist trimmed. His whole view of health changed. One of the things that he really enjoyed most was that this was something he and his wife could do together. Recently they purchased bicycles and now they cycle together as well.

"It's great to have found my way back. I can't always get to the gym, but daily I do something to boost my activity, even if it's just a brisk walk with my dog. I'm at the top of my game again. Nothing beats being in better physical shape at forty than I was at twenty!"

"T" is for Trust

7

Trust in Divine Power brings the confidence that you rest secure; it's the peace of knowing you don't have to be in control. Trusting in Divine Power allows you to keep your bearings as you navigate through the uncertainties of the world with the assurance that your life has eternal purpose.

IN THIS CHAPTER YOU WILL:

* Learn one thing you can do anytime, anywhere to find peace in the midst of crisis.

* Discover your source of immovable, unchanging strength and power.

* Learn why many doctors now believe faith heals.

"T" is for Trust

A longing for the Supernatural is natural.

C. S. Lewis

No matter how much I may desire it, I don't have a perfect track record in life. I don't get things right all the time, not for myself nor for those I love. This is the reality of my humanness. Fortunately, I don't depend totally on people or myself for safety and security. Trusting that God is in control allows me to remember to rest and only do what I can do. I've been given personal access to divine insight, understanding, awareness, and power. Trusting in God's Divine Power provides the calm assurance that he will take care of me.

As a physician, it's an awesome thing to look into the eyes of a patient, have them look back at me in preparation for surgery and have them say, "I trust you." While my patients put their confidence in me, I place my confidence in God. I have to, because in spite of all my study and preparation, there are limits to what I can do. I choose to relinquish my imperfect ability and trust God to guide me.

On the occasions that I have to travel by air (which I enjoy less and less), I put my faith in God, not in the pilot. When I'm driving, my confidence is in God. When my children are outside playing, I'm trusting God. I have confidence in his wisdom and guidance. Trusting in Divine Power doesn't mean that bad things won't happen, but it does bring rest to an anxious and stressed-out world. Trust in Divine Power centers my life and brings it into balance.

Just as I could not do my profession without trusting God, the same is true in all of life, especially when we contemplate and prepare for the future. With all the calamity surrounding us, such as natural disasters, wars, senseless crimes, and fear of what might happen to our families, we could easily be immobilized. But trusting in Divine Power provides a sense of assurance for the future and in situations that we don't clearly understand.

But more than this, research shows that trust in the divine—engaging the spiritual component of our lives—is vital to our health. With increasing evidence, medical professionals are more convinced that spirituality—one's active belief and trust in God—is a powerful aid in recovery from illness as well as an important contributing factor to health. Studies show that those who trust in God have longer, more fulfilling lives.[1]

The benefit of trusting in Divine Power reaches beyond vague ideas or perceptions. People who actively practice their faith have a lower incidence of stroke and heart disease and fewer hospitalizations. They have less depression, higher life satisfaction, and may even live longer. In his book *The Healing Power of Faith*, Harold Koenig, MD, writes, "A growing body of research shows that religious people are both physically healthier and live longer than their nonreligious counterparts. In fact, religious faith appears to protect the elderly from the two major afflictions of later life, cardiovascular disease and cancer. In this regard, one's faith may be as significant a protective factor as not smoking in terms of survival and longevity."[2]

Keep in mind, though, that developing a trust relationship with God is more than another tactic or strategy to enhance longevity. In chapter 1 we talked about the difference between *bios* and *zoë* life, and it's especially important here. While these two aspects of life fully impact each other and cannot be separated, we want more for our lives than *bios*. Strong bones and clean arteries are great, but what we're really after is *zoë* life—a life of deep fulfillment and satisfaction. When we trust in Divine Power we'll achieve greater mental, emotional, and physical well-being.

THE IMPORTANCE OF TRUST

Now with God's help, I shall become myself.
Soren Kierkegaard

"Faith" and "trust" are in their very essence relational words. Trusting is to have belief or confidence in the honesty, goodness, skill, or safety of another. It encompasses letting another know your feelings, emotions, and reactions, all the while being confident you are respected and will not be taken advantage of.[3] We may wonder why trusting in God is so important when we can place our confidence in another human being. After all, we experience trust in the context of committed human relationships: between mother and child, husband and wife, lifelong friends, physician and patient. Trust in another person leads to feelings of safety and connectedness. We can best understand our need to trust God by looking at what we gain in human relationships.

My children trust me. As hard as I try to keep margins of time available between work and picking up my girls at school, there are days when I get stuck working right up until the very last minute. In times like these, I have to zoom up to the curb to pick up my girls. They know I might be late, and though it may frustrate them, they don't ever doubt that I'll come. They rely on me, confident that I have their well-being at heart and that I'll provide a safe and secure environment for them.

Likewise, in my medical practice, my patients trust me. They rely on my expertise and believe that I have their best interests in mind—that I'll offer them the best medical science and therapies available. Ultimately they count on me to use the sharpest skills my mind and hands have to offer in times of surgical need. In the same way, I trust others. Thankfully, after seventeen years of marriage, I know my husband will never intentionally hurt me. I have faith in him and my close friends to be supportive of my welfare. Yet even with my most trusted loved ones, the reality of human relationship rings true: at some point or another I've been disappointed by those I've put my trust in, and in turn I've been a disappointment to them. Because of my own circumstances, limitations, and human frailties, I let people down. I'm not always trustworthy.

In truth, I can't always trust myself entirely! I can't always be sure that I'm going to follow through with what I've promised myself I'll do. A commitment to myself to clean the house from top to bottom on a weekend can be easily sidetracked by some other activity. I'll promise myself that I'll get a good night's rest, then get caught up in a good book, resist sleep, and finally turn in at 2 a.m. A mental promise to call someone I haven't talked to in a while can be waylaid by the day's busyness. If we can't always be trusted to come through for ourselves, it's a guarantee that we won't always be there for others.

We need a source of immovable, unchanging power and strength—someone bigger than ourselves. By design, we are in want of divine guidance and protection. Just as you would never expect your children to go day after day without ever needing your help, we're not meant to make it on our own either. With our inability to always meet expectations of ourselves or others, there is comfort in knowing and trusting one who is beyond human limitations, someone who doesn't fall prey to human frailties and failures; someone who cares deeply and has our best interests at heart; someone who is ultimately trustworthy.

In the Garden with God

From the very beginning of Creation we see God "pulling out all the stops" and extravagantly filling the world with things that were "good." He spoke stars, planets, and galaxies into space; he roared into existence mountains, valleys, lions, and elephants; whispered butterflies and lilies and guppies to life. The Creator unleashed full spectrums of colors and melody. But when it came to creating man, everything changed. God kneeled, kneaded, and gently breathed.

On the ground, in the dirt, he shaped man in the likeness of himself. And as he worked, he loved. Kneeling over Adam, he breathed his very spirit into Adam's nostrils, "and man became a living being." God is a God of relationship. He is intimately connected with humanity unlike any of his other creatures. "God makes it clear that He accepts us—more, delights in us—as individual bearers of His image."[4] He surrounded Adam and Eve with beauty and nourishment. God was their Provider and he wanted them to know that he could be relied on to care for all of their needs physically, emotionally, spiritually, and relationally. Writes the well-loved author of *The Purpose-Driven Life*, Rick Warren, "In Eden we see God's ideal relationship with us: Adam and Eve enjoyed an intimate friendship with God. There were no rituals, ceremonies, or religion—just simple loving relationship between God and the people he created. Unhindered by guilt or fear, Adam and Eve delighted in God, and he delighted in them."[5]

We were born with an innate desire to connect with God. Trusting in Divine Power is our ability to depend fully on the Creator of the Universe, who, though all-powerful, bends down to breathe life into our spirits. God, who formed our being in the image of his own, gives us stability and a sense of confidence that we don't have to know it all or be it all. And even when we make mistakes, he partners with us to make things right again.

THE OPPOSITE OF TRUST

What we believe about God is the most important thing about us.
A. W. TOZER

The attack on the World Trade Center is a tragedy that is etched in every American's memory. So too is Hurricane Katrina. Terrorism, wars, and a crushing wave of natural disasters take an emotional toll on us. And this emotional weight can have a detrimental effect on our health over time. It's not just national or international problems that weigh us down. In many ways our everyday life feels uncertain and transient. Many of us aren't afforded the luxury of lasting relationships with our neighbors, we don't know the vendors in our community, we have little to counterbalance what we see on television or hear on the news. We no longer have a sense of permanence about our jobs or our worship communities. We feel left to "white-knuckle" our way through life on our own.

Bill Hybels, best-selling author on the topic of prayer, asserts, "From birth we have been learning the rules of self-reliance as we strain and struggle to achieve self-sufficiency. [Trusting in Divine Power] . . . flies in the face of those deep-seated values. It is an assault on human autonomy, an indictment of independent living. To people in the fast lane, determined to make it on their own, [it's] an embarrassing interruption."[6]

Left to our own intellect and strength, we may be convinced that we have everything under control—for a while. It's when we stretch to make the next payment on credit card debt, or deal with what feels like impossible circumstances, that we tend to grip the wheel more tightly and power through on our own. God doesn't seem altogether present in those moments. There certainly have been times when I've felt that way. If we do consider trusting Divine Power, we wonder, "Can God really be trusted with the details of my life? How do I know he's there or that he cares?"

"In the face of doubt," says Philip Yancey, "I have learned the simple response of considering the alternatives. If there is no Creator, what then? I would have to view the world with all its suffering as well as all its beauty as a random product of a meaningless universe, the briefest flare of a match in cosmic darkness."[7] If there truly is a Creator, he is Divine Power, the source of life and health, and worthy of trust. In the face of tragedy, the power of belief may be the only way we are able to make it through seemingly insurmountable circumstances.

RESEARCH ASKS: IS THERE A GOD?

A Harris Poll of 2003 found that 79 percent of Americans believe there is a God, and that 66 percent are *absolutely certain* this is true. Only 9 percent do not believe in God, while 12 percent are not sure.[8]

THE POWER OF BELIEF

It is difficult to make a man miserable while he feels worthy of himself and claims kindred to the great God who made him.

ABRAHAM LINCOLN

Robert and his family moved from the Philippines to the United States looking for a fresh start. The cultural changes took some getting used to, and Robert found searching for employment and getting afternoon care for his children particularly stressful. After months of searching for work, his prayers were answered when he landed a good-paying construction job. Things started looking up for the family. Circumstances weren't always smooth, but okay. They found a home and began the work of settling into their new lifestyle. Then tragedy struck.

A horrible accident occurred at work. Through a series of miscommunications, a fellow worker didn't see Robert standing in his path when he was backing up the dump truck. Pinned to the ground, his legs crushed under its massive wheels, Robert lay on the ground in excruciating agony, fearing he would die. With the little strength he had, he asked God to spare him and tried to focus on the 23rd Psalm, saying the words over and over again, until emergency help arrived.

Robert needed three major surgeries to correct the damage done to his legs. His recovery has been slow and difficult. He still experiences significant pain. His doctors have advised him it's unlikely he'll ever regain his full physical strength. Exercising has helped his body recover from the accident, but he has to use a cane when he walks more than a hundred yards.

Though he struggled with feelings of anger and bitterness, Robert found a way to cope with the difficult questions. He put his trust in God's Divine Power. Every morning he set aside a time of spiritual solitude, which helped to bring him strength and peace. Now when he recalls the darkest days he says, "I believe God saved me. He's proved to me that he is with me even in the pain."

When tragedy strikes, one of the most difficult questions we all struggle with is *why*. Why me? How could God do this to me? In his best-selling book *When Bad Things Happen to Good People*, Rabbi Harold Kushner writes:

> *Innocent people do suffer misfortunes in this life. Things happen to them far worse than they deserve—they lose their jobs, they get sick, their children suffer or make them suffer. But when it happens, it does not represent God punishing them for something they did wrong. . . . Our misfortunes are none of His doing, and so we can turn to Him for help. Our question will not be [the] question, "God, why are you doing this to me?" but rather, "God, see what is happening to me. Can You help me?"* [9]

The health benefits of belief in the divine will be more fully understood in time, but we'll never be able to scientifically quantify how God interacts with individuals. If God could be fully understood and measured in scientific terms he wouldn't be God, right? Yet the data we do have available substantiate the benefits of belief and trust in Divine Power.

"Between 50 to 90 percent of all diseases can be affected by patient belief," says Herbert Benson, MD, president of the Mind/Body Medical Institute and associate professor of medicine at Harvard Medical School.[10] "We are all 'wired' for the power of belief. The most powerful belief for many people is belief in God . . . belief can heal. Belief can cure. What's important is not what the doctor believes in but what the patient believes in. It's important for doctors to listen to patients and to use the patients' own healing powers along with what we can dispense medically."[11]

DEVELOPING A TRUST RELATIONSHIP WITH GOD

We weren't put here to sink or swim on our own.
We were put here so that with a little help from a
Higher Power, we could fly.
VICTORIA MORAN

How do you go from mere belief in God to getting close to him? Developing a meaningful connection with a being you can't see may seem to be a daunting proposition. Theologians have wrestled with this question for centuries, but for our purpose here, it is enough to say that just like establishing any trusting relationship, you've got to get to know the person. The same is true of God. You start building a deeper relationship with your Creator when you spend time and communicate with him.

Spending Time with God

Like all things of value, growing good relationships take time. Knowing God is no different. Consider setting aside time when your mind is the freshest. This may be first thing in the morning or at the end of the day. It could be as short as a few minutes or more than an hour as you become more comfortable. Find a time that works for you and try to arrange your schedule so you can expect it regularly.

This is an opportunity for you to focus on thoughts or activities that will draw you closer to God. These can include: inspirational reading, spiritual study, meditation, contemplation, prayer (more on that later), praise, journaling, or even nature walks. Since this is a time to focus on your spiritual life, find a place and time where you can enjoy the quiet. I'll never forget my first experience finding "a quiet place." It was in my Lamaze class. The instructor asked us to lie on the floor with our partner and mentally envision our place of quiet and relaxation. After racking my brain for what seemed like minutes, I whispered to my husband, "Honey, I don't think I have a quiet place, I can't think of one!" He had a good chuckle. I certainly wasn't telling him something he didn't already know! But what a revealing moment for me! My type A personality wanted to immediately jump up off of the floor and write in my weekly to-do list, "Find a place of quiet." Unfortunately, that's not how it works. Finding quiet involves being still. My Huntsville experience taught me how to be still in a rather dramatic way, and I'm still learning how to incorporate stillness in my day. It's not easy to do.

Author C. S. Lewis agrees. "The real problem," he says, "comes the very moment you wake up each morning. All your wishes and hopes for the day rush at you like wild animals. Our first job each morning consists of shoving them all back; listening to that other voice, taking that other point of view, letting that other larger, stronger, quieter life come flowing in. And so on, all day. Standing back from all your natural fussings and frettings; coming in out of the wind."[12]

With the madness of our lives, each day we need to reorient ourselves to God, to open our spirits and our senses to the reality of his presence. When my day is full and I know I won't have time for spiritual reflection, I pause before I get out of bed in the morning and invite God into my day. I ask my Creator to help me see his presence in the ordinary. It never fails. When I intentionally set aside even a little time to meditate and quiet myself from all the distractions and pressures of life, I become aware of God's presence in our daily world.

How do we recognize Divine presence throughout the day? "God uses a million means to communicate with us, including circumstances, friends, enemies, nature, literature and our conscience," says Chris Blake, author of *Searching for a God to Love*.[13] Our challenge in our hurried lives is to slow down long enough to recognize it.

Prayer—Communicating with God

Prayer unites our minds, bodies, and spirits. The good news is that you don't have to be a spiritual guru to pray. Very simply, prayer is relinquishing your greatest concerns to the Maker of the Universe. It's a time to honestly talk with God about your hopes, your fears, your desires, and your needs. It's about communicating the reflections, emotions, and attitudes that lie closest to your heart. It's through prayer that you begin to experience the difference between *believing in* and *knowing* God.

The time you learn to spend in prayer and meditation has a number of immediate health benefits. Prayer lowers stress, decreases muscle tension, and provides a sense of peace. Medical internist Larry Dossey and others have published extensively on the health benefits of prayer.[14] A physical state of deep rest is experienced when you pray or meditate regularly, changing your physical and emotional responses to stress. When you pray, you also have an immediate drop in blood pressure, heart rate, and levels of stress hormones.[15]

Maybe you've never prayed before and wonder how to start. On the other hand, you may have been praying for years but you want a deeper connection with God. What can you do? I appreciate John Ortberg's book *The Life You've Always Wanted*, and found it especially helpful. With his inspiration, I suggest the following:

1. *Establish a time for focused prayer and try to be consistent with it each day.* When you're trying to establish a new behavior it always helps to have a consistent routine until it becomes natural. Choose a time when you're at your best, not when you're tired and exhausted. Morning works best for me.

2. *Create an environment for prayer.* It's helpful to have a peaceful, distraction-free environment that you can call your own.

It doesn't have to be indoors; perhaps time during your morning or evening walk will work well for you. Be creative, but be consistent.

3. *Slow down.* Before you pray take a few moments to relax. Take some deep breaths and help your mind and body to calm.

4. *Start with small increments of time and increase the minutes as your comfort grows.* When you're starting an exercise program you don't go out the first week and run a marathon. To develop a consistent prayer life, it's helpful to start with a time frame that's doable—maybe just five minutes, or even less. Gradually increase your prayer time as your comfort level grows. It's not the length of your prayers that matter—what matters most in developing a meaningful prayer life is consistency and honesty.

5. *Keep it simple.* Ortberg suggests that you "pray what's on your heart, and not what you *wish* was on your heart." Ortberg states, "Prayer simply dies from efforts to pray about 'good things' that honestly do not matter to us. The way to get to meaningful prayer is to start by praying for what you are truly interested in."[16] Noble prayers won't help you get closer to God, but honest ones will.

6. *When your mind wanders, talk to God about what your mind is wandering on.* There are very few people who have the ability to stay focused on one thought without other thoughts drifting in. Even in the morning, my mind is flooded with thoughts. I used to feel discouraged that I wasn't staying focused on "heavenly things." But truly, what drifts into my mind during those times is what I'm most concerned about for the day. These are the thoughts I've learned to talk to God about. And my experience is more meaningful now that I do.

7. *Journal.* It may be easier for you to "talk" to God by writing. You can follow these same tips should you choose to write. There are a number of reasons why I think journaling is valuable, mainly because it forces you to slow way down and it brings perspective. It's always enlightening to go back a month or two in your writing (or sometimes even years) and review your circumstances. You'll see areas where you've grown, and continued opportunities for

greater trust. Writing down answers to your prayers can also provide tangible reminders of how active God has been in your life.[17]

THE PRAYER OF RELINQUISHMENT

The Prayer of Relinquishment is an exercise of intentionally letting go of your deepest cares and concerns. It can be as easy as opening your hands, palms up in front of you, and saying, "God, I give you my [list your concerns] today. Thank you for caring." Living with your hands and hearts open rather than a desperate clutching and clinging to what you have brings freedom and a settled peace. You will trust with fresh hope and a new ability to give your cares to God.[18]

—Richard Foster, *Prayer, Finding the Heart's True Home*

Practicing God's Presence

Not all of your time with God has to be "set aside" or time alone. In his book *The Purpose-Driven Life*, Rick Warren concurs. "*Everything* you do can be 'spending time with God,' if he is invited to be a part of it and you stay aware of his presence . . . In Eden, worship was not an event to attend, but a perpetual attitude; Adam and Eve were in constant communion with God."[19] Nicolas Herman is well-known for having done just that.

Nicolas Herman, or Brother Lawrence, as he is more widely known, was a seventeenth-century cook who lived in a French monastery. For many people, Brother Lawrence's life, his experience, and his teachings express a way of relating to God that is the most significant discovery of their lives. Brother Lawrence learned to practice the presence of God throughout his day whether in worship or mundane tasks.[20]

Like Brother Lawrence, you can commit to yourself to think about God at different times in your day until it becomes more natural. Use simple triggers—perhaps certain daily activities that you regularly perform, in between scheduled appointments or when you're in your car. Don't think of these as marathon sessions or something else on the to-do list; that's the wrong motivation and you'll be doomed before you even get started. Rather, these moments are about improving your "God awareness." Go with what's comfortable for you and see it as an opportunity to stretch new muscles.

Like prayer, practicing the presence of God is a skill and habit you can develop. Consider again what life was like in the Garden of Eden. There in God's presence, man and woman never worried about how they would navigate the uncertainties of the world, instead they walked and talked with him.

FINDING A FAITH FELLOWSHIP

It is in the shelter of each other
that the people live.
IRISH PROVERB

It's wonderful to have a community where we can be with those we relate to easily and comfortably. We join health spas, boys' and girls' clubs, school fraternities, hunting lodges, volunteer groups, vacation clubs, mission trips, unions, and PTAs. The same holds true for our faith communities. The power of shared beliefs draws people closer together and provides an excellent way of connecting with others. At their best, faith communities rally around their members to provide support during hard times.

Churches, synagogues, and other worship centers also offer regular opportunities to get together for social functions to have fun together. As old-fashioned as it sounds, I love getting together for church potlucks. Often this is the only time I get to see people I don't regularly keep in touch with but whom I enjoy. "Church socials" are just plain ol' fun, and they allow my kids to see that there is excitement outside of the confines of a computer screen.

Ultimately, a faith fellowship provides opportunities for you to learn and grow in your spiritual journey. This may come through classes, seminars, speakers, or just by hearing the stories of other people. It's a wonderful way to deepen your trust.

DID YOU KNOW? CHURCH AND HEALTH

According to a *Newsweek* article published in 2003, quoting Lynda H. Powell, an epidemiologist at Rush University Medical Center in Chicago, "People who regularly attend church have a 25 percent reduction in mortality—that is, they live longer—than people who are not churchgoers."[21]

PUTTING IT ALL TOGETHER

"For countless generations, Orthodox Jews have taught six Hebrew words called the *Sh'ma* to children as soon as they are able to speak. Translated into English, they are: 'Hear O Israel, the Lord God, the Lord is One.'" Several years ago, Rachel Naomi Remen wrote these words while telling about her own Jewish heritage in her book *My Grandfather's Blessing*, and how she too learned these timeless words at a very young age. *Why?* She explains that, to her grandfather, "These words always meant that despite suffering, loss, and disappointment, God can be trusted."[22]

Across the generations, the Jewish people had many reasons to doubt God's care for them, but their trust in their Creator held firm. As you stretch your spiritual muscles, don't worry about *how much* faith or trust you have. Focus on getting close to your Creator. Read books that will encourage your spiritual growth. Spend time with others who will encourage you in your relationship. You can begin today with the 3 M's.

Maximize

Set aside daily time to nurture your relationship with God. Don't focus on the length of time, focus on being consistent. Consider joining a faith fellowship where you feel comfortable and you can participate. This will greatly enhance your spiritual growth.

Moderate

Be careful of self-sufficiency. There's a limit to what you can do in your own strength. Talk with God about your challenges and responsibilities and trust him to empower you.

Minimize

You don't have to worry about what you can control, and you shouldn't worry about the things you can't. When you're stressed or unsure, remember the Prayer of Relinquishment.

Christina's Breakthrough Story
A Miracle in the Making

"Please let me live long enough to get married," prayed Christina. Not many people fall to their knees with this prayer on their lips. At least not for Christina's reasons. But then, not many people have overcome what she has.

At age six, after she had a routine urinalysis sample at a pediatrician's office, Christina's parents were informed she had a very serious case of Type I diabetes (sometimes called juvenile diabetes). With this disease, Christina's body could not produce the insulin necessary to transport fuel (sugar) from the blood into the cells. As a result, she would be at risk for many serious health complications such as heart disease, blindness, and nerve and kidney damage. Many children diagnosed with juvenile diabetes don't live to their twenty-fifth birthday.

Not knowing where else to turn, Christina and her family relied on their faith for comfort and support. Trust and suffering don't always go hand in hand, but for Christina and her family their faith was all they had. "We knew that God would be with us," Christina's mother recalls. "We were given this child for a reason and we needed to take care of her, doing all we could to keep life as normal as possible for her and her sister."

As Christina grew she became very familiar with hospitals. During her childhood, she was admitted more than a hundred times times for various reasons, including three heart attacks, three strokes, and a kidney and pancreas transplant. To maintain her health she took sixty-seven pills a day. At the age of eighteen, Christina went blind. Within a three-year period, she underwent seventeen eye operations to restore her sight.

Determined that blindness would not rob her of a relationship with God, Christina clung to her faith. The journey was not an easy one, yet her courage and dependence on God made every step strong and focused. "Many people, friends and acquaintances, would say, 'What did you do that you're being punished by God?' And I would say, 'I'm not being punished by God. I am being taught something.'" That "something" was trust. Trust despite life's challenges and uncertainties.

Enveloped in the dark of blindness, Christina battled loneliness in her room by herself. She kept her feelings of isolation at bay through prayer—communicating with God in a deeper way than she ever had before. Prior to her blindness, Christina believed, like many others, that she needed to close her eyes and get into a certain body position to pray. But now that her world was dark all the time, she began talking to God anytime she felt like it. "I learned that I was not alone," she says. "I learned that I am never alone."

Christina's sister, Barbara, was only thirteen years old when Christina went blind. To keep her sister's spirits up, Barbara learned Braille so they could share reading and music together. They also enjoyed shopping. Christina recalls, "My mom used to take us to the mall and she would walk me around and have me sniff all the stores so I could learn where I was, making a game of it."

What about Christina's early prayer to stay alive long enough to get married? Her petition did not go unanswered. Twenty-plus years after she was first diagnosed with her life-threatening disease, Christina met and married Michael, whose love sustains her to this day. Christina believes the reason she's still alive is due to the support of her family and her faith. "God must have something for me to do because if he didn't there would be no reason for me to hang around!"

Christina's doctor is convinced of the power of prayer, especially in her life. "We've studied in medicine that there are types of situations where people have utilized prayer and received strength beyond themselves. Christina is a perfect example."

"I" is for Interpersonal Relationships

8

Relationships. We want them and we need them. Intimacy is found in those rare and treasured relationships when we allow an aspect of our true selves to be shared, when we open ourselves up to the power of one heart touching another. In so doing we discover a key to health and longevity.

IN THIS CHAPTER YOU WILL:

* Find the key that may be missing from your most intimate relationships.

* Learn the one thing you can do every day to stop surviving and start thriving.

* Discover the "disease" almost never diagnosed by doctors and how you can cure it.

"I" is for Interpersonal Relationships

The default setting for humans is to be open.

Dr. Robert Paul

I've moved five times in the past sixteen years. I've had four different jobs. My husband has had five. Our "close" family members live in the Midwest, out West, up North, and down South. If it weren't for the "family" we create as we move from place to place, we'd be a mess. In all our moving, sometimes I feel like there's something missing. I've missed connecting. I like what happens to relationships over time. Being able to openly share yourself doesn't just happen the first time you meet someone on the street. It takes time to feel comfortable.

Through science we're discovering that having strong relationships can be beneficial, even vital, to our health. The "I" in CREATION Health stands for interpersonal relationships, and we achieve our greatest benefit from the intimacy those relationships bring. Intimacy, sharing your soul and being loved and valued by another person, is one of the most important factors impacting your health today. Sheldon Cohen, PhD, at Carnegie Mellon University has found that the more friends you have, the less likely you are to catch a cold. Not only that, but if you do come down with a cold, the duration and severity of symptoms will be lessened if you have lots of social contacts. On the other hand, social isolation or loneliness can be devastating to good health. Friends not only increase your capacity for pleasure, but will enhance your ability to heal.[1]

Having grown up in a nation founded on the Declaration of Independence, our cultural tendency is to take pride in being strong and "going it alone." Our focus rests mainly on our own agendas and our ability to supply our own needs rather than being open and vulnerable to others. We are culturally anchored on the principles of rugged individualism and winning through personal achievement. These ideas are daily reinforced by the commonly held belief that our worth is not only proven by what we do, but by *doing it by ourselves.* One of the consequences is that we suffer a loss of connectedness. I'm as guilty of this as anyone.

Plenty of us have worked hard and acquired all the right "things," but we've traded our ability to deeply connect. Nothing can be more damaging to our emotional health than being isolated. Why? Because we are relational creatures; we were created to share life with others. To understand the roots of intimacy and its importance to health we need to take yet another look at the Garden.

IN THE GARDEN

Few delights can equal the mere presence
of one whom we fully trust.
GEORGE MACDONALD

After God created Adam, he made a rather remarkable statement. Remember that after each day he created, God said, "This is good." But his response was not the same after creating his first human. When he created Adam, we hear God saying for the first time that something was *not* good. It wasn't that Adam was not good, but *Adam's being alone was not good.*

In the Creation story we see the first man placed in a sanctuary where everything was made with him in mind. He was afforded the plushest comforts of nature and a lifelong position as overseer of all that surrounded him. Apprenticed to the Creator, this new man was soon absorbed in learning to preside over Eden and all its creatures. Yet at the end of the day, a feeling of incompleteness came over him. Here was Paradise, perfect in every way but one—Adam's need for human intimacy. He didn't yet have a counterpart—

another human being with whom to identify and share his thoughts, dreams, and affection.

According to the ancient account, God caused Adam to fall into a deep sleep. Then he performed the first recorded surgery. The Creator extracted a rib from Adam's side and used it to form the first woman. God could have made Eve from the dust of the ground as he did Adam, but he had something else in mind. Adam's chest was opened and a protective rib was symbolically removed to signify God's intention for Adam's heart to forever remain vulnerable to his heart-to-heart companion.[2]

Viewed in this light, companionship is the central theme of Paradise. First, after having established a loving and deep connection with God, Adam had time to explore his world long enough to know himself and discover his own strengths, needs, and desires. Only then did God give Adam another with whom to share life. Intimacy with God, self, and others has been an integral part of humanity and a central element of optimal living since the beginning of time. If it wasn't good for Adam to be alone, why would it be good for us now?

THE PROBLEM OF LONELINESS

In the West there is loneliness, which I call "the leprosy of the West."
In many ways it is worse than our poor in Calcutta.
MOTHER TERESA

Loneliness has been described as the " 'disease of the decade,' [and] perhaps every decade in our middle and late twentieth century."[3] In 1950, only 10 percent of households in America consisted of just one person, but by 2004 the number reached 26 percent. Twenty-nine million Americans now live alone.[4] According to George Gallup Jr., cochairman of the Gallup Organization, "Americans are among the loneliest people in the world. As many as one-third of us admit to frequent periods of loneliness."[5] Listen to the words of Katherine Barrett in *Ladies' Home Journal* in 1983: "In a society where most people live in impersonal cities or suburbs, where electronic entertainment often replaces one-to-one [human] conversation, where people move from job to job, state to state and marriage to marriage, loneliness has become an epidemic."[6]

In the early 1980s I remember people expressing concern about the sudden popularity of portable cassette players. We thought that seeing people on the subway or on the bus with their ears plugged, purposefully isolating themselves from us, was rude. Now? We believe it is "sanity." Today you don't have to worry about running out of music on a ninety-minute cassette tape either. Just turn on your digital music player and you have thousands of songs instantly available. You can go for hours without having to interact with another human being.

Our parents and grandparents planted themselves in one community, lived in the same house, and worked at the same job until they retired and received the gold watch. So did their neighbors. They knew each other's triumphs and sorrows, saw each other's children go off to college and get married, and they celebrated the arrival of grandchildren. They ran errands for each other. They had a sense of community.

When we're isolated, alone and disconnected, we suffer. People who feel lonely and isolated are more likely to smoke, overeat, abuse drugs, and work too hard. Studies have shown that people who are lonely have three to five times the risk of premature death not only from heart disease but from *all causes of illness* when compared to those who have a sense of connection and community. When we look at numbers like this, the magnitude of risk associated with social isolation can be compared with the risks of cigarette smoking, obesity, and lack of exercise!

DID YOU KNOW? OVERCOMING LONELINESS

We all go through periods of loneliness. You can help yourself overcome bouts of loneliness if you:

1. *Understand yourself first.* Dedicate some time to understanding yourself on a deeper level. Journal your thoughts and feelings. The more you understand about yourself the better you can relate to others.
2. *Find a hobby or explore something new.* Try joining a class or a club to develop your hobby or find a new interest. You are likely to find people with some of the same interests as you with whom you can establish a relationship. Plus, it can be fun!
3. *Serve.* Consider volunteering or giving of yourself in service to others. This is one of the most fulfilling ways to conquer loneliness. When you give your time, talents, or resources to a worthy cause you step outside yourself and make a positive contribution to someone in need. This can be a powerful antidote to loneliness.
4. *Trust in Divine Power.* People who have a strong spiritual connection with God tend to feel less isolated in the world and feel more acceptance. As a result, they have more hope and peace.
5. *Join a community of faith.* A faith fellowship can act as a surrogate family where people help and uplift each other. People who join a faith group in which they feel comfortable often find great support and encouragement. See chapter 7 for more information.
6. *Try exercising.* As we discussed in chapter 6, exercise improves your mood and feelings of well-being. This may be the added boost you need to improve your outlook and see your circumstances differently.
7. *Get professional assistance.* Sometimes your loneliness may seem bigger than you can handle. If this is the case, choose professional help to get back on track. Qualified counselors, mental health professionals, or clergy can offer the support and help you need.

LIVING BY DESIGN

You cannot be lonely if you like the person you're alone with.
WAYNE DYER

Even in Paradise, human beings were incomplete without a deep, meaningful relationship with one another. What does this mean? The Creator fashioned us to be understood at the deepest level by lifelong companions. We are meant to love and be loved for life. God's original design is for us to have intimacy with him first, and to know ourselves second, which finally opens the way for us to more completely develop intimacy with others. Let's take a look at what this means for us today.

Intimacy with Self

Just as you cannot love or trust another whom you don't know, you cannot love and trust yourself until you've taken time to acquaint yourself with *you* and know what it is that you hold dear. Being intimate with yourself means you're giving yourself quality time. You're taking inventory of all four areas of life (physical, emotional, spiritual, relational) so that you can give yourself care in any area that is lacking. What brings you joy? What gives you a deep sense of fulfillment? What hurts? What areas of life need to change? Gifting yourself with routine times of solitude and quietness will allow you to know yourself more fully.

Being in solitude is very different from being lonely. Solitude is a choice to embrace one's soul rather than to alienate it. Catherine Calvert once wrote, "Solitude is a beautiful word. It sounds like sunlight through trees, or a walk on the beach, or a soprano voice that soars. Perhaps I hear the sound of 'solace' in it, the replenishment that comes from finding what's at the center of self. . . . Solitude is for those with an ample interior, with room to roam, well-provided with supplies."[7]

Like silence, solitude is something to grow into. It won't feel comfortable at first if you're not accustomed to listening intently to your heart, but with practice and a clear sense of purpose, you will come to appreciate and even long for it.

Constant sound and visual stimulation, constant movement, has become so "normal" for us that we hardly notice it. However, moments of quiet are when we are most likely to hear our thoughts, to feel our emotions, to take our spiritual temperature. We will never be able to have a complete health breakthrough without spending some moments in solitude to allow our minds to rest, giving our emotions free expression and letting our spirits connect with God.

Again, I'm reminded of my time in Huntsville, Alabama, described in chapter 2. It proved to be a special period that I spent actively getting to know me. Recently, I was taken back in time when I found a notebook with my reflections on those months of radical restructuring and renewal:

> There is a place that is becoming mine . . . a melding with my pace, with what has become my destiny, an agreement with this active silence, with the stillness, with being. I can see it so clearly in my day now . . . in my new rhythm with God. It is no mistake that I am without a dishwasher, garbage disposal, television, and mailbox. It's the quiet that allows my movement throughout the day to be more deliberate and focused.

"What could be more comforting and luxurious than spending a few quiet hours alone?" asks Tracey McBride in her simple yet profound book on luxury.[8] I've certainly found much to appreciate in times of peaceful solitude. And I miss it when I don't have it. Through solitude, we can learn to indulge in quiet and discover intimacy with ourselves.

Intimacy with God

In the Creation story we see God walking with Adam and Eve in the cool of the day. This investment of time built a deeper relationship between them. God desires relationship with us. How do you become more intimate with God? In the same way you would develop an intimate relationship with anyone else: through the opening of your heart and allowing yourself—your thoughts and feelings—to become known to him, and then asking and allowing God to do the same with you. "In the stillness of prayer we are confronted by God's loving claim upon us—the most intense intimacy a human being can experience. Instead of having to rely on our own initiative, where we are in control, we discover that we are participating in what God has already initiated within us," says James Fenhagen, author of *Ministry and Solitude*.

For a more in-depth understanding of intimacy with God, read chapter 7.

KEEP IN MIND

Avoid stereotypes. No matter how subtle they are, preconceived ideas about people cheat us of possibilities. Don't let visible differences keep you from getting to know people for who they really are.

Intimacy with Others

Intimacy with another is found in those rare and precious moments when we allow some aspect of our truest selves to be shared, or when we open ourselves up to the power of relationship. Building and nurturing meaningful relationships is a life journey. Just like learning to choose well or rest fully, you must continue painting and bringing your picture of intimacy into full color as well.

The most rewarding health experiences in my practice—situations when I saw lasting change—came in those patients with whom I had the privilege of developing ongoing relationships over the years. Many of my patients came for doctor's visits anticipating that I would prescribe drugs to lower their cholesterol levels, reduce their blood pressure, or help them lose weight. But I learned long ago that while providing people with prescriptions and health information is important, it's not enough. I also need to address their most basic need to talk, to share, and to be known. With time, the interactions I had with my patients became less about test results and more about life. We spent time talking about the children, the job, and the stressors in their lives, which in many respects were the cause of poor choices and decreased physical and emotional well-being.

These authentic exchanges between doctor and patient were in and of themselves healthy, but in addition to that, we were able to start addressing some deeper issues. Many times people felt very alone in the problems they were facing, often without places of safety, confidence, and trust. Having someone to listen to their physical symptoms, and more importantly their life challenges, provided a platform for meaningful transformation and often provided the necessary courage for them to begin addressing serious life issues. To this day, I'll see patients from long ago and we hug each other in appreciation for what we've shared together. Our office visits, though brief and sometimes few, were powerful moments of health and healing.

True intimacy is a wonderful experience, but it requires certain elements before it can be fully realized. Similar to Maslow's hierarchy of needs,* intimacy can only become a reality in an environment where partnership, safety, and nurturing exist—where each builds upon the other.

*The famed American psychologist Abraham Maslow believed that people have certain needs that must be met in hierarchal fashion before a person's full self can be actualized.

To better understand achieving intimacy with others, consider the Relationship Pyramid.* The base of the pyramid shows the fundamental level of interpersonal relationships. As you rise in the pyramid, each level successively shows a higher stage of our relationship encounters, culminating in the highest level of sharing, intimacy.

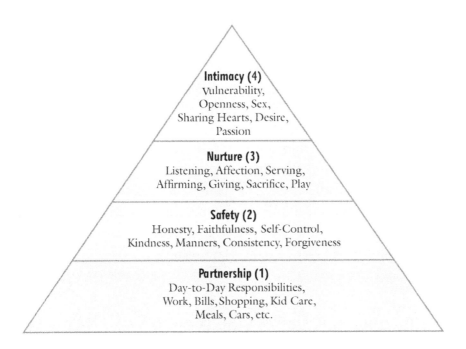

Intimacy (4)
Vulnerability,
Openness, Sex,
Sharing Hearts, Desire,
Passion

Nurture (3)
Listening, Affection, Serving,
Affirming, Giving, Sacrifice, Play

Safety (2)
Honesty, Faithfulness, Self-Control,
Kindness, Manners, Consistency, Forgiveness

Partnership (1)
Day-to-Day Responsibilities,
Work, Bills, Shopping, Kid Care,
Meals, Cars, etc.

Partnership (Level 1)

While not all of your relationships are ones in which you would reveal your innermost self—nor should they be—your interactions with the people you partner with on a daily basis can still be mean-

*The Relationship Pyramid was developed by Cathy Gibson, MA, of Vista Psychological Services, Winter Park, Florida. Used with permission.

ingful. It could be a matter of taking the time to make eye contact with the checkout clerk in the store and calling him by name (the nametag is there for a reason!), stopping to help someone who appears lost, or sharing a smile or a brief touch on the shoulder while saying "thank you." These moments we initiate interaction are fulfilling to both giver and receiver, and literally bring us life in the course of a busy day.

Partnerships are the most basic type of relationship you can have. You can't have a relationship with someone unless you are partnering in some way. Characterized by events and "to-dos," partnerships are mostly operational and are not necessarily personal. However, if the basics aren't taken care of, we are unable to share deeper levels of ourselves.

Sometimes the relationships we expect to be the most intimate get stuck in partnership mode. "Can you get the kids today?" "What time are you getting home from work?" "I need you to drop these shirts off at the cleaners." While housekeeping events in our lives need to get done, if this is the extent of "you" that is being expressed, then there is a tremendous opportunity for you to experience greater abundance in your relationships.

THE IMPORTANCE OF COMMUNITY

Judy Foreman, writer for the *Boston Globe*, penned what I found to be a fascinating article on the amazing health effects of lifelong community. "A little over a hundred years ago, a small band of Italians left Roseto Val Fortore, a village in the foothills of the Apennines, in hopes of a better life amid the slate quarries of eastern Pennsylvania.

"Naming their new village Roseto, the group soon re-created the strong community ties they had nurtured in Italy."[9] As a result of having settled in an area dominated by the English and Welsh who shunned them, the Rosetan immigrants pulled close together and not only survived, but thrived.

"They lived in three-generation households, centered their lives on family, and built their houses so close together that all it took to have a neighborly chat was a walk to the front porch."[10]

In the 1960s, medical researchers discovered a baffling statistic: in spite of the community's many commonalities with their neighbors, Rosetans died of heart attacks at a rate of only half that of the rest of America. This statistic was of special interest because the small clan of transplanted Italians led a life contrary to what the medical community would recommend for longevity.

"The men of the village smoked and drank wine freely. They spent their days in backbreaking, hazardous labor, working 200 feet down in nearby slate quarries. At home, the dinner tables each evening were laden with traditional Italian food, modified for local ingredients in ways that would drive a dietitian to despair."[11]

At it turns out, Roseto didn't have a special "protective gene," but rather a community rich in spirit, one where culture, work ethic, and celebration mattered. Most of all, "the Roseto Effect" has come to mean close ties with family and community.

Safety (Level 2)

After considering all the counseling techniques, talk shows, and magazine covers, "The easiest approach to intimacy," says Dr. Robert Paul, "is to focus on creating a safe environment for both yourself and your spouse, friend, or child. . . . When two people feel safe, they will be naturally inclined to relax and be open. Then, intimacy simply happens."[12] Safety is the fertile soil from which caring, acceptance, and affection grow. The more secure we feel in our relationships, the greater nurturance we are able to give and receive. In such a setting, we're able to share our emotions and feelings and allow others to know our hearts.

How do you move from a partnership to a more fulfilling relationship? How can we draw closer to another? Start by focusing on your relational atmosphere. Do you provide relational air for others to breathe or do you stifle them? You can begin shaping a relational "space" in which you and any other person will feel cherished, honored, and alive. By setting a safe tone, which will allow you both to feel relaxed in your relationship, you create a sanctuary for nurturance and intimacy. Start small. Make an intentional effort to maintain eye contact. Focus on care-filled, active listening. Speak words of encouragement and empathy. You don't have to go out and change the world (or an individual). But you can show you care through kindness, thoughtfulness, and being honest with others—creating a relational respite where people feel safe.[13]

Sometimes relationship pain and past hurts may make it difficult to do this by yourself. You may need the confidential sanctuary found with a counselor or clergyperson. Don't hesitate. You are meant to share in healthy, honest, accepting companionship. Don't be ashamed to seek professional help if you need it. The key is to find a place where you do feel secure; where you can share and let healing begin.

THE HEIGHT OF RELATIONSHIP: NURTURE AND INTIMACY (LEVELS 3 AND 4)

I believe the greatest gift I can conceive of having from anyone is to be seen by them, heard by them, to be understood and touched by them.
VIRGINIA SATIR

In the Genesis story we find a remarkable statement about Adam and Eve: "And they were both naked, the man and his wife, and were not ashamed."[14] This is not merely a statement of the obvious. Much more than two people walking around without clothing, these were two people totally vulnerable before each other, two people who had nothing to hide. They were embraced in an ultimate environment of safety.

When we read in the Creation story that Adam "knew" his wife, it's more than a euphemism for sex. It means that he knew his beloved without any hidden agenda—he knew her intimately— they were naked with each other in the most profound sense. Adam knew his counterpart's stories, celebrated her emotions, understood her thoughts, her motivations, and her intentions. She in turn encouraged his dreams, celebrated his triumphs, and respected his ambitions. Their physical union sprang from the heart of an ongoing emotional, mental, and spiritual union.

Notice on the pyramid that a nurturing relationship is one where there is effective listening. The ability to listen and understand the thoughts and feelings of others engages both your head and your heart. You can listen about five times as fast as a person speaks, and with that unused capacity there is a natural tendency for you to drift, daydream, and be distracted. Learning to listen well requires you to invest "you" in the conversation. Take a genuine interest in the thoughts and feelings being expressed. Be quiet and listen to understand and not just to respond. Did you get what was being said as well as the emotion behind it? Restate your understanding of what you heard, saw, and sensed. Say it in your own words. "Let me see if I understand you." And if you're confused, say so. Remember, relationships are about getting closer to one another.

A nurturing environment sets the stage for two people to come together in an extraordinary way. When two individuals who are sharing the same emotion with the same intensity open themselves to each other, something wonderful happens. "It's as if, for the moment, two souls merge into one," writes Nan Peck.[15] This is the height of intimacy. Intimacy is not limited to the physical realm. Indeed, your greatest intimate moments are ones in which all dimensions of you are involved—mind, heart, body, and soul.

Don't Invert the Pyramid

We all have a deep inborn desire to be known; however, being intimate means being open and vulnerable. Many of us struggle with not knowing whether we want to risk being open and committed to another. As a way to try to lessen the risks involved, we come up with strategies that seemingly allow us to connect "intimately" without getting hurt. One of the most common myths about relationships is that intimacy can be attained by connecting sexually without taking the time or doing the work to create a foundation of safety and nurture. Intimacy includes sex, but intimacy and sex are never one and the same. Sex is just sex when there is no established level of ongoing trust. Sex alone will not create the safety, and nurturance that allow us to know and be known. Inverting the pyramid—thinking intimacy will create partnership, safety, and nurturance—simply doesn't work. This type of relationship results in confusion and takes us farther away from a health breakthrough rather than closer. It leaves a trail of unresolved relational pain that causes us to protect ourselves and guard against letting people into our personal space. All of these actions and resulting reactions actually move us in the opposite direction from what we are ultimately seeking.

For true intimacy, no substitute will suffice. We can choose the love, affirmation, and openness we were designed for in an environment of trust and security. When we share authentically with another and in turn have them share with us, we receive one of the most spectacular wonders of Creation given to us for peace, comfort, and well-being. Intimacy.

Maintaining Intimacy: Tickles and Touches

One of the most important gifts we can give one another in life is the gift of play. How much time do you spend laughing and playing and being silly with those you love most? How much fun do you have together? These are important questions because boredom strangles relationships. We *need* ample doses of play.

"Play is the sunshine of relationships," say Jeanette and Robert Lauer in their book *The Play Solution: How to Put the Fun and Excitement Back into Your Relationship.* The Lauers interviewed three hundred couples who had been married between fifteen and sixty-one years who said they were happy in their relationship. Of those interviewed, an overwhelming majority agreed on the importance of play and humor in their relationship. This research team goes on to say, "When you play, you find the experience absorbing, an escape from everyday cares and struggles."[16]

Too often we emphasize the importance of problem-solving or talking about communication skills and tools, all the while missing one of the most simple things we all can do to make a lasting difference in our relationships. "That simple thing is just making the time for one another and in that time playing together. We live in such a busy society that it's very easy to fall through the cracks and forget that you have to make time for the relationship. It doesn't happen on its own," say Lauer and Lauer.[17]

My daughter Melanie loves to play. When she has a free moment, she'll come to me with a game of Yahtzee or checkers, or she'll want to go outside and shoot hoops. I must admit that rarely does her timing seem convenient for me. Usually I'm tired from my day and looking for a personal retreat. But what I continue to learn over and over again is that when we play together, I actually start feeling better. The game relaxes me and brings energy. We laugh and have a good time; it refreshes me and keeps me feeling young. The laughter in those moments usually results in spontaneous hugs, kisses, and moments of "I love you, Mommy." And when you've been hugged by Melanie, you have really been hugged! Our hearts open to each other and relationship magic happens.

We need to play more in our spousal relationships as well. We are far too adult-ish, occupied with life's many concerns. Play is a welcome escape into our child-selves, which brings balance to the worries of the day. And when the whole family gets outside together and plays, what great moments are created! Our play together reminds us that "these kids aren't half bad," and neither are we. These "tickles" are pathways for sharing our hearts and creating some of our favorite memories.

Touch

A partner to play and an important aspect of intimacy is affectionate touch. One of the things I love to do is to teach people how to hug. There is something wonderful about a full-body squeeze and it's so easy to give. Psychotherapist Virginia Satir, the "Mother of Family System Therapy," is well-known for saying that we need four hugs a day for survival, eight hugs a day for maintenance, and twelve hugs a day for growth. For most of us, that means we need more touch.

What a difference touch makes for both me and my patients when we've talked together—especially in moments of crisis. The ability to hold hands or to lay a hand on the shoulder of the one in pain makes a profound impact on the experience. What a difference it makes in my day when I step out of my corporate persona and give or receive a hug from a fellow coworker between meetings. Touch conveys so much: acceptance, companionship, concern, and through touch we affirm our care for one another, communicating what words can never say. We come closer to optimal health when we share our affection through gentle touch.

MINI QUIZ

How many hugs have you received today? How many have you given?

RESOLVING PAIN AND RESTORING INTIMACY

Forgiveness does not change the past,
but it does enlarge the future.
PAUL BOESE

The quality of your relationships determines to a large extent the quality of your lives. Some people can actually create such stress that when you are around them you feel nervous or anxious. These types of relationships obviously work against your health. We've all had relationships in our lives that create stress; phone numbers that pop up on the caller ID that we dread answering; people we actively avoid; acquaintances we find draining. At the time, we may feel badly about protecting ourselves from such people, but science supports the notion that building healthy relational boundaries is in fact very beneficial.

Research indicates that poor relationships can make you physically ill as a direct result of ongoing conflict. Stressful relationships are a factor in serious illness and degenerative disease to the degree they impact your life. While this does not give license to sever close ties recklessly, seriously consider whether that significant person is safe and trustworthy. If not, and this relationship is valuable, you should take a step down on the pyramid and reestablish a safe zone. Once there is mutual safety, you can ascend the pyramid again.

Forgiveness

Regardless of race, creed, color, or background, everyone has been hurt by someone in the past. It may have been a parent, spouse, child, friend, relative, boss, or coworker. Each of us has experienced the pain of wounding words or unkind actions. Too often, that pain leads to strong negative emotions—such as anger—that can linger for years.

According to Dr. Dick Tibbits in his book *Forgive to Live*, when you are emotionally injured, a "grievance story" is created.[18] This is a story you repeat over and over again in your mind (consciously or subconsciously) about the injustice done to you. It may sound innocent enough, but in the end your grievance story will destroy not only your happiness but your health also. The longer you hold on to such a story, the greater the negative impact it has on your health. The consequences include an increased risk of heart disease, a lack of mental and emotional peace, feelings of loneliness, social isolation, and a shorter life span. Cardiologist Dr. Redford Williams of Duke University Medical Center demonstrates that repressed anger can kill you. His studies show how anger can influence the progression of heart disease and as a result of his work, the American Heart Association (AHA) added anger to the known risk factors for heart disease.[19]

What's the solution for unresolved anger? Forgiveness.

Forgiveness is a way of learning how to handle life rather than being overwhelmed by it. Forgiveness focuses on the ability to let go of a painful past and replace it with something better. In his classic book *Forgive and Forget*, Lewis Smedes, late professor of philosophy at Fuller Graduate School of Psychology, points out that forgiveness is not just something righteous or religious people need to do, but an essential exercise for everyone.[20] Forgiveness helps a person emotionally and physically by dealing with the anger and the hurt that's been inflicted by others. Forgiveness helps a person socially because people who retain anger are usually not much fun to be around. These people tend to isolate themselves (or be isolated by society) and can end up experiencing loneliness.

KEEP IN MIND

Two things should be kept in mind when it comes to forgiveness.

1. Forgiveness is a choice that only you can make.
2. Forgiveness is a learned skill you can use effectively with practice.

While encouraging choosing to forgive and learning how to do so more effectively, Dr. Tibbits further asserts that forgiveness can take place at any one of three levels. Each has a different approach and a different benefit. The first level of forgiveness takes place "within myself." This is where I come to terms with the fact that I am not perfect, but I can forgive my own imperfections. This level of forgiveness is not dependent upon anything another person may or may not do. Yet by practicing forgiveness here, I move from victim to victor. The second level of forgiveness is "between myself and the offender." This requires joint participation and mutual understanding. This may or may not occur. Reconciliation is not always possible, but when it is, it can change lives like nothing else. The third level of forgiveness is spiritual, and takes place "between God and myself." This is where I understand the impact and meaning of his forgiveness toward me. As a result, I am more understanding of the shortcomings and failures of others, and thus I am more willing to forgive.

As with learning to connect with self, others, and God, each level of forgiveness is related yet independent. Therefore, I can forgive even if reconciliation is not possible. I can heal my pain even if the pain between me and the other person cannot be resolved. The essential question of forgiveness is not "who did what?" but "will I allow this event that occurred to ruin my life or enrich it?" Though forgiveness is hard, the alternative is worse. When you don't forgive, you are the one left suffering. Once you understand this, it's easier to see that forgiveness is for your own good.[21]

Gathering Intimacy by Giving

I've heard of an old English proverb that says, "The heart that gives . . . gathers." I find these words especially timely for today. It's a natural reaction to "shut down" after a painful experience. Be careful about keeping parts of yourself closed for extensive periods of time or ignoring/denying how you actually feel. You may feel that walls keep pain out of your life, but those same walls also keep joy from entering in. If you have erected walls of emotional protection, you may be surviving but you're not *thriving*, and it's not a healthy place to live for any length of time.

What can you do to develop meaningful connections once you've begun to heal? Consider volunteering. In my own life, I've found that reaching out to others can create the kind of meaning that sustains me not only through a process of recovery but throughout my life. At various times I recall tutoring high school and college students, feeding the homeless in Los Angeles, and giving my time with the PTA at my children's school. These times of serving others have always helped me to round out my life and allowed me to see a bigger picture than just my own story. So many times I've intended to give a little bowl of soup to support someone else and have returned home with an emotional feast for myself.

"Sometimes we look for intimacy in all the wrong places," says Renita Weems, author of *I Asked for Intimacy*. "Sometimes it is to be found in the strangest of places and with the most unlikely people. . . . The relationship may not be a permanent one—nor does it have to be. But the experience of intimacy is always a lasting one."[22]

We are meant to share life with others. We were never meant to survive alone. Knowing yourself, drawing close to God, and reaching out to others are truly secrets to living a long and fulfilled life.

SCIENCE SAYS

"It would seem fairly intuitive that helping others would make you feel good, but what about actual health benefits? Studies have shown that volunteering can play a role in increasing your overall sense of well-being, alleviating chronic pain, and even reducing depression," writes Patricia Griffin Kellicker.[23]

PUTTING IT ALL TOGETHER

Intimacy is a relational continuum reaching from basic partnerships to finding the freedom of embracing another without inhibition or fear. What we may have accomplished in one relationship we may not yet have in another. There is no better time than the present to grow healthier in our interpersonal relationships.

Eden was indeed Paradise, not merely because of its beauty and bounty, but because it was a supremely safe place for relationships to grow. The first man and woman felt no fear or inhibitions. They enjoyed an amazing relationship with God, themselves, and each other. You don't need to wait passively to see what becomes of your relationships. You can actively engage in knowing yourself, God, and others starting today with the 3 M's.

Maximize

Make the most of the moments you spend with people you care deeply about. Listen, laugh, play, and hug up! Remember that safety is the soil in which intimacy grows. Listen, affirm, and "do unto others as you would have them do unto you."

Moderate

Watch for feelings of loneliness. Start a new hobby, volunteer, take a class. If you feel alone more than is comfortable, take the time to discover why. Talk with a trusted family member, friend, or professional.

Minimize

Don't hold on to unresolved hurt and pain in your life. Forgive yourself and others. It's a choice you can make and a skill you can learn with practice.

Jim & Sally's Breakthrough Story
First I Gave Him My Heart

Jim had been feeling unusually tired. Sensing there might be something wrong physically, he went to the hospital for an exam and some answers. Sadly, the news wasn't good. After living with a chronic illness for more than thirty-seven years, his kidneys were nearly worn out. In fact, they were in the process of shutting down, and not much time remained. It would take a kidney transplant to save his life.

As doctors talked with Jim and his wife, Sally, they explained that the best donor would likely be one of Jim's siblings. He had four brothers and sisters, but to the doctors' surprise, Sally wanted to be tested first. She wanted to be the donor herself. The doctors explained that the chances of a good kidney match were far greater with a blood relative. But Sally insisted on being tested anyway, and the doctors finally agreed to give it a try.

The results were remarkable. Sally's and Jim's blood makeup turned out to be very similar, making the chance of a successful transplant very high. So the surgery was quickly approved. She realized the risks involved, and what could potentially happen if both she and her husband suffered complications either during or after surgery. The operation would last over three hours, and recovery would take at least two months. The time away from work would be financially tough, and their three children would have to be cared for by others. Despite the risks and challenges and an unknown future, Sally was undaunted. She would give her kidney to her husband.

The surgery was successful, and the couple even got to recover in side-by-side beds after the operation. Since then, life has returned to normal with one exception, Jim and Sally are now a one-heart, three-kidney marriage.

When asked why she insisted on being the donor for Jim, her reply was simple. "I gave him my heart nineteen years ago," she said. "What's a kidney?"

"O" is for Outlook

9

Outlook is how you see the world. It's the colors on the palette with which you paint your life. A healthy outlook belongs to those who choose to open their minds to learn, stretch, and grow. Outlook is a powerful, invisible force influencing your body's health and healing.

IN THIS CHAPTER YOU WILL:

* Understand how to transform your thoughts to ensure your success.

* Discover the secret to boosting creativity and brilliance.

* Learn to conquer attitudes that limit your potential.

"O" is for Outlook

Inside yourself or outside,
you never have to change what you see,
only the way you see it.

THADDEUS GOLAS

A friend of mine traveled overseas and was now on his way home to America. Stopping off in several countries, he passed through various customs offices. At each of these checkpoints he found he was regularly being searched and sometimes even harassed. One particularly rude customs official shouted at him for no apparent reason. Another took him to a security room where he was searched and questioned. A third official pulled apart his suitcase and went through every item, going so far as to open shampoo and lotion bottles and sticking his finger in them. After the search was completed, Ben's suitcase was tossed aside and he was told to repack it himself, even if it meant missing his next flight.

As I listened to the story, I could feel myself getting riled. Ben is a friend and a talented, poised professional with brilliant business sense. "How did you endure that?!" I asked. Looking me straight in the eye, he said, "Monica, these guys were doing their jobs. It wasn't about me—or at least I chose not to think so. Yes, it was frustrating, but I had to keep telling myself and remembering, they don't know me. They're paid to make sure that their countries remain secure. I was just the *lucky* one that day."

Outlook. Famous author Chuck Swindoll says that the single most significant decision he can make on a day-to-day basis is his choice of attitude. "It is more important than my past, my education, my bankroll, my success or failures. . . . Attitude . . . keeps me going or cripples my progress. It alone fuels my fire or assaults my hope. When my attitudes are right, there's no barrier too high, no valley too deep, no dream too extreme, no challenge too great for me."[1]

THE MIND-BODY CONNECTION

If you want your life to be more rewarding,
you have to change the way you think.
OPRAH

Have you ever been around a person who always expects the best? We all know people who have weathered similar life experiences to ours, but no matter what happens, they always seem to naturally find the bright side. Most of us "normal people" tend to find these eternal optimists somewhat annoying. But maybe we're just jealous. *Can life really be that good?* we wonder. *If so, why isn't mine so great?* Can it really be just a matter of perspective? Research says, probably so. Looking at the bright side is a skill that can be learned. And that's good news, because seeing the bright side not only adds years but also flavor to your life.

Optimists paint their world with bright colors. Built-in coping mechanisms, such as the "every cloud has a silver lining" mentality, enable upbeat people to better weather stress and difficulty. Support systems are also paramount to bright optimists. Mental health research supports that strong relational ties and social networks are a central factor for people with positive outlook.

We also know what it's like to be around people who can't see a silver lining anywhere at any time. Think about how it makes you feel to be in their presence. They pull you down, take away your energy; they're simply not fun to be around. If their negative outlook is having that effect on your bodies just by hearing it, can you imagine what it must do to the body of the one who is living it?

A sour outlook does affect your health; people who perpetually see the glass "half empty" are more prone to isolation, worry, and depression. When you're depressed, certain brain hormones are depleted, creating a chain of biochemical events that ends up slowing down the activity of the whole immune system.[2] You're more inclined to sickness and even earlier death.

SCIENCE SAYS

T cells and NK cells are key players in your immune system. When your T cells recognize viruses, they begin multiplying to ward off the dangerous invaders. Your NK cells are important in fighting against cancer. According to researchers, pessimists' T cells don't multiply as quickly as optimists' do, and while pessimists' NK cells recognize dangerous cells, they're less effective in destroying them, making a person more vulnerable to disease.[3]

No one would describe me as Miss Pollyanna, but I really do try to make a conscious effort to speak words of hope, or at least words of possibility. I learned this the hard way. Early in my career I had a front-office manager who never "saw the light at the end of the tunnel." Every time she sought me out, no matter what the issue, her sentence always started with, "Dr. Reed, we have a problem . . ." I grew to hate the word "problem," especially when it was preceded by "we." I avoided her like the plague—not really a good thing to do when you're running an office practice. Finally I decided it was time for a chat. We exchanged business pleasantries, and then I dove in. "Lucille," I said, "please don't ever use the word 'problem' with me again. Tell me you have a challenge, tell me you are giving an issue some thought, tell me you have a question, but please don't tell me that 'we have a problem'!" She was stunned, but she got it. I don't know if she was happier for it, but I sure was!

Optimism, Pessimism, Realism: Which "Ism" Is Best?

Is there life between the two extremes? What about the realist? "I just call it like I see it," the realist may argue. "Sometimes you just can't make lemonade when circumstances give you lemons." "Life is not all bad, but it's not all good, either."

If you consider yourself a realist and think that optimists aren't always in touch with reality, you're right! Actually, realists and pessimists are more often right . . . but optimists *accomplish more in life*. Well-respected researcher Martin Seligman, PhD, in his book *Learned Optimism* holds that "optimists have a strong sense of belief that whatever the odds, they can be overcome—regardless of the condition of the water, one can still swim across. Realists want to test the water before they leap, while people who are fully pessimistic don't believe things will work out for them, and so they never even jump in. Pessimists don't get a chance to find out if they can or can't do it," says Seligman.[4]

THE IMPORTANCE OF STAYING MENTALLY FIT

A merry heart doeth good like medicine.
KING SOLOMON

Outlook is your ability to stay "mentally fit." Your outlook has a far-reaching influence on everything, from your day-to-day life, selection of mate and friends, choice of career, and even your long-term success and happiness. Unfortunately, research shows that we Americans are as out of shape mentally as we are physically. Depression is a critical health care problem in our nation. Almost 20 million American adults in a given year have a depressive disorder, and as many as one in every eight Americans will experience an episode of depression requiring treatment in their lifetime. Prescription drug sales for anxiety and depression are at an all-time high. In fact, clinical depression is about ten times as frequent now as it was fifty years ago and depressive disorders may be appearing earlier in life in people born in recent decades compared to the past.[5]

While the incidence of depression does cause concern, even greater numbers of people live just under the depression radar chronically "stressed out." When you face significant life changes, a loss of a loved one, or an uncertain future, anxiety is expected. But much of the stress we experience is because what we *plan* to do exceeds what we have the *ability* to do. In a 2003 Gallup poll, half of U.S. adults stated that they lacked the time they needed to do the things they wanted. In addition, three-quarters of adult Americans said they were "sometimes" stressed in their daily lives, including one in three who experienced stress "frequently."[6]

Misplaced Expectations

Expectations are a powerful force in your life. What you think life should be was imprinted in your early life. As you get older, what you read, who you listen to, and what you choose to believe shapes your expectations. These expectations will either gently *nudge* you along or *drive* you headlong. Your preconceived ideas and expectations determine whether you see your life as a success or a failure. They determine your degree of anxiety. When expectations are misplaced or are unrealistic, you can be sure frustration, anger, and a dismal perspective on life will result.

Destructive Patterns

With each life experience, we automatically perform a mental evaluation. If the situation is threatening, we determine how to best deal with it, and what skills we can use. If we decide the demands of the situation outweigh the skills we have, then we label the situation as "stressful" and react with the classic stress response. This "fight-or-flight" stress response results in the release of stress hormones into the bloodstream, preparing us for action. Stress hormones, if left unchecked, can have a very damaging effect on our bodies.

When you have multiple work assignments, or you're squeezing one more appointment into an already crammed schedule, when you're juggling competing responsibilities, you get tense, anxious, and sick. Living stressed out is not a way to live. It really is the way of illness. You know what it looks like. From the blues to insomnia, ulcers, irritable bowel, and chronic headaches and more, our bodies are screaming for us to take a different approach—to ease up on the tension.

How can you step away from destructive patterns and thought processes? By staying mentally fit, you alter the course of your life and bring added vitality. I want you to do more than whisper positive thoughts. Positive thinking in and of itself is not enough to make us mentally fit. You can have a positive outlook because you have access to a mentally fit, eternally optimistic Creator who is involved and interested in the details of your life. Willing yourself to have a good attitude will help for a while. But when your inspiration comes from a Divine Power established from an intimate trust in God, yourself, and loved ones, it doesn't have to be conjured up. You don't have to rely on your own power of positive thinking.

ARE YOU MENTALLY FIT?

According to Ian Pike, people who are mentally fit live longer and are more resistant to depression. Take a moment to assess your mental fitness.

Do You:
* Live in the here and now, and respond to people and events in a genuine way?
* Know the difference between what you can and cannot change?
* Take steps to control what you can change and take responsibility for your actions and feelings?
* Give and receive love, share your feelings with others?

* Gauge people by their individual merits and not according to race, sex, age, or economic background?
* Lead as well as follow, judge as well as empathize?
* Take pleasure in family, community, work, and leisure without expecting perfection?
* Feel good in your own skin and have a sense of being worthwhile?

Adapted from Ian Pike, "Mental Health Pivotal Dimension of Optimal Health," *Visions: BC's Mental Health Journal* 4 (1998): 2–3, www.cmha-bc.org/content/resources/visions/issues/04.pdf.

THROUGH EYES OF EDEN

The best is yet to be.
ROBERT BROWNING

You may have anticipated by now that scientific discoveries about mental fitness have their roots in a story dating back thousands of years.

In the very beginning the Creator looked out on a vast, empty space of nothingness and envisioned a glorious universe filled with promise. With each brushstroke of Creation, the Master Artist exclaimed, "This is good! This is good! This is very good!" And finally, with Adam at his side, I can imagine he turned and asked, "What do you think?"

I have a hard time picturing Adam shaking his head and saying, "I don't know, I just don't like it." No. Spurred on with contagious enthusiasm, Adam must have stood awestruck, and then with full eagerness began exploring this Garden of wonder and possibility.

In essence God said, "This is your home. This is where you will be master of your domain . . . work and play with all your heart, live with all your life and love with all your being." "But," you may say, "that was then, this is now . . . that was Paradise! Now our world is war-torn, famine-plagued, filled with illness, disease, and death. Evil seems to have the upper hand." Remember, evil soon existed in Eden as well. And like the first man and woman, our outlook is directly connected to our ability to trust a God who can look at empty space and see a universe. We are empowered to live freely and fully. Evil does exist, but it doesn't have to be our focus and it doesn't have to control us.

In Charge of Your Beliefs

Launching into strategies to develop a healthier outlook and ongoing mental fitness requires us to start at the very beginning, the genesis, or what scholars call the apriority of the thought or idea. Mental fitness starts with our beliefs. What we believe about ourselves and life in general can either hold us hostage or set us free. Belief is more than just an idea. According to Talmudic teaching, "We do not see things as they are. We see them *as we are.*" We see life through the lenses of our own beliefs, and depending on the conviction of our beliefs it can be difficult to convince ourselves that what we see is not what is real. My husband is always reminding me of the templates I have in my head of how "life is supposed to be." My way of thinking is not necessarily his way. The less willing I am to change my lenses every once in a while, or maybe even borrow his glasses, the poorer my perspective. The good news is that we can be in charge of our beliefs. We'll explore some pointers to do just that.

Avoid Self-Fulfilling Prophecies

Henry Ford once said, "Whether you think you can, or that you can't, you are usually right." If you believe you will fail, chances are high that you will. Expect the worst from people and that's what you will get. Belief is very powerful, and we have much more control over our views than we first anticipate. If you allow yourself to focus on a negative outcome, you will most likely fall into the trap of a self-fulfilling prophecy—unconsciously you may set yourself up for failure. If you go to a party, for example, assuming that you will have a bad time, you're probably not going to be extremely friendly or open-minded. You will create your own bad time. And of course the opposite is true: if you go expecting to meet new people and enjoy yourself, chances are you will.

SCIENCE SAYS: HOW YOU SEE THE WORLD IS MORE IMPORTANT THAN HOW THE WORLD IS

David Niven, PhD, writes about a study wherein scientists showed people a deck of playing cards. Each card had something out of the ordinary. For example, the clubs were red, the five of diamonds had four. People were then shown the cards and asked to tell what they saw. "Were the people surprised to see these obviously error-filled cards? They were not, because they didn't notice. When asked to describe the cards they were looking at, people answered they were looking at the five of diamonds or the four of clubs. They didn't mention that the cards were mismarked. Why did this happen? Because what we see is a function not only of what is really there, but also of what we are looking for—our expectations (our beliefs), our assumptions."[7]

Practice TSE

Martin Seligman's research shows that pessimists see problems as being permanent, pervasive, and personal. In contrast, optimists see life's unpleasantries as temporary, specific, and external (TSE),[8] Seligman explains. Imagine your boss is not pleased with your last project. Instead of thinking, "I'll never be able to please him" (permanent), realize that you can talk with your boss, clarify his expectations, and improve the project (temporary). Instead of thinking, "I never do a good job," recognize the possibility that you may not have given this project your best effort (specific). And finally, instead of thinking, "I'm a lousy performer" (personal), tell yourself "the boss didn't get what he wanted and that can be fixed" (external).[9]

Choose Happiness

If you believe you can be happy, you will be. Sometimes a bit of intentionality will help. We can all afford to put on some rose-colored glasses from time to time. "Choosing happiness will energize you, mobilize your strength, and motivate you to keep you going during the hard times."[10] In other words, just as we discussed in the chapter on Choice, our behavior can have a profound effect on our beliefs. For an overall sense of happiness, you can afford to turn on a little optimism from time to time. You may be surprised to see how happy you really can be.

STRATEGIES FOR OPTIMISM

Always direct your thoughts to those truths that will give you confidence,
hope, joy, love, thanksgiving, and turn away your mind from
those that inspire you with fear, sadness, depression.
BERTRAND WILBERTFORCE

Just as we incorporate activity into our lives to increase our physical fitness, we need to develop and maintain specific exercises for our mental well-being. The most fitting strategy to improve optimism and mental fitness is to simplify and clarify your purpose in life. Once you identify what's really important you can let go of standards of living and demands that don't fit into your mission for life. Being free of these pressures is an inspiring and freeing proposition.

Sometimes the propositions can also be a bit scary. My health and well-being are my most important priority. And after three years back at the hospital in a new administrative role, I was mentally exhausted. I was overloaded, cranky, and I needed a break.

Not just a two-week vacation—I needed some serious time off. I tried out the idea on my husband. "Honey," I said, "I'm gonna ask for three months off. I need it. My mind is tired." Now you have to understand, this is a man who has heard some rather unconventional ideas from me. He's learned to survive these conversations with the necessary first step—validation. "Okay, honey," he said politely. I knew he was alarmed, though, because his voice was a little higher than usual.

"And what will you do if they deny your request?" he asked too calmly.

I'd already thought it through. "I'll just quit!"

He looked at me for a long minute, paused, and said, "Okay, honey."

You can feel sorry for him. I do. The man really shouldn't have to deal with such stress.

Later on we came back to the topic and really talked it through. We agreed that health was most important, and instead of trying to figure out the "what ifs," we would start with the request for extended time and take it from there. We were both relieved when it was approved—no doubt for slightly different reasons! Something quite remarkable happened after I made the decision to take time off. Coworkers freely shared their personal stories of burnout with me, sometimes in tears. Some of them took much-needed time off. When you clarify your priorities, everyone wins—you, your family, and your workplace.

Clarifying Priorities

To live wholly and freely, you must have a clear sense of what matters most to you, and align your daily actions with those things that you say are truly important. If you need some help determining what really is important to you, take a look at your weekly schedule and your checkbook! That helps to clarify things rather quickly, and then you can spend some time with what your life is, and what you want your life to be. In his best-selling book *The Purpose-Driven Life,* Rick Warren points out:

> Knowing your purpose simplifies your life. It defines what you do and what you don't do. Your purpose becomes the standard you use to evaluate which activities are essential and which aren't. . . . Without a clear purpose you have no foundation on which you base decisions, allocate your time, and use your resources. You will tend to make choices based on circumstances, pressures, and your mood at that moment. People who don't know their purpose try to do too much—and *that* causes stress, fatigue, and conflict.[11]

Take some time to think about your purpose. Make sure your purpose is in line with your overall vision and that it is a true reflection of what you really want and were created for. Develop a personal mission statement. The Three-Day Rejuvenation Therapy is a perfect time to do this. You'll be giving yourself permission to spend your days doing what you most want to do—not only what others expect of you.

Simplifying Your Life

There is a big difference between being busy and being productive. An important step in improving your mental fitness is to stop the busyness; do less and enjoy it more. If you feel overburdened, look at your schedule to see where you can eliminate all nonessential commitments. Declutter your life and your environment to create space. More space will automatically give you the feeling of more time. Simplify your life. Savor and appreciate what you have now rather than working harder to have more. Joy is most often found in appreciation for what we already have, not wanting what we don't have.

Developing the Practice of Solitude

Schedule time in your calendar set aside just for you. Stretch, dance, walk in nature, read, journal, do yoga or tai chi, paint or draw, meditate, focus on your breathing—do something that allows you to be quiet but alive.

Peter Suedfeld, PhD, a recognized expert on the science of solitude, states, "When you are alone and quiet, your degree of negativity decreases while your degree of alertness increases. As a result, solitude and reduced stimulation can restore your ability to think clearly, be creative, and maintain emotional calm."[12]

Try to take at least fifteen minutes a day to be in complete silence with no distractions or interruptions. If fifteen minutes of silence makes you feel like you're going to go crazy, start with five and gradually increase. You don't need to do anything during this time. Practicing silence, or quiet contemplation, allows clarity, order, and a sense of ease and peace to emerge. Set the tone of your day and recenter on your purpose. Don't forget to express gratitude for what you have.

Once you become comfortable with silence, a sense of peaceful energy and a natural order comes into your life that doesn't require as much of your effort and control. After a period of creative silence, you will find it takes less time to accomplish tasks. Your true values and priorities emerge and take precedence over competing demands on your time. You will find direction and answers to questions you've been thinking about.

Relaxation Exercise: Deep Belly Breathing

One of the simplest forms of stress management is deep belly breathing. When we get stressed or worried one of the physical symptoms is shorter, more shallow breaths. This actually adds to feelings of anxiety. Learning deep belly breathing techniques helps to balance your nervous system, calm you down, and make you feel more peaceful and relaxed. In the book *Stress Free for Good*, Stanford University researchers Dr. Fred Luskin and Dr. Kenneth Pelletier advise, "Breathing slowly and deeply into and out of your belly is a signal to your mind and body to let go of stress and improve your health and happiness." The authors give the following steps to learn the best technique:

1. Inhale and imagine that your belly is a big balloon that you're slowly filling with air.
2. Place your hands on your belly while you slowly inhale.
3. Watch your hands as they rise with your in-breath.
4. Watch your hands fall as you slowly breathe out, letting the air out of the balloon.
5. Exhale, making sure your belly stays relaxed.
6. Take at least two or three more slow and deep breaths, making sure to keep your attention on the rise and fall of your belly.[13]

The best time to deep belly breathe is whenever you feel anxious, nervous, stressed, or angry. But it's also good to practice this skill every day whether you are anxious or not. The benefits of deep breathing can be yours anytime.

Take Brain Breaks

Quiet times such as a yearly vacation, a weekly day of rest, or my three-month sabbatical reorient and center our lives. But what about during the workday? My boss asked me an important question before approving my time: "What are you going to do differently when you get back?" I've learned. If I need to think through a work issue, instead of staying late at the office and working away until the wee hours, I leave and try to find a quiet, relaxing place to catch my thoughts. Even if it means going to bed. Your brain needs time for recovery. I guarantee you the solution will come quicker and more creatively with a fresh mind.

As the day wears on, your productivity decreases. The reason is simple—you need a break. Next time you feel the blahs coming on, instead of ignoring them or grabbing a Coke and powering your way through, acknowledge that your tank is running on empty. Take a Brain Break by stepping away from your work for a three-minute stretch. Take a few deep belly breaths and focus on a pleasant thought. You can also revitalize yourself with quiet time outdoors or by looking at relaxing pictures or listening to sounds of nature. An even simpler method for a time-out is to put your head down on your desk for a few moments. Remember doing that in the first grade when the teacher thought things were getting out of control? After turning the lights down, what did she say? "Everyone put your heads down!" What we perceived as punishment was actually a quiet time that allowed everyone to regroup. If we needed quiet time in the first grade, we certainly need it now!

Without a break, our lives can get just as unruly as a class of disorderly first-graders. In the end, an overtaxed, ridiculous schedule will wear out strategy any day. We simply can't smile our way through a forty-hour workweek that has eighty hours worth of "to-dos." Overtaxed schedules and unrealistic goals will consistently rob us of our joy and peace. A positive outlook is not the fixer-upper for a harried, pressured life—to paste on a smile and keep driving yourself into the ground. Instead, true optimism is the "can-do" outlook that allows you to say, "Because I choose to make this better, it will be better and this is how." *That's* something you can smile about!

Play and Laughter

Not all of your mental fitness activity needs to be purpose-filled and goal-oriented—nor should it be. Picture kids playing in a yard or garden or just lying on their backs looking up at cloud formations. Where are the adults? It's time to join in the fun!

DID YOU KNOW?

Psychologist and author Kay Redfield Jamison suggests, "Play increases performance on a variety of measures of intelligence. Adults as well as children who play engage in a number of valuable cognitive activities: they strategize and learn to take risks in a safe setting. With nothing at stake, they learn flexibility in response to changing situations and are brought into situations that encourage dopamine-inducing laughter. People who play, especially those who play regularly with good friends, enjoy better communication skills and closer relationships."[14]

There's nothing better than a good laugh to bring a smile to your spirit. The release of endorphins makes us feel good inside and decreases stress and tension. We talked about the importance of laughter in our intimate relationships, but being able to laugh at yourself helps keep your life in perspective. It helps us not to take ourselves—or life—too seriously. And laughter is not only good for your spirit. It's actually good for your heart.

Researchers at the University of Maryland School of Medicine in Baltimore have shown for the first time that laughter is linked to healthy function of blood vessels. They assert that laughter appears to cause the tissue that forms the inner lining of blood vessels to expand. This helps increase blood flow, which has a healthy effect on your arteries and reduces your risk of cardiovascular disease. Says principal investigator Michael Miller, MD, director of preventive cardiology at the University of Maryland Medical Center, "At the very least, laughter offsets the impact of mental stress, which is harmful to the endothelium. . . . We recommend that you try to laugh on a regular basis. Thirty minutes of physical exercise three times a week, and 15 minutes of laughter on a daily basis is strongly recommended for the vascular system."[15]

PUTTING IT ALL TOGETHER

Many people neglect to appreciate the gentle kindnesses and tender mercies that touch their lives on a daily basis. Your positive mental outlook begins the moment you determine to make the most of any situation in which you find yourself. Begin by designing an attitude, home, and lifestyle that appeals to your sense of well-being. Choose to embellish ordinary days with intelligence, comfort, beauty, and a renewed faith that God created your life with you in mind. In the words of Tracey McBride, "Choose now to become quietly privileged."[16] You'll be well on your way when you practice the 3 M's.

Maximize

Expect good and you will find it! Take daily Brain Breaks, practice daily deep belly breathing, and laugh. Surround yourself with the positive forces that lift your spirit. Set the tone of your day with positive thoughts—pick a simple sentence that reflects your vision and purpose with which you can start each day.

Moderate

Want what you can have—align your desires with your purpose. Embrace the beauty and gifts that are already yours. Journal to keep yourself accountable to you. Maintain a schedule that reflects your values.

Minimize

Monitor yourself for burnout. Don't let competing technology or distractions keep you from enjoying the moment. Be present, centering your focus on the task or relationship at hand. This will bring greater fulfillment and minimize stress.

Rachel's Breakthrough Story
I Wanted to Live

Rachel was young, vivacious, and pretty. A typical teenager, she enjoyed spending time with family and friends and just having fun. Unfortunately, her life took a rather drastic turn. An unexpected accident left her a quadriplegic.

When she realized she'd be paralyzed and would spend the rest of her life in a wheelchair everything turned upside down. At first she didn't believe it. Maybe the doctors were mistaken. But nothing changed. And yet in that same moment everything changed. She was depressed for months. It seemed like her life, her dreams, her aspirations—everything—had come to a screeching halt. Was this life now? It didn't seem she could go on. In truth, she didn't want to.

In the quietness of those months, Rachel slowly began to realize that she didn't want to spend her life angry and isolated either. She had to go on, somehow. It took time, but she started coming to grips with her new reality. She realized that despite the changes in her body and her limitations, she was still Rachel. She still wanted to have fun. She really did have dreams and she thought she still wanted to pursue them. She didn't know how that was going to happen, but she knew she could at least start with today.

She started going to physical therapy. Eventually, although wheelchair-dependent, she learned to bathe and dress herself. In time, with special equipment she learned to make her own food. She even learned how to drive with a specially equipped van. With each new accomplishment her confidence level increased. She had some bad days, but she didn't allow them to overwhelm her. She started enjoying life again with her family and friends and she learned how to share her struggles. She even started pursuing her dream career as a model. Slowly, life started coming together again. Illness and disability stopped consuming her every thought. She was living. Going through physical therapy opened her eyes to people who were trying to manage just like her. She started speaking to groups of other disabled patients, encouraging them by sharing her triumphs and pitfalls.

Rachel is the first to tell you that her life is not easy, but she quickly adds, "Whose is? It took me some time to get to this point—a lot of it. But once it hit me that I was still gifted to have life, I wanted it. I wanted to live. I focus on what I do have, and it's so much. Realizing that helps me get through the difficulties. Looking back, I'd have to say that a changed outlook has made all the difference."

"N" is for Nutrition

10

Providing what our bodies need for fuel and pleasure, nutrition is the highest form of art and science converging. No other species on the planet has been given such vast variety and choice for sustenance.

We've been gifted with a myriad of choices for daily sustenance, yet when we hear the word "nutrition" we feel twinges of misgiving. We've come to believe, "If it is good for us, it's bound to be tasteless."

Nothing could be further from the truth.

IN THIS CHAPTER YOU WILL:

* Find out two truths about food that can save your life . . . or ruin it.

* Learn the ultimate disease-fighting diet.

* Discover the way to lose weight without counting calories or fat grams.

"N" is for Nutrition

One cannot think well, love well, sleep well,
if one has not dined well.

Virginia Woolf

I love the above quote. I use it every time I give presentations on nutrition and the Breakthrough principles, and as soon as it flashes on the screen I get plenty of nods and murmurs of approval. After using it so many times and getting the same response, I know why I get such an emphatic response; we like eating. The thought of dining well conjures up all kinds of images of sumptuous holiday feasts. We envision good food and plenty of it! Now, I don't know about your family, but once my family is done with a holiday meal, we definitely *can't* think, love, or sleep! We can't even move! As a society, we have some serious misconceptions about "dining well." Actually, we wouldn't do too badly if we ate the balanced meals that characterize our American Thanksgiving dinner (as long as we cut the portion sizes in half!). But with our lifestyles today we are routinely challenged by both the *quantity* and the *quality* of the food we eat. We love our food . . . or do we?

ENJOYING FOOD TOO MUCH, OR TOO LITTLE?

He who distinguishes the true savor of his food can never be a glutton;
He who does not cannot be otherwise.

Thoreau

It's a common belief that America is overweight as a result of her love affair with food. I disagree. I believe *people enjoy food too little, not too much*. In fact, it's the lack of finding real pleasure in our dining that threatens our ability to eat healthfully and well. Let's face it—our food receives very little of our attention.

Our meals rarely require the use of fork, knife, and spoon. Shamefully, my own children don't remember how to formally set a table. Every time we have a cooked meal together I have to remind them. I'm not talking salad forks and bread plates. I'm just talking about a napkin, fork, knife, plate, and a glass. As I go over and over the proper way to set a table, each time their expressions clearly say, "How would we know that you fold a napkin with the point going away from the plate? We're used to those skinny little rectangular napkins that come in a paper bag with our meals!" I laugh to keep from crying.

We don't take time to creatively plan our meals. We eat on the run, barely taking the time to register the aroma and flavor of the food before it's gone. Think about how often you eat while doing something else. Have you stopped to consider how often you eat while

* watching TV?
* running out the door to work or school?
* driving in a car between appointments?
* working on a computer?
* reading a newspaper, book, or magazine?
* catching up on some business-related work?

It's not terrible if this happens once in a while. But when this eating pattern is the norm rather than the exception, it has a profound effect on what we eat, how we eat, and the quantities we consume.

We go for fast food because it's quick or we opt for prepackaged food when we're short on time even though we know it's not the best choice. Eating on the run or eating while preoccupied with other things robs us of the pleasure of eating. It also causes us to frequently overeat—more on that later.

By and large, we've slipped away from taking the time to celebrate our sustenance. The dinner hour falls right at our most hectic time of day, when our career and family lives are colliding. Eating is just another task to be done in the transition between the office, the dry cleaner's, and home. We'll begin to end our nutritional woes when we recapture the experience of truly enjoying our food.

The Gain and the Drain

Have you ever paused and thought about how the foods you eat make you feel? Your meal will either trigger an energy gain or an energy drain. The drain comes from eating low-quality foods in great quantity. On the other hand, we receive a natural energy gain from eating high-quality foods in moderate quantities.

Low-quality foods are foods with limited nutritional value. Generally, these are high-calorie, highly processed foods. They usually offer little in terms of protein, vitamins, or minerals. They contain high quantities of sugar, salt, fat, or calories with low nutrient content. Eating a lot of low-quality foods can lead to moodiness, trouble concentrating, sleepiness, and low energy.

On the other hand, high-quality foods have excellent nutritional value and provide an energy gain. Generally, such foods are less processed. High-quality foods contain naturally occurring vitamins, minerals, and fiber that are essential to good health. They're lower in sugar, unhealthy fats, and calories. These include whole foods such as fruits, vegetables, nuts, grains, legumes, and some lean meats.

Research shows that when you eat higher-quality foods, you're less susceptible to lifestyle diseases such as heart disease, cancer, diabetes, and stroke. You're more likely to live a longer, healthier life. Because high-quality foods are so nutritionally dense, it's also less likely you'll overeat. When you eat higher-quality foods you have more energy, you can think more clearly, you feel more positive, and you'll naturally lose weight.

Very few Americans are satisfied with their weight. It's not for lack of trying. The average American goes on a diet three to four times per year. It's estimated that over $30 billion is spent on pills, remedies, and diets each year in the United States. For too many people, food is a demon of mythological proportions—a dragon that must be slain—and the sword we wield is the only weapon we know . . . diets.

Instead of describing our eating style, the word "diet" has become synonymous with an extreme eating program that one uses for a period of time to lose weight. Of course, most people will give up on their program because it is too miserable and unrealistic as an eating lifestyle. And you know what happens next: the moment those drastic restrictions come to an end, you gradually fall right back into your poor eating habits. "We cannot repair a lifetime of poor choices with a quick fix," says Dr. Ray Strand in his book *Healthy for Life*. "The very phrase, 'going on a diet' reveals our greatest downfall—if you 'go on a diet' to lose weight, you are planning to 'come off' that diet sometime in the near future—usually sooner than you even planned."[1]

RESEARCH SAYS

It has been well documented that even in controlled settings most individuals who remain in a weight-loss program lose a maximum of 10 percent of their weight. However, approximately two-thirds of the weight is regained within one year and often it increases over the next five years.[2]

Too Big to Swing

My friend and collaborator Donna Wallace told me of a visit she made to the home of a couple she'd been close friends with in college. While they were sharing old memories and catching up on the latest in each other's lives, Donna was having fun getting acquainted with their young daughter whom she'd just met.

As the hot summer day cooled into evening, she took the four-year-old out to the backyard to play while her friends prepared dinner. Together she and her new friend explored the playhouse and toys. Donna then went over to an elaborate play structure and perched on a swing. She leaned back and started pumping her legs to pick up momentum. Caught up in the revelry of the moment, several minutes passed before she realized the little girl had stopped playing and was standing stock-still, watching her with eyes open wide.

"What *are* you doing?" the child demanded.

Donna laughed and said, "I'm swinging. Would you like a turn?"

The four-year-old stood there another moment looking confused before shaking her head. "Mommy and Daddy *never* do that!"

It wasn't just that Mom and Dad were too busy to play. Since Donna had last seen her friends, both had gained such a remarkable amount of weight that swinging was out of the question. When this little girl's parents were children, I'm sure they never anticipated they would ever be too big to fit on a swing, a slide . . . or an airplane seat.

I'm not at all interested in offering you another short-term fix with temporary results. I am interested in helping you take a firm grasp of freedom—in rediscovering nutrition as it was meant to be. Your body is made up of living cells, which respond immediately when given the nutrition they need. Regardless of your shape or size, your body can be restored by following the simple guidelines for eating provided for us in the Garden.

FROM THE GARDEN OF "EATIN'"

In the Garden of Eden, the Creator presented precisely what we need to live fully in all aspects of our health, including our diets.

"See, I have given you every herb that yields seed which is on the face of all the earth, and every tree whose fruit yields seed; to you it shall be for food."[3]

The Creator provided every herb that yields seed—in other words, edible plants. He went on to recommend "every tree whose fruit yields seed." A vast variety of fruits, vegetables, nuts, seeds, grains, herbs, and flavorful seasonings were theirs to enjoy. In Eden, the original diet was intended to sustain optimal health: living foods for living bodies, natural foods for natural health. A little later in this chapter we will take a look at how contemporary science is verifying the wisdom of this natural diet, but first let's take a moment to notice the beauty and benefits of Eden's bounty.

Think of the many flavors and textures of natural foods. We've been given enough variety to make meals interesting and enjoyable for an entire lifetime, especially when these tastes and textures are combined in interesting ways. "But it's inconvenient," you say. "Why didn't God create fast food?" Actually he did, just not the deep-fried kind. Fresh fruits, veggies, nuts, and seeds are the optimal fast food. For most natural foods, little preparation is required other than cleaning and peeling. They do, however, offer great flexibility and variety with soaking, juicing, and cooking, which opens up a whole new spectrum of possibilities for texture and mixes of flavor.

Science continues to support the benefits of a natural, plant-based diet. A properly prepared plant-based meal provides the basic nutritional components you need for healthy living. In his book *SuperFoods Rx,* Steven Pratt, MD, identifies a number of foods that are so nutrient-dense and beneficial for people to eat that he calls them "SuperFoods." Of course, these were on the Creator's list. They include beans, blueberries, broccoli, oats, oranges, spinach, tomatoes, walnuts, and many others. Packed with antioxidants and phytonutrients, these natural foods can put you on the road to super health when eaten regularly.[4]

THE GARDEN DIET

When I use the word "diet," I'm talking about a healthy eating style that can be used for life. This is not about a fad that you start, stay on for a short while, and then go back to the old ways because it was too difficult to maintain. The Garden Diet is another key to your breakthrough. I have two simple strategies for healthy eating that will help you live longer, reduce your risk for disease, boost your energy, keep your mind clear, and help you lose excess weight:

Eat Close to the Ground
and
Mind Your Portions.

Strategy 1: Eat Close to the Ground

A quick review of what Adam and Eve ate in the Garden provides the perfect model of what we should be eating: fruits and vegetables, nuts and seeds, legumes, beans, herbs, whole grains, and fresh water to drink. Whole foods that grow close to the ground are packed with living vitamins, minerals, water, fiber, and the enzymes needed to digest the food itself; they are the exact fit for the cells of our bodies and for nurturing the body in just the right amounts and balance. For this reason, I recommend that this simple strategy guide your food choices. The reverse is also true: the farther away you move from foods that are naturally grown in the ground, the farther away you move from those foods that add health and longevity.

Scientific support abounds in the area of natural foods and their ability to provide optimal nutrition. For example, well over two hundred studies show the benefits of phytochemicals for fighting disease. Phytochemicals such as lycopene, beta-carotene, and isoflavones are found in fruits, vegetables, and grains and help reduce your risk for disease. Multiple epidemiological studies prove that eating fresh fruits and veggies can substantially reduce the risk of cancer, as well as lower your risk for high blood pressure and high cholesterol.

According to nutritionist Sherri Flynt, MPH, RD, LD, "The phytochemicals (we like to call them 'fighter chemicals') in fruits and veggies act like soldiers. They protect you and your children against disease. Some fighter chemicals battle heart disease, others fight or protect from cancer, and still others promote healthy immune systems. Daily consumption of fruits and vegetables not only reduces the risk of [disease] but also helps in weight control."[5]

Fruits and Veggies

Since different colors contain different phytochemicals, be sure to eat a wide variety of colors; the deeper the color the better. Here are a few suggestions:

* Blue—blueberries, eggplant, purple cabbage, plums, raisins
* Orange—cantaloupe, carrots, sweet potatoes, oranges, pumpkin
* Green—spinach, kiwifruit, honeydew, peas, avocados, broccoli
* Yellow—grapefruit, squash, yellow peppers, pineapple, lemon, mango
* Red—cherries, strawberries, tomatoes, red peppers, raspberries, red apples, beets
* White—cauliflower, bananas, white mushrooms, pears, onions, potatoes

For maximum benefit, eat two to four servings (2 cups) of fruit *and* three to five servings (2 cups) of vegetables each day. Haven't had a vegetable in a while? You don't have to get to the finish line in the first week, but do make a commitment to start. Gradually increase your serving sizes. Do a mix of fresh, frozen, and canned. Be sure to watch the sugar content of canned fruits and the salt content of canned vegetables.

Grains

One of the primary sources of energy for the body is complex carbohydrates. In general, 50 percent of the body's energy should be supplied by carbohydrates. An excellent source of quality carbohydrates is whole grains. They are also a good source of protein, fiber, vitamins, and minerals. They keep our digestive system moving and healthy. Some of the best whole grains are whole wheat, oats, barley, millet, rye, corn, and brown rice.

On the other hand, if your food label lists "enriched flour," this typically means the good parts of the grain have been milled out and the flour has been bleached. This results in a fine white flour that makes light, fluffy pastries but leaves no nutritional benefit. Therefore, the flour is "enriched" to put nutrients back in. Make a conscious effort to choose fewer refined products and look for whole grain instead. The total recommended daily allowance for grains is six to eleven servings a day. Women should stay closer to six; if you're physically active, shoot more for midrange. Very few people need eleven servings of grains a day.

Fiber

The coarse, fibrous parts of grains, fruits, and vegetables aid in digestion and keep your intestines working regularly. Fiber also lowers cholesterol and reduces your risk for colon cancer. To get these benefits, you need to eat approximately 35 grams of fiber a day. In this case, more is not necessarily better; too much (greater than 35 grams) can interfere with the absorption of other essential nutrients. However, this usually isn't a problem—most Americans eat far less fiber than they should. We average only 11 grams of fiber every day.[6] Use the table below for ideas on how you can increase your daily servings of fiber.

FIBER FOODS

FOOD	SERVING SIZE	TOTAL FIBER (GRAMS)
Apple (with skin)	1 medium	3.5
Apricots (dried)	5 halves	1.4
Banana	1 medium	2.4
Blueberries	½ cup	2.0
Bread (whole wheat)	1 slice	1.4
Broccoli	½ cup	2.3
Chickpeas (garbanzo beans)	½ cup	7.0
Corn	1 ear or ½ cup	5.0
Grapefruit (with membrane)	half	1.6
High-fiber cereals	1 ounce (½ cup)	10–14
Kidney beans	½ cup	7.3
Lentils (such as in soup)	½ cup	3.7
Lima beans	½ cup	4.5
Navy beans	½ cup	6.0
Oat bran	¼ cup	4.0
Orange (with membrane)	1 medium	2.6
Peas	½ cup	3.6
Pita bread (whole wheat)	1 piece	5.0
Potatoes (with skin)	1 medium	2.5
Prunes	3 medium	3.0
Spaghetti (whole wheat)	1 cup	3.9
Spinach	½ cup	2.1
Sweet potato	½ cup	3.0

Adapted from William Sears, "Fantastic Fiber," *AskDrSears.com: Family Nutrition,* http://www.askdrsears.com/html/4/T041500.asp, accessed June 15, 2005.

Where's the Beef?

In the Garden Diet there is no mention of meat. It was absent from the original diet of Paradise. I realize meat eating can be an emotionally charged issue—something many of us hold dear, even sacred. Without arguing whether you should or shouldn't, I want you to realize that everything you need for health and well-being can be found in a diet that does not include meat. In many ways a plant-based diet is more beneficial to your health.* Registered dietitian Johanna Dwyer, of Tufts University Medical School and the New England Medical Center Hospital, has found substantive data that vegetarians are at lesser risk for obesity, constipation, lung cancer, and alcoholism. Evidence is good that their risks for hypertension, coronary artery disease, Type II diabetes, and gallstones are lower as well.[7]

Those who choose to eat meat need to remember to eat more fruits and vegetables, and ironically so do many vegetarians. I know many a vegetarian who doesn't like vegetables! (These people are in effect, non–meat eaters, more than they are vegetarians.) Caught up in the rush, vegetarians often default to quick, easy meals such as grilled cheese sandwiches, french fries, and pizza.

While reading this chapter, take inventory of your food choices and see where you can bring healthy change. The bottom line is this: regardless of your foundational premise for abstaining from or eating meat, the more fruits and vegetables you consume on a daily basis, the better health you'll experience.

Protein

It is important for us to have protein in our diet as a necessary building block for body growth and repair. Research has shown that eating too much meat, particularly meat high in fat, clearly raises cholesterol and increases our risk for heart disease and various forms of cancer. In a definitive five-year study of the eating habits of half a million people from various countries, researchers found that

---

*The American Dietetic Association (ADA) 1997 position paper states that appropriately planned vegetarian diets are healthful, are nutritionally adequate, and provide health benefits in the prevention and treatment of certain diseases.

those who regularly ate red meat such as beef, lamb, pork, veal, and processed varieties such as ham and bacon were shown to have increased risk for bowel cancer.[8]

This is cause for concern since the average American diet gets 34 percent of its calories from fat, much of which comes from animal products and most often from red meat. The evidence for this is so compelling that the American Dietetic Association is now recommending that we eat no more than *four to six ounces of meat per day.*

As a general rule, if you're eating meat you need to eat lean cuts, keep serving sizes reasonable, and purchase meats that are free-range (not supplemented with hormones). I recommend minimizing the use of animal proteins whenever possible, and focusing on adequate protein obtained from eating more beans, legumes, nuts, and seeds. For ideas of plant-based sources of protein see the table below.

PROTEIN FINDER

	SERVINGS	GRAMS
Almost all veggies	1 cup	2
Avocado, medium	1	4
Banana, small	1	1.2
Berries	1 cup	2
Bread, whole grain	2 slices	6
Chicken breast, skinless	3 oz.	26
Cottage cheese, no fat	½ cup	14
Eggs	1	6
Halibut, broiled	3 oz.	23
Lentils, cooked	½ cup	18
Oatmeal	1 cup	8
Pasta, whole grain	1 cup	6
Pinto beans, cooked	½ cup	14
Rice milk, fortified	1 cup	2.1
Rice, brown	1 cup	3
Salmon, broiled	3 oz.	20
Skim milk	1 cup	8

	SERVINGS	GRAMS
Soy milk, fortified	1 cup	6.6
Soybeans, cooked	½ cup	28
Sweet potato, baked	1 med.	2
Tofu, firm, cooked; 4 oz. is normal serving	½ cup	20
Trout, broiled	3 oz.	24
Wild game	3 oz.	28
Yogurt, plain, nonfat	½ cup	5

Adapted from Netzer, Corrine T., *The Complete Book of Food Counts* (New York: Dell Publishing, 1997).

Beans/Legumes

Beans and legumes are a good source of high-quality protein and a rich source of fiber and nutrients. Because of their heartiness, both can function as meat substitutes. As with fruits and vegetables, your greatest benefit comes with expanded variety: lentils, soybeans, red beans, kidney beans, black beans, garbanzo, navy, and pinto beans are all delicious and simple to prepare. The total recommended daily allowance for beans is two to three servings a day.

Nuts/Seeds

Nuts and seeds are excellent sources of fiber, protein, and healthy fats. Try to have a small serving of unsalted raw nuts at least three to five times per week, especially if you have heart disease. Instead of peanuts, which are high in saturated fats, experiment with almonds, walnuts, soybeans, pecans, and so on. Pumpkin and sunflower seeds are a great addition to your salads for texture, variety, and nutritional value.

Water

All the above food categories are important, but the body absolutely cannot survive without water. We all know this, yet most of us fail to drink enough of it. Drinking water every day is important to flush out the metabolic by-products we are consuming and producing daily.

How much water should you consume? The general recommendation is to drink eight 8-ounce glasses of water per day (64 ounces). For a more customized recommendation, take your body weight and divide it in half to give you the number of ounces you need each day. For example, a 150-pound female would need 75 ounces, or a bit more than half a gallon a day. Remember, for people living in drier climates or for those involved in physically demanding work or sports, you'll need to drink more.

This may sound like a lot, but there are several tricks that can help. As always, start gradually. If you haven't typically enjoyed one glass of water at a sitting, you certainly are not going to sit down and enjoy eight! The same general rule of thumb applies here: always start small and work your way up.

TIPS FOR ENJOYING WATER

Tip #1: Find a temperature of water that is most appealing to you.

Tip #2: Purchase a size and shape of container that works for you mentally. I can swig down an 8-ounce glass pretty quick and feel accomplished. The thought of parking a half gallon of water on my desk at work is overwhelming for me. Find what suits you best.

Tip #3: Establish a routine to your water drinking until it becomes natural. Consider bathroom breaks. If you're too busy to go to the bathroom, then you are too busy! It will get better. Once your body develops a capacity for water, you won't need to go nearly as often.

When you boost your water consumption up to where it should be, you'll find that your body wants it. You'll also notice that you drink less caffeine, sugary drinks, or colas with artificial sweeteners. Your skin will be smoother, your complexion clearer, and you'll feel less bloated. You'll feel substantially improved when your body is being flushed daily with adequate amounts of water.

Strategy 2: Mind Your Portions

In addition to improving what you eat, a strategy guaranteed to improve your health and enable you to live longer is *eating less.* Dr. Robert Good has conducted research showing in both animals and humans that by reducing caloric intake, almost every aspect of the immune system will improve. Not only that, but illnesses stemming from an unbalanced immune system become easier to manage.

Whenever you reach a point during a meal where you'd like more, instead push the plate away and wait fifteen to twenty minutes rather than automatically reaching for a second helping. It takes that long for your stomach to "tell" your brain you're full. If you give your body time to begin digesting your food, the hunger usually subsides and you'll be exactly where you need to be for optimal health.

Eating out poses its own unique challenges. When we order food in public places we often think about getting the best deal for our money. But when it comes to eating, *more* is not always the best deal. Your greatest meal value is when you purchase a moderate order of food. Since you don't want to *be* "supersized," don't *eat* supersized! This rule of thumb is not just limited to fast-food restaurants. Many restaurants stake their claim on giving you massive quantities of food. Fine. Halve your order and get closer to a regular serving size (at some restaurants, it's closer to a third). Ask for a to-go box right up front and remove the excess from your plate before you start eating. You won't miss it, you'll be proud of yourself, and you'll have another meal for the following day. Now that's a great deal!

In order to mind your portion sizes it's helpful to know what constitutes a serving. The only way to learn portion sizes is to measure your food. This will help readjust your eyes to appropriate serving sizes, and will give you more of a feel for how much you're eating. The right-hand column on the table below is a good everyday guide to help you as well.

SERVING SIZES

FOOD GROUP	SERVING SIZE	ABOUT THE SIZE OF
Whole Grains 6–11 servings a day	1 slice 4-inch bread ½ cup of cooked cereal, grain, or pasta ½ –1 cup of breakfast cereal	½ cup = small light bulb 1 cup = tennis ball
Vegetables 3–5 servings a day	½ cup of cooked vegetables 1 cup raw vegetables; 4 lettuce leaves	½ cup = small light bulb 1 cup = tennis ball

Fruits
2–4 servings a day
	1 medium fruit
	½ cup of canned, cooked,
	    or chopped
	4 ounces of 100% juice
		1 medium fruit = size of
		    your fist
		½ cup = small light bulb

Protein
4–6 ounces a day
	3 ounces of meat
	1 ounce of meat protein
	    is the same as:
	½ cup of tofu
	1 egg
	1 tablespoon of
	    peanut or
	    almond butter
		3 ounces = deck of cards, or
		    the size of a computer
		    mouse
		½ cup = small light bulb
		1 tablespoon = the size of
		    the tip of your thumb

Beans/Legumes 2–3 servings a day	½ cup cooked beans, lentils, peas	½ cup = small light bulb

Adapted from David L. Katz, "Health Promotion: Estimating Serving Sizes," *The Way to Eat* (Naperville, IL: Sourcebooks, Inc., 2002), and National Center on Physical Activity and Disability (NCPAD), http://www.ncpad.org/nutrition/fact_sheet.php?sheet=91.

CREATING A NEW CULTURE—
LIVING *ABUNDANTLY*

Practice yourself . . . in little things; and thence proceed to greater.
EPICTETUS

For many of us who go through the daily rigors of work, kids, or parents, food is a break from it all. We're unwilling to give up our welcome reprieve for a tasteless diet that leaves us feeling hungry and with little satisfaction. Life is already hard, and we don't have the energy to bring something else into the mix that is complicated or unfulfilling.

Successfully changing your eating lifestyle is a matter of taste and workability. It can be doable and fun if you keep an open mind and agree that you won't force yourself—or your kids—to eat foods you (or they) hate. The transition should be gradual. My family changed to brown rice, which we didn't mind, and whole wheat pasta tasted the same to us as the more highly processed white pasta. Buckwheat waffles didn't go over so well—the color and texture change was too dramatic—but it wasn't so bad when I added fresh blueberries to the batter. I gradually started adding more color to our family plates: sweet potatoes, collard greens, carrots, and broccoli. We've tried to make it fun for the kids, and established a family mantra: "Always try it once."

Most importantly, I am convinced we must resist taking the extreme measures we're so geared to do in our American culture. We not only want immediate food, we want immediate results. We must keep in mind that what took several years (if not a decade or two) to accumulate will not go away safely or permanently in a matter of several weeks. The objective is not merely to live longer, but to live well—*to live abundantly.*

Eating is a cultural experience. Just as we associate celebrations such as the Fourth of July, birthdays, weddings, and Christmas with specific foods, our daily meals define our culture even more. If you are someone who is in the habit of scarfing down food while sitting behind the steering wheel, a new cultural ideal may seem ridiculously out of reach.

Upon her return from Europe, a friend was shocked to discover how rushed and unromantic our lives seem in contrast to our counterparts across the sea. "Their pace is remarkably slower," she said. "We walked to the markets where the locals buy fresh bread and produce daily. Each meal is a sensuous experience—prepared with delight. People there talk about food and its preparation with great passion. It was like living inside the pages of a novel."

We may not be able to celebrate with trips to the market every day like they do in France or Italy, but we can each make steps toward positive and worthwhile change! We may not be able to attain a calm, beautiful meal with our family and friends every day, but we certainly can make small consistent changes toward our picture of healthy living and commit to incremental improvements. How about having a lovely meal once a week?

Our motivation may wax and wane, but remember that our inspiration for life comes from the Garden. The CREATION acronym provides a beautiful outline for our picture of health and culture of eating:

Choice

"Healthy choices beget healthy choices," and you have wonderful choices when it comes to choosing what you will eat. Why waste time blaming the fast-food industry for our choices? There is a world of variety available for us to choose from, why not break out of those same meals you've been eating week after week and choose something healthy and different?

Rest

Sitting down to a meal is a time for us to take a load off of our feet, to relax and enjoy. Sitting down is not usually the problem; planning and preparing the meal is. If you come home exhausted from work like I do, Monday through Friday at 6:00 p.m. is not the time to be planning your evening meal. We have only so many hours of energy to expend. Wait until you are rested to do a bit of preplanning. The girls and I like to do this on Sundays. Everybody gets to pick a complete meal. You can avoid taking shortcuts on your food planning and preparation, which will bring you rest during your meals, as it should be.

Environment

Consider your eating environment. Is it restful? Do what you can to bring peace to your "table." Again, keep in mind each of the five senses during your meals. And remember, mealtime can be a wonderful time for family bonding. You probably won't be able to do it every day, but choose a day consistently and create an experience!

Activity

Nutrition and activity are virtually impossible to separate. When it comes to improving your health, a well-balanced diet and appropriate activity is the gold standard for reducing your risk for harmful diseases, increasing your longevity, and adding vitality to your life. Physical activity helps to keep your appetite under control. When you're active, you're not sitting and being entertained by food and television. Sometimes I'll exercise in the evening to avoid grazing, which I do when I'm stressed or tired. After a walk, my focus changes and I'm able to choose better.

Trust

Do you ever slip into the mentality of eating as if this is your last meal? I do. Sometimes we must intentionally tell ourselves that we can save a little appetite for next time. Allow your meals to be a time of gratitude, a time of giving thanks for the abundance that has been given to you.

Intimacy

Mealtime is an intimate time of sharing. Our bodies have been created to be fueled in any number of ways, but as relational beings there's pleasure in eating together. Making changes in the way you eat is always more fun when you have someone to talk and share with. Find a friend or family member and partner together. You can strengthen and support each other while making healthy living more fun for both of you. "Breaking bread" together deepens relationships and nourishes our souls.

Outlook

We need a radically new outlook on our eating. It's a journey, not a formula; a time of replenishment, not of deprivation. Mealtimes bring opportunity to try new things, to learn how to nurture our bodies, to pay attention to how our minds and emotions influence our eating. Our bodies merely need fuel. We decide what type of fuel to give it, how much to put in, and how often.

Tips to Create and Live By

We've looked at nutrition in very broad terms, examining principles that can lead and guide you for a lifetime. However, there are a few specifics that I think are important for you to implement (or perhaps continue) to have a healthy eating lifestyle.

* Eat breakfast every day. If you are not a breakfast eater, start small. A small, balanced breakfast brings all the needed benefits to start your day. Though it sounds like a cliché, not eating breakfast is starting out your physical race for the day with the "needle on

empty." Your brain cannot store energy like muscles can. Each day, choose to bless yourself, your family, your employer, and all those around you: eat breakfast.

* Add one fruit or vegetable every couple of weeks until you've reached the desired portions. Try new varieties of fruit and veggies. Try to stay in season (you can usually tell by the price if it's in season). Be mindful of eating darker colors in your fruits and vegetables. If you are accustomed to eating iceberg lettuce, switch to romaine. Try other delicious greens.

* Give your body an occasional break from animal protein with a vegetarian day. Experiment with different types of beans and lentils. Hummus spreads and miso for soups are also excellent sources of protein.

* Have a cutoff time for eating. This should be two to three hours prior to bedtime.

* Socialize with people and eat with those who are interested in their health.

PUTTING IT ALL TOGETHER

Food is part of the Creator's great plan for our pleasure and to make us whole. I don't believe God tossed Adam an apple in midstride and said, "Come on, there's work to be done." No, God delighted in his creation, displayed his handiwork, and taught man and woman to feast on every color and variety of fruit, vegetable, whole grain, nut, and herb known—the same diet that has been shown over and over again in scientific studies to lower heart disease, blood pressure, and our risk for certain cancers.

I want you to establish the picture for a healthier lifestyle, and we've been given every color of the rainbow to do so in our food. Remember, when you get out of sync you can tweak your lifestyle and get back to how you want to live. Give yourself plenty of grace. Life is too short for guilt trips (the dieter mentality is definitely a loser mentality). Make it your mission to create a culture of healthy, enjoyable eating by minding your portions and staying close to the ground.

As with any other of our CREATION Health principles, it only takes the 3 M's to get started.

Maximize

Choose to live by the two most important principles of healthy eating: (1) eat close to the ground, and (2) mind your portions. Fill your plate with whole grains, beans, and colorful fruits and veggies. When you do eat, don't overdo it!

Moderate

Monitor your intake of meat, processed foods, caffeine, and artificial sweeteners. Regularly choose a day each week to fast from meat, processed foods, and fast foods. You can do it!

Minimize

Banish the typical dieter's mentality. No more extreme programs that you can't sustain. Instead, establish a healthy eating lifestyle. Coupled with appropriate exercise, you'll achieve your goals.

Beth's Breakthrough Story
How to Become a Salad Queen

The first thing you notice about Beth is her energy. When she speaks her hands and eyes communicate enthusiasm as much as her words. She enjoys talking animatedly about her family, her friends, and her work. But she especially enjoys talking about how she became a queen.

Eighteen months ago the most accurate description of Beth might have been "worn out." She continually felt tired and wasn't entirely sure why. True, there were times she didn't get enough sleep at night due to one project or another, but she suspected there might be something more. She often experienced a general feeling of weariness that hit her about midmorning and stayed with her throughout the rest of the day. Going to her doctor, Beth received a full physical that uncovered no serious illness or disease.

After talking about her frustration with a friend, Beth concluded she needed to take better care of her health. Enlisting her friend, the two decided to encourage each other to make some lifestyle changes—starting with their diet. Since both had done numerous diets before, they decided not to jump on the latest fad diet on TV and instead focused on eating more fresh foods. To make the changes fun, the two decided to become "salad queens." Together they started collecting salad recipes and making them for their families. The number one criteria for the salads was that they had to be made primarily of fresh ingredients.

Beth found a local farmers' market where she could buy fresh fruits, vegetables, herbs, and nuts. She learned how to make green salads, bean salads, fruit salads, ethnic salads, layered salads, and pasta salads. She discovered how to make delicious dressings that contained healthy oils and vinaigrettes rather than using high-fat creamy dressings.

Salads were not the only thing she and her family ate. But they became a staple of almost every meal. Did it ever get boring eating salads? Not really. Variety was the key. Beth and her friend were constantly trying and trading new salad recipes. The variety kept things interesting and allowed Beth to exercise some creativity, which she enjoyed.

Becoming a salad queen wasn't her only lifestyle change. Beth has an office job where she spends much of her day behind a desk, so she also adopted a simple plan to get more active. She bought a pedometer that counted the number of steps she took every day. At first she was averaging only 2,000–3,000 steps daily. But by making a few small efforts she was able to increase her daily steps to an average of 6,000–8,000. At least twice a day (once in the morning and once in the afternoon) she would walk downstairs and once around her office building. It took less than five minutes but gave her a refreshing break. Sometimes she would take a ten-minute walk at the end of her lunchtime or when she got home in the evening. She even signed up to do a few "5K fun walks" to raise money for charity.

Over the course of a year Beth lost almost twenty pounds. The weight came off slowly but naturally. And now Beth says she sleeps better at night, feels more rested during the day, and has more energy than ever. Not bad for a salad queen.

The CREATION
Health Plan

11

My friend Will needed a break.

Some call him a hard worker, others a workaholic. If you talk to him, he'll just tell you he loves his job. Either way, Will was tired. He needed a health breakthrough and was open to examining his options. Since I had recently completed the manuscript for this book I asked Will to consider doing my Three-Day Rejuvenation Therapy. He agreed.

I gave Will a copy of the book and he followed the steps I will be sharing with you shortly. One of Will's friends had a condo on the beach and agreed to let him use it for a getaway weekend. Will took Friday off work so he could spend three days at the beach. But rather than seeking the traditional fun in the sun, Will used the time to focus on personal reading, understanding, growth, and rest. Over the course of the weekend he read the entire *CREATION Health Breakthrough* book and completed the exercises and activities recommended. During the three days he ate healthy, got more sleep, exercised a bit more, explored his personal values, and learned the basics of good health.

The result? A life-transforming experience.

Will reports that experiencing the Three-Day Rejuvenation Therapy helped him to slow down enough to understand what was missing in his life—balance. Now he takes time to regularly focus on the most important areas of his life. His health has improved, he has dropped a few pounds, his relationships are stronger, and his outlook is more upbeat. In fact, Will reports that the Three-Day Rejuvenation Therapy was such a positive experience that he plans to do it at least once a year.

I believe you could experience similar results. The CREATION Health Plan is your guide to experiencing a breakthrough. It is a three-phase plan that will move you from *knowing* what it means to be healthy, to actually *experiencing* what it means to be healthy. You will achieve lasting health benefits and a renewed sense of living as you complete all three phases of the plan.

Phase 1 is an intensive Three-Day Rejuvenation Therapy. Think of it as a mini-vacation with a mission. Or a personal retreat with a purpose. It's an opportunity to experience deep rest and rejuvenation. The Three-Day Rejuvenation Therapy is a lifestyle detox weekend. It's a time for you to completely exhale from the stressors of daily of life that are so often the source of our dis-ease.

During the therapy you *won't* do many of the things you might normally do during a weekend—be it laundry, housework, yard work, going to the mall, or just playing catch-up. You will step away from the things that deplete you of energy so you can begin to experience the things that refill you. Why is the program three full days? Because in my experience it takes about three days to calm our inner and outer world to the point where we can truly unwind.

Phase 2 of the CREATION Health Plan is the Eight-Week Lifestyle Transformation Plan. Phase 2 builds off of the healthy foundation you established during your getaway so that you can begin a life of health and well-being "in the real world." It will allow you to incorporate each element of CREATION Health into your life in a way that's doable but keeps you appropriately challenged to make new and better choices. Ideally, Phase 2 should follow Phase 1, but they are designed to also function independently. I'm more interested in you receiving the benefits available to you now. If your rejuvenation weekend won't be for a while, you can start right away on Phase 2.

Phase 3, CREATION Health for Life, provides the necessary guides you need to maintain healthy, vibrant living. As I described in my own story (see chapter 2), we will never be in a place where life is perfectly balanced all of the time. There will always be some event that will tip the scales. Even if we all quit our jobs and moved to isolated monasteries, we would still have opportunities to embrace life more fully and to experience better health. Using CREATION Health for Life, you can perform your own self-checks to ensure you're living life as it was intended.

Phase 1
The CREATION Health Three-Day Rejuvenation Therapy

The three-day therapy is specifically designed to help you slow down and break some of the habits that put additional stress into your life. You may want to read the entire book and then do the three-day therapy. Or your life may seem so busy that you don't have time to read the whole book. If this is true for you, jump right to the Three-Day Rejuvenation Therapy and you can read the book as part of the weekend.

You'll be asked to do some unique things, ranging from power naps and stretching routines to reading assignments and personal journaling. To get the most out of the experience you will need to undergo some advance planning. In the section entitled "Before You Go" you will find several checklists to help you prepare for the weekend. The next section, entitled "While You're There," gives the specific activities you will engage in during the three days. Finally, there is a short section called "When You Return." Also included is a question-and-answer section addressing some of the most frequently asked questions about the three-day weekend.

BEFORE YOU GO

Preflight Plan

- [ ] Pick a date (preferably over a weekend) where you can get away for three full days. You may need to factor in additional travel time to and from your selected location.
- [ ] Make arrangements for things to be taken care of while you're gone (i.e., work, family, home, etc.) so your mind can be comfortably free. Be sure to request time off work if necessary.
- [ ] Plan your workload so you don't come back to an overly loaded schedule.
- [ ] Leave all work-related material at work. This is your time to rejuvenate. Leave your laptop or other electronic work accessories at home.
- [ ] If you haven't already, read the first two chapters of this book before your three-day weekend. As part of the weekend you will have the opportunity to read or reread the eight CREATION chapters (chapters 3 through 10).
- [ ] Part of the three-day weekend includes fun/relaxing time. Plan to bring a personal hobby, activity, or recreational reading you enjoy. If you are doing this weekend with a partner, you might want to consider bringing a game or activity to enjoy together.
- [ ] Carefully read through the activities for the three-day plan so you'll know what to expect.
- [ ] **Optional but Optimal**—For best results I recommend you spend three days and four nights on the retreat. For example, if you traveled to your destination on Thursday evening, you would stay through Sunday and travel home on Monday morning. However, if this is not workable with your schedule you may choose to travel home on Sunday evening. For this reason the activities scheduled for Sunday evening are optional after 4:00 p.m.

Destination

- ☐ Choose a place to stay where you can have plenty of quiet time to relax, read, write, reflect, and feel at peace. Ideally the place would include a comfortable spot to sit and read.
- ☐ Preferably choose somewhere near nature that inspires you and creates an atmosphere of relaxation for you.
- ☐ If you're going alone, be sure to let someone know where you are and when you'll be back.
- ☐ Plan your transportation to and from your selected location.

Clothing

Plan appropriate clothing for the following activities:
- ☐ Exercise clothing and shoes.
- ☐ Comfortable shoes and clothing for walking.
- ☐ Comfortable clothing for lounging.
- ☐ Extra clothing in case of inclement weather.

Food

- ☐ Your food choices are an integral part of this weekend. You need to spend time in advance to ensure you will be able to eat as we've outlined. Poor planning in this area will diminish the value of the weekend. Either bring your food, plan to buy it nearby, or make sure there are options available for healthy dining as we've outlined.
- ☐ Bring food that you can easily prepare.
- ☐ Plan to eat as many meals as you can without going out to eat.
- ☐ Keep processed foods to a minimum. Go fresh!
- ☐ No fast-food eating while on this weekend.
- ☐ Plenty of water to drink.
- ☐ Healthy snacks such as nuts, fruits, carrots, etc. Avoid processed food snacks.

- □ You will also need to consider whether the place you are going to has refrigeration available or not.
- □ See the suggested menu listed on individual days.

Other Items to Take

- □ Book—*The CREATION Health Breakthrough*
- □ Journal—bound journal, spiral-bound paper, or notepad, no laptops
- □ Writing implements—pens, pencils, and highlighters
- □ Music player—boom box, portable stereo, or digital music player
- □ Music—instrumental, inspirational, peaceful, relaxing
- □ Aromatherapy—candles, oils, incense, potpourri, lotions, etc.
- □ Inspirational reading—spiritual book(s) to inspire you
- □ Extra paper—stationery or legal pad
- □ Pictures of loved ones (optional)

THE THREE-DAY REJUVENATION THERAPY

Arrival Day

EVENING

ARRIVAL—Plan to arrive at your destination in the early evening so you have time to unpack your things and get settled for the next three days.

FOOD—If you planned to buy your food locally for the weekend, this would be a good time to go shopping for it so you don't have to worry about it later.

ENVIRONMENT—In preparation for the next several days, set up as inviting an environment as you can. If you brought peaceful music to enjoy, set it up in a central place. If you brought aromatherapy items such as scented candles, incense, or potpourri, use them to their best effect. If you brought any family pictures, set them up where you will be reading or next to your bed.

BEDTIME—Lights out by 10:00 p.m.

Day 1

MORNING

RISE TIME—8:00 a.m. You should be out of bed no later than eight o'clock, though you may, of course, rise earlier if you wish. The goal is to enjoy at least eight hours of sleep.

PRAYER/MEDITATION—To begin your day think of someone special and offer a prayer of blessing for them. You can also use this prayer time to acknowledge God's guidance in your life.

WATER—Upon rising drink one full glass of water. *Note: 8-ounce glass is recommended.*

EXERCISE—Take a brisk walk outdoors for 30–45 minutes. The first five minutes should be a slow walk to warm up. The last five minutes should be a slow walk to cool down. *Note: This is a minimum requirement. If you are currently engaged in a more vigorous exercise routine you may feel free to substitute it during this weekend. But don't overdo it. This is intended to be a rejuvenating weekend.*

WATER—After your exercise drink one full glass of water.

STRETCHING—After exercising, spend 10–15 minutes stretching the major muscle groups of your body. Do two or three 30-second stretches for every major muscle group. See chapter 6 for a list of major muscle groups. *Note: Stretching should be slow, relaxed, and to the point where you feel some slight discomfort in the muscle but not pain. Breathe freely while stretching and don't bounce.*

FOOD NOTE: *The theme for the day is "Back to the Garden." Today you will eat foods grown in the ground. This is a meat-free day (no red meat, poultry, fish, etc.). Focus on fruits, vegetables, nuts, beans, grains, soy, etc.*

BREAKFAST—Whole grain cereals, granola, hot cereals, fruits, whole grain breads. If you haven't tried it before, consider using soymilk in place of regular milk on your cereal. *Eating Tips: Eat while sitting at a table. Eat slowly. Enjoy the taste of your food. Don't do anything else while eating (i.e., reading, writing, TV, etc.). Eat enough to satisfy yourself, but don't overeat.*

WATER—During your morning activities drink two full glasses of water.

ASSESSMENT—Complete the CREATION Health Self-Assessment in appendix A of this book. This will give you an idea of your current level of whole-person health. *Note: if you have already completed the self-assessment, take time here to review your answers and results.*

READ—Read chapter 3, "'C' is for Choice," of this book. Mark up the chapter by highlighting important passages. Write notes to yourself in the margins for things you would like to remember or do. *Note: if you have previously read the chapter, review it and mark it up.*

SNACK—If you get hungry during the morning or afternoon, have a handful of nuts (almonds, walnuts, cashews, etc.) and some fruit (apple, banana, orange, grapes, etc.). Avoid processed snacks high in sugar, salt, and fat.

AFTERNOON

LUNCH—Start with a hearty, healthy salad including a wide variety of fresh ingredients. Your meal can also include protein (soy, tofu), grains (rice, pilaf, etc.), beans (canned or fresh), soups (vegetarian), or other cooked or fresh vegetables. *Note: see "Eating Tips" from breakfast.*

WATER—During your afternoon activities drink two full glasses of water.

POWER NAP—Take a 30- to 60-minute "power nap" sometime during the afternoon. Even if you cannot sleep, enjoy the time by closing your eyes and resting peacefully.

READ—Read chapter 4, " 'R' is for Rest," of this book. Mark up the chapter by highlighting important passages. Write notes to yourself in the margins for things you would like to remember or do. *Note: if you have previously read the chapter, review it and mark it up.*

SNACK—If you get hungry during the morning or afternoon, have a handful of nuts (almonds, walnuts, cashews, etc.) and some fruit (apple, banana, orange, grapes, etc.) or veggies (carrots, cucumber, radishes, celery, etc.). Avoid processed snacks high in sugar, salt, and fat.

MISSION—Write a personal mission statement that describes your vision and values. This mission statement can be used as a guide in the daily decisions you make. *Note: for more information on how to write a mission statement see chapter 3.*

WALK—Before dinner go on a short walk.

EVENING

DINNER—Start with a hearty, healthy salad including a wide variety of fresh ingredients. Your meal can also include protein (soy, tofu), grains (rice, pilaf, etc.), beans (canned or fresh), soups (vegetarian), or other cooked or fresh vegetables. *Note: see "Eating Tips" from breakfast.*

READ—Read chapter 5, " 'E' is for Environment," of this book. Mark up the chapter by highlighting important passages. Write notes to yourself in the margins for things you would like to remember or do. *Note: if you have previously read the chapter, review it and mark it up.*

FUN TIME—Enjoy some evening fun time by participating in a personal hobby, activity, or recreational reading you enjoy. *Note: if you are doing this weekend with a partner, you might want to consider bringing a game or activity to enjoy together.*

WATER—During the evening drink two full glasses of water.

PRAYER/MEDITATION—End your day by counting your blessings. Think of some things you are thankful for or have been blessed with and offer a prayer of thanksgiving.

BEDTIME—Lights out by 10:00 p.m.

Day 2

MORNING

RISE TIME—8:00 a.m. You should be out of bed no later than eight o'clock, though you may, of course, rise earlier if you wish. The goal is to enjoy at least eight hours of sleep.

PRAYER/MEDITATION—To begin your day think of someone special and offer a prayer of blessing for them. You can also use this prayer time to acknowledge God's guidance in your life.

WATER—Upon rising drink one full glass of water.

EXERCISE—Take a brisk walk outdoors for 30–45 minutes. The first five minutes should be a slow walk to warm up. The last five minutes should be a slow walk to cool down. *Note: see day 1 for additional notes.*

WATER—After your exercise drink one full glass of water.

STRETCHING—After exercising, spend 10–15 minutes stretching the major muscle groups of your body. Do two or three 30-second stretches for every major muscle group. See chapter 6 for a list of major muscle groups. *Note: see day 1 for additional notes.*

FOOD NOTE: *The theme for the day is "Fruits and Veggies." This is a mild nutritional detox day. Today you will eat only fruits or vegetables, including beverages (no soft drinks or fruit punches). 100 percent pure fruit and vegetable juices are okay. This is a meat-free day (no red meat, poultry, fish, etc.).*

BREAKFAST—For breakfast enjoy as many varieties of fruits as you like. *Note: see "Eating Tips" from day 1 for additional notes.*

WATER—During your morning activities drink two full glasses of water.

READ—Read chapter 6, "'A' is for Activity," of this book. Mark up the chapter by highlighting important passages. Write notes to yourself in the margins for things you would like to remember or do. *Note: if you have previously read the chapter, review it and mark it up.*

SNACKS—If you get hungry during the day, stick to fruits or veggies only.

JOURNAL—Journaling is a time for introspection. You can use your journal time to explore your thoughts and feelings on your health, family, worries or concerns, dreams and aspirations, etc.

AFTERNOON

LUNCH—Enjoy a hearty, healthy salad comprised of only vegetables. Eat until satisfied.

POWER NAP—Take a 30- to 60-minute "power nap" sometime during the afternoon. Even if you cannot sleep, enjoy the time by closing your eyes and resting peacefully.

WATER—During your afternoon activities drink two full glasses of water.

READ—Read chapter 7, "'T' is for Trust," of this book. Mark up the chapter by highlighting important passages. Write notes to yourself in the margins for things you would like to remember or do. *Note: if you have previously read the chapter, review it and mark it up.*

GOALS—Write three goals you would like to achieve in your life. Be specific. *Note: see chapter 3, "'C' is for Choice," for guidelines.*

WALK—Before dinner go on a short walk.

EVENING

DINNER—Enjoy a hearty, healthy salad comprised of only vegetables or cut-up fruit. Eat until satisfied.

READ—Read chapter 8, "'I' is for Interpersonal Relationships," of this book. Mark up the chapter by highlighting important passages. Write notes to yourself in the margins for things you would like to remember or do. *Note: if you have previously read the chapter, review it and mark it up.*

FUN TIME—Enjoy some evening fun time by participating in a personal hobby, activity, or recreational reading you enjoy. *Note: if you are doing this weekend with a partner, you might want to consider bringing a game or activity to enjoy together.*

WATER—During the evening drink two full glasses of water.

PRAYER/MEDITATION—End your day by counting your blessings. Think of some things you are thankful for or have been blessed with. Now offer a prayer of thanksgiving.

BEDTIME—Lights out by 10:00 p.m.

Day 3

MORNING

RISE TIME—8:00 a.m. You should be out of bed no later than eight o'clock, though you may, of course, rise earlier if you wish. The goal is to enjoy at least eight hours of sleep.

PRAYER/MEDITATION—To begin your day think of someone special and offer a prayer of blessing for them. You can also use this prayer time to acknowledge God's guidance in your life.

WATER—Upon rising drink one full glass of water.

EXERCISE—Take a brisk walk outdoors for 30–45 minutes. The first five minutes should be a slow walk to warm up. The last five minutes should be a slow walk to cool down. *Note: see day 1 for additional notes.*

WATER—After your exercise drink one full glass of water.

STRETCHING—After exercising, spend 10–15 minutes stretching the major muscle groups of your body. Do two or three 30-second stretches for every major muscle group. See chapter 6 for a list of major muscle groups. *Note: see day 1 for additional notes.*

FOOD NOTE: *The theme for the day is "Whole Foods Day." Today you will focus on healthy, satisfying, unprocessed foods.*

BREAKFAST—Whole grain cereals, granola, hot cereals, fruits, whole grain breads. If you haven't tried it before, consider using soymilk in place of regular milk on your cereal. *Note: see "Eating Tips" from day 1 for additional notes.*

READ—Read chapter 9, "'O' is for Outlook," of this book. Mark up the chapter by highlighting important passages. Write notes to yourself in the margins for things you would like to remember or do. *Note: if you have previously read the chapter, review it and mark it up.*

WATER—During your morning activities drink two full glasses of water.

SNACK—If you get hungry during the morning or afternoon, have a handful of nuts (almonds, walnuts, cashews, etc.) and some fruit (apple, banana, orange, grapes, etc.). Avoid processed snacks high in sugar, salt, and fat.

JOURNAL—Write a letter to a friend thanking them for the role they play in your life. Be specific.

AFTERNOON

LUNCH—Start with a hearty, healthy salad including a wide variety of fresh ingredients. Your meal can also include protein (soy, tofu, chicken, or fish only), grains (rice, pilaf, etc.), beans (canned or fresh), soups, or other cooked or fresh vegetables. For protein, be sure to keep portion size to 4–6 ounces. *Note: see "Eating Tips" from day 1 for additional notes.*

POWER NAP—Take a 30- to 60-minute "power nap" sometime during the afternoon. Even if you cannot sleep, enjoy the time by closing your eyes and resting peacefully.

WATER—During your afternoon activities drink two full glasses of water.

READ—Read chapter 10, "'N' is for Nutrition," of this book. Mark up the chapter by highlighting important passages. Write notes to yourself in the margins for things you would like to remember or do. *Note: if you have previously read the chapter, review it and mark it up.*

OPTIONAL BUT OPTIMAL (AFTER 4 P.M.)

LOCAL—Find something to do locally that would be enjoyable and relaxing, such as visiting a park, museum, garden, zoo, etc.

WALK—Before dinner go on a short walk.

EVENING

DINNER—Start with a hearty, healthy salad including a wide variety of fresh ingredients. Your meal can also include protein (soy, tofu, chicken, or fish only), grains (rice, pilaf, etc.), beans (canned or fresh), soups, or other cooked or fresh vegetables. For protein, be sure to keep portion size to 4–6 ounces. *Note: see "Eating Tips" from day 1 for additional notes.*

READ—Read chapter 11, "The CREATION Health Plan," of this book. Mark up the chapter by highlighting important passages. Write notes to yourself in the margins for things you would like to remember or do. *Note: if you have previously read the chapter, review it and mark it up.*

FUN TIME—Enjoy some evening fun time by participating in a personal hobby, activity, or recreational reading you enjoy. *Note: if you are doing this weekend with a partner, you might want to consider bringing a game or activity to enjoy together.*

WATER—During the evening drink two full glasses of water.

PRAYER/MEDITATION—End your day by counting your blessings. Think of some things you are thankful for or have been blessed with. Now offer a prayer of thanksgiving. *Note: you can do this before climbing into bed or once you have turned out the light.*

BEDTIME— Lights out by 10:00 p.m.

WHEN YOU RETURN

☐ Don't jump right back into the fast pace of life. Ease back into your responsibilities.

☐ Continue some of the habits you have started, especially the ones you found most beneficial during the weekend.

☐ Start the CREATION Health Eight-Week Lifestyle Transformation Plan.

Three-Day Rejuvenation Therapy Weekend Q&A

Should I do this weekend alone or with someone else?

If you feel comfortable doing so, I recommend experiencing the Three-Day Rejuvenation Therapy alone. Nevertheless, it is perfectly fine to do it with another person. You might be able to share some expenses and encourage each other along the way. One word of caution: this weekend is not really intended as a vacation trip or buddy get-together. Its purpose is to give you an opportunity to rest, reflect, and rejuvenate. So if you go with someone else, be sure you have separate rooms you can retreat to for private time.

Where should I go?

Pick a comfortable spot that is within your budget. This could be a cabin, condo, hotel, retreat center, campground, or even a vacationing friend's empty home. Some may also consider going on a camping trip. While more difficult (and not quite as comfortable), camping is certainly a possibility for hearty outdoor types. If you choose to go camping, examine the suggested list of things to take very carefully and bring only the most essential.

How does this program change if I'm doing it with a partner?

You can certainly enjoy your meals and exercise together. You can also share your free time together in the evening. But your reading and contemplative time should be done alone.

How can I get more information on CREATION Health programs, seminars, and retreats?

Go to www.CREATIONhealth.com.

Phase 2
The CREATION Health Eight-Week Lifestyle Transformation Plan

The CREATION Health Lifestyle Transformation Plan is an eight-week program that doesn't require you to go through boot-camp-like physical and mental training. Each week there are eight tasks for you to accomplish sometime during the week. Most of the tasks are quite simple, such as drinking more water, finding new ways to laugh, and buying attractive plants to beautify your personal space. Some others are a bit more challenging, such as practicing anti-stress techniques, eating more healthfully, and committing to some weekly activity goals. You will be able to do the majority of these things at home. Some tasks ask you to spend a little money, but most simply require you to set aside some time to do them.

The aim of this eight-week plan is to introduce you to a number of healthy behaviors that can improve your life and your relationships. Some of the suggestions build on what you have done in the previous week. This is true primarily of the eating and activity guidelines. After finishing the program you will have built a solid foundation for a lifetime of healthy living.

For every week of the program you will have eight assignments. Sixty-four assignments in all. In a perfect world, you would complete the whole program in the suggested time frame. However, since we don't live in a perfect world, you may have to take a bit longer. Don't be discouraged. If you need two weeks to do all the assignments I've listed here for one week, take the extra time. It's very important to try all of these lifestyle changes and see which ones you can incorporate into your everyday life.

Going through the program, you will likely find some of the tasks to be surprising, enjoyable, annoying, or humorous. You may not resonate with all of them. But hopefully you will find the majority to be life-enhancing experiences that you will want to continue to practice. This is especially important in areas like rest, eating, and activity.

Throughout the book, there are many additional lifestyle tips that are not included in this formal eight-week plan. This is intentional. I didn't want to use this eight-week plan to overload your life with so many new things that you give up completing it. So after you have finished with the eight-week plan, be sure to check back in the book for other helpful ideas you may want to try out.

Finally, a few quick notes about Phases 1 and 2 of the CREATION Health Plan.

* There may be some who choose to do the eight-week plan first before doing the Three-Day Rejuvenation Therapy. It is fine to do this if your schedule does not allow you to do the weekend right away.

* If you have completed the Three-Day Rejuvenation Therapy you may notice that a few of the tasks you did on that weekend are repeated in this eight-week program. I chose to do so with some of the most important tasks (such as writing a personal mission statement) because they are so important that I did not want someone to miss out on the experience if they chose to only complete Phase 1 or Phase 2 of the plan. If you have already completed one of the tasks, use the time in the eight-week program to refine it.

Included are eight blank weekly calendar pages you can use to plot out your activities for each week. This will help you to stay on course as you successfully complete each week. I thought you might find it helpful to see a sample of one of my weeks as I went through the program. Here is my page from week 3 of the program:

MONICA REED SAMPLE PAGE FROM THE CREATION HEALTH EIGHT-WEEK LIFESTYLE TRANSFORMATION PLAN

WEEK 3

DATE: April 12	A.M.	P.M.
Sun	One fruit (N) This week I'll cut my caffeine consumption in half from 1 cup a day to only 3 cups this week (C)	One veggie (N) Get a card for Wendy and Stan (I) Plan menu with kids and shop (N)
Mon	One fruit (N) Practice deep belly breathing during lunchtime (O)	One veggie (N) Drink 3 glasses of water (N)
Tue	One fruit (N) Morning inspiration (T) Start stretching routine (A)	One veggie (N) Drink 3 glasses of water (N)
Wed	One fruit (N)	One veggie (N) Have you practiced your breathing exercises? (O) Drink 3 glasses of water (N)
Thu	One fruit (N) Morning inspiration (T) Media fast day—no TV, radio, or Internet today (R)	One veggie (N) Drink 3 glasses of water (N)
Fri	One fruit (N) Stretching routine (A)	One veggie (N) Massage at 3:00 p.m. (E) Drink 3 glasses of water (N)
Sat	One fruit (N) Morning inspiration (T)	One veggie (N) Write and mail cards today (I) Drink 3 glasses of water (N)

You'll notice that I'm fairly thorough in my approach; I write down everything. Use the calendar in a way that works best for you, while keeping yourself accountable.

Now you're ready to begin. Pick a start date and enjoy your eight-week experience!

WEEK 1

PRINCIPLE	EXPERIENCE
C—Choice	Commit to finishing the eight-week program.
R—Rest	Go to bed 30 minutes earlier than you normally do three times this week.
E—Environment	Add some plants to your home or office.
A—Activity	This week find simple ways to increase your movement. This could include: taking stairs instead of elevators, parking at the far end of the parking lot, washing your car, mowing the lawn (not with a riding mower).
T—Trust	Before you get out of bed in the morning take a few minutes to acknowledge God and talk to him about your day.
I—Interpersonal Relationships	Think about the number of daily hugs you give to family and friends. Double it this week.
O—Outlook	Promote laughter in your life. Watch a funny movie, learn a new joke and share it, tell a humorous personal story to a friend, etc.
N—Nutrition	Have a full breakfast at least four days this week (see Nutrition chapter). Drink at least *one* 8-ounce glass of water every day this week. Familiarize yourself with serving sizes by measuring your portions at least three times this week (see chart in Nutrition chapter, page 202).

WEEK 1

DATE:	A.M.	P.M.
Sun		
Mon		
Tue		
Wed		
Thu		
Fri		
Sat		

WEEK 2

PRINCIPLE	EXPERIENCE
C—Choice	If you haven't done so already, start a personal journal or diary.
R—Rest	Be in bed with lights off by 10:00 p.m. three times this week.
E—Environment	Purchase peaceful music CDs and listen for at least 30 minutes three times this week. This can be done while doing other activities, such as drive time to work, during bedtime routine, or before going to bed. Relaxing music could include: instrumental music, solo piano, guitar, violin, orchestra, light jazz, etc.
A—Activity	Participate in aerobic activity for at least 20 minutes at a time for three days this week. This could include: walking, biking, swimming, jogging.
T—Trust	Purchase an inspirational or devotional book.
I—Interpersonal Relationships	Send flowers with a personal note to someone you love.
O—Outlook	Count your blessings! Pull out a piece of paper (or grab your journal) and in five minutes list as many blessings as you can.
N—Nutrition	Eat at least one fruit and vegetable every day. Drink at least *two* 8-ounce glasses of water every day. Limit the number of sugary desserts you eat this week to four.

WEEK 2

DATE:	A.M.	P.M.
Sun		
Mon		
Tue		
Wed		
Thu		
Fri		
Sat		

WEEK 3

PRINCIPLE	EXPERIENCE
C—Choice	Select one unhealthy habit you have and make a plan to reduce or eliminate it. This could be something that is already being done in the eight-week plan.
R—Rest	Try fasting from all media for one day this week. This includes no television, radio, Internet, newspapers, etc.
E—Environment	Get a massage.
A—Activity	Begin doing stretching exercises at least twice this week. Continue with your aerobic activity from last week.
T—Trust	Set aside some regular quiet time to read from your new inspirational/devotional book.
I—Interpersonal Relationships	Write a card, send a note, or call a friend to thank them for the acceptance, support, and encouragement they've given you in hard times.
O—Outlook	Practice performing the deep belly breathing exercise whenever you feel stress coming on (see Outlook chapter, p. 179).
N—Nutrition	Make up a menu of at least five simple, healthy meals and keep it posted on the refrigerator or in your planner. Try shopping at a health food store. Drink at least *three* 8-ounce glasses of water every day. Continue to eat at least one serving of fruits and vegetables every day.

WEEK 3

DATE:	A.M.	P.M.
Sun		
Mon		
Tue		
Wed		
Thu		
Fri		
Sat		

WEEK 4

PRINCIPLE	EXPERIENCE
C—Choice	Set aside a half hour to write about one new personal goal for your life.
R—Rest	Pick a healthy time to leave work and then stick to it all week.
E—Environment	Purchase a scent-producing device for creating a relaxing scent for your home. Examples include: scented candles, potpourri, aromatherapy, scent diffuser, incense, room spray, air freshener. Refer to the chart on page 87.
A—Activity	Begin doing strength (or resistance) training twice this week. Continue with your aerobic activity and stretching exercises from last week.
T—Trust	Experience something beautiful such as a sunset, natural vista, etc., and recognize it as a gift from God.
I—Interpersonal Relationships	Set aside a half hour to relive a forgiveness experience. Remember a time when you were hurt by another person and you forgave them. Write down what you learned about yourself and how it can help you more easily forgive others in the future.
O—Outlook	End your day with a positive thought. Find a book of life-affirming thoughts or quotations and read one every night before turning off the light.
N—Nutrition	Increase your intake of fruits and vegetables to at least two servings every day. Drink at least *four* 8-ounce glasses of water every day. If you drink fruit juices, try diluting the content by a third or a half with water or sparkling water.

WEEK 4

DATE:	A.M.	P.M.
Sun		
Mon		
Tue		
Wed		
Thu		
Fri		
Sat		

WEEK 5

PRINCIPLE	EXPERIENCE
C—Choice	Set aside a half hour this week and write about the changes you have experienced in the first four weeks of the CREATION Heath Plan.
R—Rest	Plan a relaxing vacation that you will take in the calendar year. This vacation should not be filled with activities, but rather be a time of rest.
E—Environment	Bring beautiful nature images into your home and work environment. This could include: art, photography, calendars, screen savers, etc. Alternatively, bring in natural objects that you find beautiful such as: seashells, stones . . .
A—Activity	Increase aerobic activity to 30 minutes three times per week. Maintain your stretching exercises twice this week and strength training twice.
T—Trust	Talk honestly with God about one specific challenge or worry in your life.
I—Interpersonal Relationships	Make an effort to meet a new neighbor. Consider taking a token of your hospitality such as a plant, cookies, bread, etc.
O—Outlook	Remember the fun games you played as a child? Pick one of your favorite childhood games and play it this week. It could be a board game, card game, building toys, a yo-yo, an outdoor game, etc. The important thing is to play and have fun!
N—Nutrition	Continue to eat your two servings of fruits and veggies every day. Drink at least *five* 8-ounce glasses of water every day. Try avoiding red meat two or three days this week.

WEEK 5

DATE:	A.M.	P.M.
Sun		
Mon		
Tue		
Wed		
Thu		
Fri		
Sat		

WEEK 6

PRINCIPLE	EXPERIENCE
C—Choice	Set aside a half hour to write about one new professional goal for your life.
R—Rest	Have one hour of media-free relaxation time before going to bed (i.e., no TV, computer, radio, etc.). This includes no household chores such as dishes, cleaning, bills, etc. Try to do this at least three times this week.
E—Environment	Find ways to bring relaxing nature sounds into your life. This could include: sound generators, CDs of nature sounds (like birds, ocean waves, etc.), tabletop fountain, nature alarm clock, pet songbird.
A—Activity	Maintain your 30 minutes of aerobic activity three times per week. Add one additional 60-minute aerobic session (this means four days of aerobic activity). Continue with your stretching exercises twice this week and strength training twice.
T—Trust	Write a prayer to God this week asking for a blessing for someone you know.
I—Interpersonal Relationships	Make an effort to truly listen to someone who is sharing with you. This could include a coworker, spouse, child, family member, or friend. Don't try to solve their problem; instead listen to understand and empathize with how they feel.
O—Outlook	Take intentional Brain Breaks whenever you feel stress coming on (see Outlook chapter, p. 180).
N—Nutrition	Increase the number of fruits and veggies you eat to three servings a day. Drink at least *six* 8-ounce glasses of water every day. Try reducing your caffeine consumption (this includes coffee, tea, or caffeinated cola).

WEEK 6

DATE:	A.M.	P.M.
Sun		
Mon		
Tue		
Wed		
Thu		
Fri		
Sat		

WEEK 7

PRINCIPLE	EXPERIENCE
C—Choice	Set aside a half hour to write about one new relational goal for your life. This could include spouse, child, coworker, family, or friend.
R—Rest	This weekend take a 30- to 60-minute power nap on Saturday, Sunday, or both days.
E—Environment	Simplify and declutter a closet or room at home. Give away unneeded stuff to an organization or a person in need.
A—Activity	Experiment with a different aerobic activity from what you have been doing. For example, if you've been walking, try biking, swimming, or Rollerblading. Maintain your 30 minutes of aerobic activity three times this week. Maintain your one additional 60-minute aerobic session. Continue with your stretching exercises twice this week and strength training twice.
T—Trust	Go out in nature for a prayer walk. Connect with God by talking with him.
I—Interpersonal Relationships	Make special time for a child who is important in your life. Choose an activity that allows you to share with each other. Go for a walk, go out for ice cream, play a game, etc.
O—Outlook	Think about an area in your life in which you are less than perfect. Write a statement acknowledging your faults in this area and accepting yourself despite your limitations.
N—Nutrition	Increase the number of fruits and veggies you eat to four servings a day. Drink at least *seven* 8-ounce glasses of water every day. Refrain from eating two to three hours prior to bedtime. For three days this week eat fresh—avoid eating meals that come out of a box or can (in other words, avoid processed food).

WEEK 7

DATE:	A.M.	P.M.
Sun		
Mon		
Tue		
Wed		
Thu		
Fri		
Sat		

WEEK 8

PRINCIPLE	EXPERIENCE
C—Choice	If you haven't already, write a personal mission statement that describes your values. Use your mission statement as a guide for the decisions you make.
R—Rest	This week take a day of Sabbath rest, a day in which you set aside all business activities, household chores, and major projects and rest. Activities could include: rest, picnics, nurture relationships, enjoy nature, visit a house of worship, etc. The idea is to relax, nurture relationships, and experience the divine.
E—Environment	Plan a trip to a place where you can experience and enjoy the wonders of nature, such as a park, beach, zoo, forest, garden, lake, etc.
A—Activity	Find someone (family or friend) to partner with in setting and achieving your future activity goals.
T—Trust	Find a church, temple, synagogue, or other place of worship that will support and encourage your spiritual growth.
I—Interpersonal Relationships	Find an activity in which you can volunteer your time and talents in serving others. This may include charity work, community service, mission trips, spiritual out reach, etc.
O—Outlook	Continuous learning keeps your mind fresh. Plan to do something new you've always wanted to do. Make plans to take up a new hobby, take a class, attend a seminar, learn a new language, learn to sew, learn to bake bread, learn to play a new game, etc.
N—Nutrition	Plan three meat-free days this week. Increase the number of fruits and veggies you eat to five servings a day. Drink at least *eight* 8-ounce glasses of water every day. Determine your healthy weight and body mass index (BMI).

WEEK 8

DATE:	A.M.	P.M.
Sun		
Mon		
Tue		
Wed		
Thu		
Fri		
Sat		

Congratulations on completing the eight-week program! You have successfully taken steps to create a lifestyle that will help you live longer and live better. Try and incorporate as many of these healthy experiences as you can; you are ready to enter Phase 3— CREATION Health for Life.

Phase 3
CREATION Health for Life

You've completed Phase 1 and Phase 2 of the CREATION Health Plan. You now have a firm foundation for your own CREATION Health Breakthrough. Your greatest benefits will come as you ingrain the healthy behaviors you've learned into your daily life.

The following steps will help you to maintain CREATION Health for Life.

Commit to Success

* Make a CREATION Health commitment for each of the eight elements that will help you to maintain a healthy mind, body, and spirit.
* Write down your commitments on paper. Review them frequently. Live them daily.
* Consider using the eight-week plan on a continuing basis. Keep yourself challenged by upping the ante. For example, in week 1 under Interpersonal Relationships you doubled your number of daily hugs. You can double it again (or at least increase it).

Perform Periodic Lifestyle Checkups

* Do the CREATION Health Self-Assessment twice a year to reevaluate your overall health and well-being. Try to select two times of

the year that will be easy for you to remember. I use my birthday and New Year's.

* Consider doing the CREATION Health Self-Assessment during a personal retreat you take once a year similar to the Three-Day Rejuvenation Therapy weekend. If this isn't possible, do the assessment when you can get away for a short period of time by yourself.
* Identify the elements in your assessment that need improvement.

Regain Your Balance

* Reread the chapter(s) that will help you address the elements that need improvement.
* Implement the 3 M's at the end of the chapter.
* Reexamine the eight-week plan and focus on the specific elements you need. Renew the positive behaviors you learned previously.

Form a Success Group

* Form your own CREATION Health group, network, or community. Your family and friends will enjoy doing the program with you. Long-term success is frequently found in groups where people support and challenge each other.
* Go through the book together. Discuss and commit to lifestyle changes that you can encourage each other to follow through on.

Get Free Online Resources

Come and visit us on the Web at www.CREATIONhealth.com. You'll have access to many free resources and ideas to make the principles of CREATION Health practical in your life. Here are a few of the things you'll find available online:

* *CREATION Health for work groups.* Print out directions and an implementation plan for doing a CREATION Health program

at work. Your colleagues and employees will benefit from finding a better balance to life through whole-person health.

❋ *CREATION Health for church groups.* Many churches are looking for ways to help their members live life to the fullest. CREATION Health gets to the heart of the matter by focusing on being whole mentally, physically, spiritually, and socially. Find out how your church can host a CREATION Health seminar or set up classes for small groups and study teams.

❋ *CREATION Health seminars.* On the Web you can find the latest information about a CREATION Health seminar coming to your area or how you can visit Orlando, Florida, for a national CREATION Health seminar.

❋ *Inspirational stories.* You can read inspirational stories of others who have successfully used these life-changing principles to transform their lives. You can also share your story with us. We'd love to hear it!

❋ *Resources.* On the Web you can find additional resources such as books, videos, music, and other products to enhance your CREATION Health Breakthrough experience. There are also author interviews, event information, and health links to other Web sites you may find beneficial.

Stay CREATION healthy for life!

The Breakthrough
Solution for a New You

12

fear less, hope more;
eat less, chew more;
whine less, breathe more;
talk less, say more;
hate less, love more,
and all good things will be yours.
SWEDISH PROVERB

The Breakthrough is about living. It's about *experiencing* new choices, not just *doing* them. The last thing I want is for you to reduce this to just another program—another task on your daily to-do list. Even though I've written the book on it, it's something I continue to learn myself.

My tendency is to slip into overdrive and start doing instead of experiencing. It's great when I can catch it myself, but sometimes I require a gentle nudge from someone else to let me know when I'm off course.

Recently I had a particularly hectic couple of weeks. I was keeping late hours, neglecting my personal time, stress eating, and trying to run away from my kids and husband for a moment's peace. That evening I went to bed disgruntled, wondering why I couldn't get people to obey me at home or at work! I knew tomorrow wouldn't be any better (I was definitely having an "Outlook" problem). The new day started with a 6 a.m. bang and my morning was filled with back-to-back appointments. Around noon I flew into my office for the first time to pick up some papers for my next meeting. What I saw stopped me in my tracks. In the midst of my sea of papers stood a breathtaking bouquet of tropical flowers. Next to it was a warm meal and a card. I smiled to myself realizing my husband, Stan, knew what I needed better than I knew myself.

Sitting down, I opened the card, which read:

Honey,

I don't know exactly when you did it, but you did:

You misplaced CREATION!

You've surrendered your power of Choice to the world of business and its demands.

You've refused to give your mind, body, emotions, and spirit the Rest it needs.

You've overlooked the elements in your Environment that naturally invigorate and restore you.

Needless to say, the lack of good choices, rest, and a healthy environment will impact your Activity.

Your eyes have become dim to Trusting in Divine Power no matter the cost.

When you don't C-R-E-A-T your Interpersonal Relationships become lifeless.

Dark clouds of fatigue and stress are blurring your Outlook.

You've neglected key Nutritional ingredients that energize and rejuvenate your body and soul.

Eat the food from the earth to soothe your body and the warm soup to comfort your heart.

May the flowers impact your outlook and reconnect your trust in Divine Power.

Love, Your Soul Mate . . .

I slowly ate my lunch, absorbed the smell and the beauty of the flowers, and called my husband to thank him for knowing me and for loving me as I am. What a beautiful nudge; it was just what I needed. And you know what I thought was really cool? Ever the teacher, I was thrilled that Stan knew and truly understood CRE-ATION Health. I was so proud of him! With my spirits lifted, I taped that wonderful card to my computer so I could read it every day.

I worked with my assistant to readjust my calendar for the remainder of the week in order to have a little more breathing room. I made it home at a reasonable hour and had a wonderful time with my family. Later that evening, Megan and I made a date to go to the mall. I'm not much of a shopper, but she is. I knew it would be a time for us to laugh, talk, and have a great time together. I tucked Melanie into bed for the night and it was wonderful to receive her special hugs and kisses. She has a way of loving that is uniquely her own. As the girls get older, my shared times with them are increasingly precious. It had really been a great day.

I know this sounds like a fairy tale. The only thing missing is the "happily ever after" ending. But you know what? Life can be filled with many happily-ever-after moments. Right now, you may not be able to say that you have a happily-ever-after *life*. I can't either. With all of the stressors we face, there will always be times when life gets a bit crazy and off course. But as you grow in your understanding of life as it was intended, you will have more of those happily-ever-after moments. The CREATION Health Breakthrough gives you what you need to succeed.

PUTTING IT ALL TOGETHER— ONE LAST TIME

Life as it's intended. Full. Rich. Fragrant. It's not something you have to figure out and put together on your own. It was perfectly designed by the Creator at the beginning of time. The CRE-ATION Health Breakthrough provides the picture of that life. It's

a life that will revitalize your body, rejuvenate your mind, and restore your spirit.

There is no doubt in my mind that it can be yours. You want to
know how I know? Because it's mine. As I told you in the very beginning, my life is really not much different than yours; we both
have daily challenges. We want to be healthy. We both have decisions to make. And we want to make right ones. With a changed
mind-set and a changed toolset you can have a changed way of life.
The CREATION Health Breakthrough has given you what you
need.

The CREATION Health Self-Assessment

ARE YOU LIVING CREATION HEALTHY?

CREATION Health is an exciting plan for achieving whole-person health mentally, physically, spiritually, and socially. Each letter of the word CREATION stands for one of the eight principles of health drawn from the Genesis story of Creation. For a concise definition of each letter in the CREATION Health acronym see chapter 1.

CREATION Health is about living a longer, fuller, freer life. To know how to achieve this, it's important to know where you are now. Utilizing the scale below, rate yourself on the following statements based on your past year.

SCORING
5 = Excellent
4 = Above Average
3 = Average
2 = Below Average
1 = Poor

Choice

———— **Responsibility**: I take responsibility for my feelings and actions and do not blame others.

———— **Goals**: I regularly establish written goals for myself in the most important areas of my life and review my progress.

———— **Discipline**: I am good at delaying gratification until I achieve the goals I set.

———— **Habits**: I am able to curb unhealthy habits and replace them with more beneficial alternatives.

———— **Mission**: I have a personal mission statement that describes my values and guides the decisions I make on a daily basis.

CHOICE Total ————

Rest

———— **Sleep**: I sleep soundly through the night, getting at least seven to eight hours of rest every night.

———— **Work**: I minimize excessive work hours. I determine the time I will go home at the beginning of the day and stick to it.

———— **Media Break**: At least once a week I have a media-free night where I give my mind a rest by avoiding TV, radio, newspapers, magazines, video games, computers, and the Internet.

———— **Rest Day**: Once a week I take a day of rest in which I don't do my regular work and instead focus on inspiration, rest, and relationships.

———— **Vacation**: At least once or twice a year I take a vacation that allows me to "slow down" or "get away from it all" and experience relaxation and rejuvenation.

REST Total ————

Environment

———— **Declutter**: I declutter and simplify my home once or twice a year, getting rid of unused, unneeded, or excess items.

———— **Sight**: I have added beautiful things to my home (and/or work space) that inspire me and give me a sense of well-being. These may include plants, personal photographs, art, nature scenes, or other inspirational things.

———— **Sound**: I have found ways to make my home and work environment more peaceful and relaxing through the use of music, nature sounds, and sometimes just silence.

———— **Smell**: I have found ways to overcome offensive odors at my work, home, and during my commute. I regularly incorporate fragrances that are enjoyable and relaxing.

———— **Nature**: At least once a month I go to a place where I can experience and enjoy the wonders of nature, such as a park, beach, zoo, forest, garden, lake, etc.

ENVIRONMENT Total ————

Activity

———— **Aerobic**: I get 30–60 minutes of aerobic exercise (such as walking, running, cycling, swimming, etc.) 3–6 days per week.

———— **Strength**: I have a muscle development routine (such as weightlifting, resistance training, core strengthening, etc.) that challenges me at least two times per week.

———— **Stretching**: I have a stretching routine I use at least two times a week.

———— **Movement**: I take every opportunity to increase my daily movement (i.e., taking stairs instead of the elevator, walking instead of driving, etc.).

———— **Support**: I have family or friends who support my activity goals and encourage me to follow through on my commitments. This may include an exercise partner who helps keep me accountable and makes the activity more enjoyable.

ACTIVITY Total ————

Trust

———— **Faith**: I believe there is a Divine Power ultimately in control of the universe.

———— **Prayer**: I talk honestly with God about my life, including my hopes, fears, desires, and needs. I believe God hears my prayers.

———— **Acceptance**: I know God accepts me and is with me. As a result, I have hope.

———— **Contemplation**: I regularly set aside time for personal spiritual development. Such time might include study, meditation, prayer, praise, journaling, etc.

———— **Fellowship**: I participate in a faith fellowship (such as church, temple, synagogue, etc.) that supports and encourages my spiritual growth.

TRUST Total ____

Interpersonal Relationships

———— **Family**: I have a good relationship with my immediate family in which I give and receive love. We are able to share honestly and still accept each other.

———— **Friendship**: I have friends with whom I can be myself. I share my true thoughts and feelings with at least one close friend. I can count on at least one friend for acceptance, support, and encouragement in hard times.

———— **Time**: I do what it takes to nurture and grow the most important relationships in my life.

———— **Forgiveness**: When someone hurts me I can forgive them. When I hurt someone else, I am able to seek forgiveness.

———— **Service**: I am involved in *volunteer* activities where I can serve others. This may include charity work, community service, mission trips, spiritual outreach, etc.

INTERPERSONAL RELATIONSHIPS Total ____

Outlook

———— **Attitude**: I am generally optimistic, with a positive attitude that impacts the way I view life, the world, and the people I interact with.

———— **Acceptance**: I accept myself despite my faults and limitations. I do not expect perfection in my life.

———— **Mental Fitness**: I keep my mind alert through continuous learning. Mental challenges are regular and rewarding experiences for me.

———— **Humor**: I have adequate doses of play and laughter in my life.

———— **Stress**: I have several stress-reduction techniques I use throughout the day to lower my stress level (such as deep breathing, Brain Breaks, stretching, visualization, walks, etc.)

OUTLOOK Total ——

Nutrition

———— **Fresh**: I eat at least five servings of fresh fruits and vegetables every day.

———— **Portions**: I am aware of the appropriate serving sizes of the major food groups and eat accordingly.

———— **Processed Food**: I avoid processed and fast food whenever possible.

———— **Water**: I drink 6–8 glasses of water every day.

———— **Weight**: My body mass index (BMI) and my weight are within healthy guidelines.

NUTRITION Total ——

TALLY YOUR SCORE

Add the scores for the five questions from each letter and place them in the spaces provided at the end of each section. There are 25 points possible in each section. Transcribe the subtotals for each letter below. Finally, add all the subtotal scores together to derive your total CREATION Health score.

C _____

R _____

E _____

A _____

T _____

I _____

O _____

N _____

Total _____

WHAT YOUR CREATION HEALTH SCORE MEANS

CREATION = 200 (Excellent)

Congratulations on your score! Keep healthy living a priority in your life and share your healthy lifestyle with others. Allow each element of the CREATION Health Breakthrough to help you develop lasting health and well-being.

CREATION = 160–199 (Above Average)

Your experience of life is rewarding and well balanced. Use each element of the CREATION Health Breakthrough as a launching point for long-term wellness strategies as well as equipping yourself for challenging or stressful times as they come.

CREATION = 120–159 (Average)

Your life experience is routine and moderately acceptable in comparison with others, but there are areas in your life that you can improve. Review your CREATION letter scores to reveal ideal areas to begin enhancing your health and lifestyle.

CREATION = 80–119 (Below Average)

Your life experience isn't satisfactory and there are significant areas needing marked improvement. Your candid analysis of your circumstance is an excellent first step to making changes. Note elements that need particular attention and focus on these areas first.

CREATION = 40–79 (Poor)

Your life experience is marked by disappointment and dissatisfaction. Review your CREATION letter scores to determine areas that need more intensified focus and consider the assistance of professional coaching in areas where your scores are critically low.

PUTTING IT ALL TOGETHER

Now that you know your CREATION Health score, consider how you can improve it. Any single letter score under 12 deserves your specific focus and attention. Plan your Three-Day Rejuvenation Therapy and follow this with the Eight-Week Lifestyle Transformation Plan and the CREATION Health for Life plan to achieve the health your body, mind, and spirit need.

APPENDIX B

Body Mass Index (BMI) Chart

BMI	13	14	15	16	17	18	19	20	21	22	23	24	25	26	27	28	29	30	31	32	33	34	35	36
33"	20	22	23	25	26	28	29	31	33	34	36	37	39	40	42	43	45	46	48	50	51	53	54	56
34"	21	23	25	26	28	30	31	33	35	36	38	39	41	43	44	46	48	49	51	53	54	56	58	59
35"	23	24	26	28	30	31	33	35	37	38	40	42	44	45	47	49	51	52	54	56	58	59	61	63
36"	24	26	28	29	31	33	35	37	39	41	42	44	46	48	50	52	53	55	57	59	61	63	65	66
37"	25	27	29	31	33	35	37	39	41	43	45	47	49	51	53	55	56	58	60	62	64	66	68	70
38"	27	29	31	33	35	37	39	41	43	45	47	49	51	53	55	58	60	62	64	66	68	70	72	74
39"	28	30	32	35	37	39	41	43	45	48	50	52	54	56	58	61	63	65	67	69	71	74	76	78
40"	30	32	34	36	39	41	43	46	48	50	52	55	57	59	61	64	66	68	71	73	75	77	80	82
41"	31	33	36	38	41	43	45	48	50	53	55	57	60	62	65	67	69	72	74	77	79	81	84	86
42"	33	35	38	40	43	45	48	50	53	55	58	60	63	65	68	70	73	75	78	80	83	85	88	90
43"	34	37	39	42	45	47	50	53	55	58	60	63	66	68	71	74	76	79	82	84	87	89	92	95
44"	36	39	41	44	47	50	52	55	58	61	63	66	69	72	74	77	80	83	85	88	91	94	96	99
45"	37	40	43	46	49	52	55	58	60	63	66	69	72	75	78	81	84	86	89	92	95	98	101	104
46"	39	42	45	48	51	54	57	60	63	66	69	72	75	78	81	84	87	90	93	96	99	102	105	108
47"	41	44	47	50	53	57	60	63	66	69	72	75	79	82	85	88	91	94	97	101	104	107	110	113
48"	43	46	49	52	56	59	62	66	69	72	75	79	82	85	88	92	95	98	102	105	108	111	115	118
49"	44	48	51	55	58	61	65	68	72	75	79	82	85	89	92	96	99	102	106	109	113	116	120	123
50"	46	50	53	57	60	64	68	71	75	78	82	85	89	92	96	100	103	107	110	114	117	121	124	128
51"	48	52	55	59	63	67	70	74	78	81	85	89	92	96	100	104	107	111	115	118	122	126	129	133
52"	50	54	58	62	65	69	73	77	81	85	88	92	96	100	104	108	112	115	119	123	127	131	135	138
53"	52	56	60	64	68	72	76	80	84	88	92	96	100	104	108	112	116	120	124	128	132	136	140	144
54"	54	58	62	66	71	75	79	83	87	91	95	100	104	108	112	116	120	124	129	133	137	141	145	149
55"	56	60	65	69	73	77	82	86	90	95	99	103	108	112	116	120	125	129	133	138	142	146	151	155
56"	58	62	67	71	76	80	85	89	94	98	103	107	112	116	120	125	129	134	138	143	147	152	156	161
57"	60	65	69	74	79	83	88	92	97	102	106	111	116	120	125	129	134	139	143	148	153	157	162	166
58"	62	67	72	77	81	86	91	96	100	105	110	115	120	124	129	134	139	144	148	153	158	163	167	172
59"	64	69	74	79	84	89	94	99	104	109	114	119	124	129	134	139	144	149	154	158	163	168	173	178
60"	67	72	77	82	87	92	97	102	108	113	118	123	128	133	138	143	149	154	159	164	169	174	179	184

Ht. in inches

Weight in pounds

BMI	13	14	15	16	17	18	19	20	21	22	23	24	25	26	27	28	29	30	31	32	33	34	35	36
Ht. in inches																								
61"	69	74	79	85	90	95	101	106	111	116	122	127	132	138	143	148	153	159	164	169	175	180	185	191
62"	71	77	82	87	93	98	104	109	115	120	126	131	137	142	148	153	159	164	170	175	180	186	191	197
63"	73	79	85	90	96	102	107	113	119	124	130	135	141	147	152	158	164	169	175	181	186	192	198	203
64"	76	82	87	93	99	105	111	117	122	128	134	140	146	151	157	163	169	175	181	186	192	198	204	210
65"	78	84	90	96	102	108	114	120	126	132	138	144	150	156	162	168	174	180	186	192	198	204	210	216
66"	81	87	93	99	105	112	118	124	130	136	143	149	155	161	167	173	180	186	192	198	204	211	217	223
67"	83	89	96	102	109	115	121	128	134	140	147	153	160	166	172	179	185	192	198	204	211	217	223	230
68"	86	92	99	105	112	118	125	132	138	145	151	158	164	171	178	184	191	197	204	210	217	224	230	237
69"	88	95	102	108	115	122	129	135	142	149	156	163	169	176	183	190	196	203	210	217	223	230	237	244
70"	91	98	105	112	118	125	132	139	146	153	160	167	174	181	188	195	202	209	216	223	230	237	244	251
71"	93	100	108	115	122	129	136	143	151	158	165	172	179	186	194	201	208	215	222	229	237	244	251	258
72"	96	103	111	118	125	133	140	147	155	162	170	177	184	192	199	206	214	221	229	236	243	251	258	265
73"	99	106	114	121	129	136	144	152	159	167	174	182	190	197	205	212	220	227	235	243	250	258	265	273
74"	101	109	117	125	132	140	148	156	164	171	179	187	195	203	210	218	226	234	241	249	257	265	273	280
75"	104	112	120	128	136	144	152	160	168	176	184	192	200	208	216	224	232	240	248	256	264	272	280	288
76"	107	115	123	131	140	148	156	164	173	181	189	197	205	214	222	230	238	246	255	263	271	279	288	296
77"	110	118	127	135	143	152	160	169	177	186	194	202	211	219	228	236	245	253	261	270	278	287	295	304

Weight in pounds

Notes

BEFORE YOU BEGIN

1. I have adapted the Lifestyle Learning Continuum from a concept commonly referred to as the Conscious Competence Learning Matrix. It is not clear who originated this matrix. However, it has been used by a variety of modern scholars and writers. Adapted from Lyndsay Swinton, "Smooth Your Learning Journey with the Learning Matrix," *Management for the Rest of Us*, http://www.mftrou.com/learning-matrix.html, accessed December 14, 2005.

CHAPTER 1: FINDING YOUR BREAKTHROUGH

1. Bill Ewing, *Rest Assured* (Rapid City, SD: Real Life, 2003), 16–17.
2. Dan Buettner, "The Secrets of Long Life," *National Geographic*, Nov. 2005, 2–27.
3. Dean Ornish, MD, Forward, *Kitchen Table Wisdom* (New York: Riverhead, 1996), xvii.
4. Ibid.

CHAPTER 3: "C" IS FOR CHOICE

1. Mary Anne Radmacher, *ThinkExist.com*, original quote, http://en.thinkexist.com/quotes/mary_anne_radmacher, accessed Jan. 4, 2006.
2. Richard Swenson, *Hurtling Toward Oblivion* (Colorado Springs: NavPress, 1999), 31.
3. William Andress and Winnie Gohde, *Grandma Whitney: Queen of the Mountain* (Brushton, New York: Teach Services, Inc., 1996), 53.
4. Jim Russell, "The Backpacking Octogenarian—Hulda Crooks," *Find Articles: Aging*, Oct./Nov. 1984, http://www.findarticles.com/p/articles/mi_m1000/is_1984_Oct-Nov/ai_3450351, accessed Jan. 4, 2006.
5. Ibid.
6. Loma Linda University, "Hulda Crook Passes Away at 101," *Loma Linda University News*, Dec. 3, 1997, http://www.llu.edu/news/today/dec3/llu, accessed Jan. 4, 2006.
7. Milton L. Creagh, Creagh & Associates.
8. Gary Smalley, *The DNA of Relationships* (Wheaton, IL: Tyndale, 2004), 35.
9. Chris Blake, *Searching for a God to Love* (Nashville: W Publishing Group, 2000), 31. In 1964, psychologist Leon Festinger concluded this in his groundbreaking research regarding cognitive dissonance.

10. Ann Greybiel, a world-renowned neuroanatomist at MIT, is known for her work regarding the basal ganglia and its involvement in not only habits but obsessive-compulsive and mood disorders, addictions, and motor disorders such as Parkinson's disease.

11. The twenty one-day time period first appeared in pop psychology: Maltz Maxwell, *The Power of Psycho Cybernetics* (New York: Simon & Schuster, 1960).

CHAPTER 4: "R" IS FOR REST

1. "Cut to the Heart," *Nova Online*, http://www.pbs.org/wgbh/nova/heart/heartfacts.html, accessed May 4, 2005.

2. Richard W. Schwarz, *John Harvey Kellogg: Father of the Health Food Industry* (Nashville: Southern Publishing Association, 1970), 132–33.

3. Boyé Lafayette De Mente, "Asia's Business Codewords," *Asia Pacific Management Forum*, May 2002, http://www.apmforum.com/columns/boye5115, accessed Dec. 15, 2005.

4. Wikipedia, http://en.wikipedia.org/wiki/Karoshi, accessed Dec. 15, 2005, and Katsuo Nishiyama and Jeffrey V. Johnson, "Karoshi-death from overwork: occupational health consequences of the Japanese production management," *International Journal of Health Services*, Feb. 4, 1997, www.workhealth.org/whatsnew/lpkarosh.html, accessed Dec. 15, 2005.

5. K. Spiegel, R. Leproult and E. Van Cauter, "Impact of a sleep debt on metabolic and endocrine function," *Lancet* 354 (1999): 1435–39.

6. Judith Owens, MD, MPH, et al., "Television Viewing Habits and Sleep Disturbance in School Children," *Pediatrics* 104:3 (1999): e27, http://pediatrics.aappublications.org/cgi/content/full/104/3/e27, accessed June 6, 2005.

7. Washington State University, "Caffeine," Health and Wellness Services Patient Education Brochure, http://www.hws.wsu.edu/brochures/caffeine.htm, accessed March 27, 2006.

8. "Information About Caffeine Dependence," Johns Hopkins Bayview Medical Center. Adapted from R. R. Griffiths, L. M. Juliano, and A. L. Chausmer, *Caffeine Pharmacology and Clinical Effects*, 2003, http://www.caffeinedependence.org/caffeine_dependence.html, accessed July 1, 2005.

9. Genesis 2:2. The Sabbath was such an important element to health and well-being that it is actually memorialized in the biblical Ten Commandments. "Remember the Sabbath day, to keep it holy. Six days you shall labor and do all your work, but the seventh day is the Sabbath of the LORD your God. In it you shall do no work." (Exodus 20:8–11).

10. Wayne Mueller, *Sabbath: Restoring the Sacred Rhythm of Rest* (New York: Bantam, 1999), 8–10.

11. Ibid., 6.

12. E. D. Eaker, J. Pinsky, and W. P. Castelli, "Myocardial infarction and coronary death among women: Psychosocial predictors from a 20-year follow-up of women in the Framingham study," *American Journal of Epidemiology* 135 (1992): 854–64.

13. B. B. Gump, and K. A. Matthews, "Are vacations good for your health? The nine-year mortality experience after multiple risk factor intervention trial," *Psychosomatic Medicine* 62 (2000): 608–12.

CHAPTER 5: "E" IS FOR ENVIRONMENT

1. Edward O. Wilson, *Biophilia: The Human Bond with Other Species* (Cambridge, MA: Harvard University Press, 1984).

2. Roger Ulrich, "View through a window may influence recovery from surgery," *Science* 224 (1984): 420–21.

3. Michael Waldholz, "Flower Power: How Gardens Improve Your Mental Health," *Wall Street Journal*, Aug. 26, 2003: D1.

4. Judith Dancoff, "WebMD: Gardening for Health," *MedicineNet.com*, Oct. 30, 2000, http://www.medicinenet.com/script/main/art.asp?articlekey=51498, accessed Dec. 15, 2005.

5. "The Inside Story: A Guide to Indoor Air Quality," U.S. Environmental Protection Agency and the U.S. Consumer Product Safety Commission Office of Radiation and Indoor Air (6604J) EPA Doc. number 402-K-93-007, April 1995, http://www.epa.gov/iaq/pubs/insidest, accessed Jan. 10, 2006.

6. Debbie Nelson, "Fight Indoor Air Pollution with Plants," *Camden Community News*, http://www.camdenews.org/news/templates/camdenoutdoors.asp?articleid=1272&zoneid=19, accessed June 6, 2005.

7. V. I. Lohr, C. H. Pearson-Mims, and G. K. Goodwin, "Interior plants may improve worker productivity and reduce stress in a windowless environment," *Journal of Environmental Horticulture* 14:2 (1996): 97–100.

8. Porter Anderson, "Study: U.S. employees put in the most hours," *CNN Career*, http://archives.cnn.com/2001/CAREER/trends/08/30/ilo.study, accessed Aug. 15, 2005.

9. H. Gordon Ainsleigh, "Beneficial effects of sun exposure on cancer mortality," *Preventive Medicine* (Jan. 1993): 132–40.

10. "The Benefits of Sunlight," www.whatreallyworks.co/uk3, accessed March 3, 2005.

11. Ibid.

12. "Flowers and Plant Care—Scent-sational Effects," *Florist.com*, http://www.florist.com/10171/content/resources/scenteffects.epl, accessed March 3, 2005.

13. Tracey McBride, *Frugal Luxuries: Simple Pleasures to Enhance Your Life and Comfort Your Soul* (New York: Bantam Books, 1997).

14. Alan Beck, ScD, as quoted by Patricia Wagner, "Surprising Health Benefits for Pet Owners," http://www.wagner-articles.com/pet.html, accessed May 3, 2005.

15. Don Miller, *In Search of God Knows What* (Nashville: Thomas Nelson, 2004), 61.

16. T. Takano et al., "Urban Residential Environments and Senior Citizens' Longevity in Megacity Areas: The Importance of Walkable Green Spaces," *Journal of Epidemiology and Community Health* 56 (December 2002): 913–18.

CHAPTER 6: "A" IS FOR ACTIVITY

1. Sarah Yang, "Americans spend more energy and time watching TV than on exercise, finds new study," *UC Berkeley News*, March 10, 2004, http://www.berkeley.edu/news/media/releases/2004/03/10_amtv.shtml, accessed March 17, 2005.

2. S. J. Olshansky, PhD, et al., "A Potential Decline in Life Expectancy in the U.S. in the 21st Century," *New England Journal of Medicine* 352 (2005): 1138–45, accessed March 17, 2005.

3. Walt Larimore, MD, and Sherri Flynt, *SuperSized Kids* (New York: Warner Books, 2005).

4. Mike Adams, "Sedentary Lifestyle Causes More Death than Smoking, Says Study," *News Target*, July 28, 2004, www.newstarget.com/001547.html, accessed March 30, 2005.

5. American Heart Association, "Physical Activity and Cardiovascular Health: Questions and Answers," www.americanheart.org/presenter.jhtml?identifier=830, accessed March 29, 2006.

6. Jonathan Myers, PhD, leading physician in a study cited in the July 2003 issue of *Prevention* magazine.

7. "Exercise Helps Keep Your Psyche Fit," *American Psychological Association Online*, http://www.psychologymatters.org/exercise.html, accessed March 23, 2005.

8. "The Heart," *International Sports Sciences Association*, www.issaonline.com/trial/unit/unit19.html, accessed March 23, 2005.

9. I. M. Lee, C. C. Hsieh, and R. S. Paffenbarger Jr., "Exercise intensity and longevity in men. The Harvard Alumni Health Study," *Journal of the American Medical Association* 273:15 (April 19, 1995), http://jama.ama-assn.org/cgi/content/abstract/273/15/1179, accessed March 14, 2006.

10. Bob Greene and Oprah Winfrey, *Make the Connection* (New York: Hyperion, 1996), 140.

11. AetnaInteliHealth, "Heart and Circulatory: Sedentary Lifestyle," http://www.intelihealth.com/IH/ihtIH/WSIHW000/8059/8052/152207.html, accessed July 2006.

12. Ray Strand, MD, *Healthy for Life* (Rapid City, SD: Real Life Press, 2005), 199.

13. Julia Sommerfeld, "Benefits of stretching may be overstretched," *Seattle Times*, March 25, 2005, http://seattletimes.nwsource.com/html/dietandfitness/2002208437_stretch16.html.

14. "Stretching: Focus on Flexibility," http://www.mayoclinic.com/health/stretching/HQ01447.

15. A. Arbab-Zadeh, E. Dijk, et al.,"Effect of aging and physical activity on left ventricular compliance," *Circulation* 110:13 (Sept. 28, 2004): 1799–805.

CHAPTER 7: "T" IS FOR TRUST

1. In the past decade, more than one thousand research studies have been conducted by researchers from Harvard, Duke, and Yale universities on the effects of faith, prayer, and meditation.

2. Harold Koenig, *The Healing Power of Faith* (New York: Simon & Schuster, 1999), 24.

3. James J. Messina and Constance M. Messina, *Tools for Coping Series*, http://www.coping.org/growth/trust, accessed Dec. 15, 2005.

4. Philip Yancey, *Reaching for the Invisible God* (Grand Rapids, MI: Zondervan, 2000), 164.

5. Rick Warren, *The Purpose-Driven Life* (Grand Rapids, MI: Zondervan, 2002), 85.

6. Bill Hybels, *Too Busy Not to Pray* (Downers Grove, IL: InterVarsity, 1998), 9.

7. Philip Yancey, *Rumors of Another World: What Are We Missing?* (Grand Rapids, MI: Zondervan, 2003), 50.

8. Harris Poll #59, http://www.harrisinteractive.com/harris_poll/index.asp?PID=408, accessed Oct. 15, 2003.

9. Harold S. Kushner, *When Bad Things Happen to Good People* (New York: Avon, 1983), 44.

10. Lonny J. Brown, PhD, "The Power of Belief: Surprising Studies on Faith and Health," Lupus Foundation of Minnesota, http://www.lupusmn.org/Education/Articles.html, accessed June 5, 2005.

11. Larry Dossey et al., *Healing Through Prayer* (Toronto: Anglican Book Centre, 1999), 47–49.

12. C. S. Lewis, *Letters to Malcolm: Chiefly on Prayer* (New York: Harcourt, 1963), 114.

13. Chris Blake, *Searching for a God to Love* (Nashville: W Publishing Group, 2000), 53.

14. Larry Dossey, *Prayer Is Good Medicine* (San Francisco: Harper, 1996).

15. Herbert Benson, *The Relaxation Response* (New York: HarperTouch, 1976), and *Beyond the Relaxation Response* (New York: Times Books), 1984.

16. Adapted from John Ortberg, *The Life You've Always Wanted* (Grand Rapids, MI: Zondervan, 2002), 91–106.

17. Ibid.

18. Richard Foster, *Prayer: Finding the Heart's True Home* (San Francisco: Harper, 1992).

19. Rick Warren, *The Purpose-Driven Life*, 88.

20. Brother Lawrence, *The Practice of the Presence of God*, excerpted in *Devotional Classics* (San Francisco: Harper, 1993), 84.

21. Claudia Kalb, "Faith & Healing: Can religion improve health?" *Newsweek* (Society section, international ed.), Nov. 12, 2003, http://www.msnbc.msn.com/id/3474967, accessed June 2005.

22. Rachel Naomi Remen, *My Grandfather's Blessing: Stories of Strength, Refuge, and Belonging* (New York: Riverhead, 2000), 175–76.

CHAPTER 8: "I" IS FOR INTERPERSONAL RELATIONSHIPS

1. Dr. Cohen's work on this topic has been summarized by Susan M. Persons, "Social Support, Stress and the Common Cold," *NIHRecord*, Dec. 2, 1997, http://obssr.od.nih.gov/Content/Publications/Articles/socsup.html, accessed June 2, 2005.

2. Genesis 2:23.

3. Katherine Barrett, as quoted by Edward Watke Jr., "The Problem of Loneliness," *Revival in the Home Ministries, Inc.*, 2001, http://www.watke.org/cou_helps.htm, accessed June 5, 2005.

4. "Households by Size: 1960–Present," *U.S. Census Bureau Annual Social and Economic Supplement: 2003 Current Population Survey*, Internet release date Sept. 15, 2004, http://www.census.gov/population/socdemo/hh-fam/tabHH-4.pdf, accessed June 1, 2005.

5. George Gallup Jr., "Will the Vitality of the Churches Be the Surprise of the Next Century?" Program #3915, Jan. 14, 1996, http://www.csec/sermon/gallup_3195.htm #anchor610088, accessed June 3, 2005.

6. Edward Watke Jr., "The Problem of Loneliness," *Revival in the Home Ministries, Inc.*, 2001, http://www.watke.org/cou_helps.htm, accessed June 3, 2005.

7. Catherine Calvert, source unknown.

8. Tracey McBride, *Frugal Luxuries*, 219.

9. Judy Foreman, "Loneliness can be the death of us," *Boston Globe*, April 22, 1996, 25, http://www.boston.com/globe/search/stories/health/health_sense/042296.htm.

10. Ibid.

11. "The Roseto Effect," http://www.uic.edu/classes/osci/osci590/14_2%20The %20Roseto%20Effect.htm, accessed June 1, 2005.

12. Robert Paul and Donna Wallace, "Intimacy," *Gesundheit! With Jacobus*, News Radio 1450 KMMS, Bozeman, MT, May 29, 2005, http://www.jacobusproductions.com/gwj/live/index.html, accessed June 1, 2005.

13. Adapted from concepts taught at the National Institute of Marriage, Branson, MO, by Dr. Robert Paul, April 2005.

14. Genesis 2:25.

15. Nan Peck, "The Levels of Communication: A Cheat Sheet," http://www.nvcc.edu/home/npeck/Handouts/communicationlevels.htm, accessed June 3, 2005.

16. Jeanette C. Lauer and Robert Lauer, *The Play Solution: How to Put the Fun and Excitement Back into Your Relationship* (New York: Contemporary Books, 2003).

17. Ibid.

18. I am grateful to my colleague Dr. Dick Tibbits for his insights into the healing power of forgiveness. This subsection titled "Forgiveness" was cowritten with him. For further information, see his book *Forgive to Live* (Nashville: Integrity Publishers, 2006).

19. R. Williams and V. Williams, *Anger Kills* (New York: HarperCollins, 1998).

20. Lewis Smedes, *Forgive and Forget* (San Francisco: HarperSanFrancisco, 1984).

21. Dick Tibbits, *Forgive to Live*.

22. Renita Weems, *I Asked for Intimacy* (San Diego: LuraMedia, 1993), 85.

23. Patricia Griffin Kellicker, BSN, "Volunteer Vacations: The Health Benefits of Helping Others," *Swedish Medical Center: Travel & Health*, 2005, http://www.swedish.org/19201.cfm, accessed June 3, 2005.

CHAPTER 9: "O" IS FOR OUTLOOK

1. Charles Swindoll, *Wisdom for the Way* (Nashville: Thomas Nelson, 2001), 238.

2. Martin Seligman, *Learned Optimism: How to Change Your Mind and Your Life* (New York: Alfred A. Knopf, 1991).

3. Adam Kahn, "Optimism: The Key to a Good Life," http://www.thisisawar.com/HealthOptimism.htm, accessed June 15, 2005.

4. Martin Seligman, *Learned Optimism*.

5. Mental Health Association, "MHIC: Mental Illness and the Family," http://www.nmha.org/infoctr/factsheets/15.cfm, accessed June 15, 2005.

6. The Gallup Organization, "December 2003 Gallup Poll," http://www.gallup.com/poll/content/login.aspx?ci=11545, accessed June 15, 2005.

7. David Niven, PhD, *The 100 Simple Secrets of Happy People* (New York: HarperCollins, 2000), 121.

8. Martin Seligman, *Learned Optimism*.

9. Ibid.

10. http://psychologytoday.psychtests.com/cgi-bin/tests/optimism_pessimism, accessed June 15, 2005.

11. Rick Warren, *The Purpose-Driven Life*, 31.

12. Henrylito D. Tacio, "Stress Management," http://www.sunstar.com.ph/static/dav/2006/05/13/feat/stress. management.html, accessed July 2006.

13. Fred Luskin and Kenneth Pelletier, *Stress Free for Good* (New York: HarperCollins, 2005), 73.

14. Kay Redfield Jamison, *Exuberance: The Passion for Life* (New York: Alfred A. Knopf, 2004), cited from Marianna Krejci-Papa, "Adults: Stay a kid at heart with some 'Exuberance,'" *Science and Theology News*, April 4, 2005, http://www.stnews.org/Books-255.htm, accessed June 17, 2005.

15. Michael Miller, MD, "University of Maryland School of Medicine study shows laughter helps blood vessels function better," http://www.umm.edu/news/releases/laughter2.html, accessed June 15, 2005.

16. Tracey McBride, *Frugal Luxuries*.

CHAPTER 10: "N" IS FOR NUTRITION

1. Ray Strand, *Healthy for Life* (Rapid City, SD: Real Life Press, 2005), 124.

2. NIH Technology Assessment Conference Panel, "Methods for Voluntary Weight Loss and Control," *Annals of Internal Medicine* 119 (1993): 764–70.

3. Genesis 1:29.

4. Steven Pratt and Kathy Matthews, *SuperFoods Rx* (New York: HarperCollins, 2004), 2.

5. W. Larimore, S. Flynt, and S. Halliday, *SuperSized Kids* (New York: Center Street, 2005), 132–33.

6. William Sears, "Fantastic Fiber," *AskDrSears.com: Family Nutrition*, http://www.askdrsears.com/html/4/TO41500.asp, accessed June 15, 2005.

7. Dixie Farley, "More People Trying Vegetarian Diets," U.S. FDA, *FDA Consumer*, January 1996, http://www.fda.gov/fdac/features/895_vegdiet.html, accessed June 15, 2005.

8. Sarah Bosley, "Big study links red meat diet to cancer," *Guardian* (UK), Nov. 10, 2005, http://society.guardian.co.uk/print/0,3858,5215963-106702,00.html, accessed June 15, 2005.

About the Authors

MONICA REED

As the senior medical officer for the 2,000 physicians at the largest hospital in America—Florida Hospital—Monica Reed, MD, a graduate of Loma Linda University School of Medicine, is a board-certified obstetrician/gynecologist who has dedicated her medical career to promoting health, healing, and wellness.

In 1992, with a passion to reach a broader audience than her patients in the examination room, Dr. Reed became the associate director of Florida Hospital's Family Practice Residency Program helping to train physicians in all aspects of female health. Also in 1992 she assumed directorship of the Loch Haven OBGYN group, a hospital-based practice dedicated to comprehensive women's health care. During this time Dr. Reed served as medical adviser for Florida Hospital's women's programs and frequently taught in the community on a variety of health-related and lifestyle issues. She has been a featured speaker at annual meetings of both the National Medical Association and the American Academy of Family Practitioners.

Harnessing her gifts of education and public speaking and her passion for lifestyle behavioral change, in 1997 she became the medical news reporter for WFTV (ABC affiliate) in Orlando, and later WAFF (NBC affiliate) in Huntsville, Alabama. Her tenure on television included a weight reduction and fitness program for the greater Orlando area. The ability to reach thousands of people with important health news and information remains one of her greatest joys.

While serving as a medical news reporter, Dr. Reed concurrently became the medical director of women's medicine at Celebration Health, a state-of-the-art medical facility whose focus is not only on curing disease but also on promoting wellness. As director, she established a clinical foundation of care that gave equal emphasis to physical, mental, emotional, and spiritual dimensions of health.

In 2001, Dr. Reed accepted the position of senior medical officer for Florida Hospital. Her varied responsibilities include physician strategic planning, research and innovation, graduate medical education, risk management, and the medical affairs of the hospital's 2,000 physicians.

In recognition of her contributions, Dr. Reed was voted Orlando's "Downtown Woman of the Year" by the Women's Executive Council in 1996, Alumna of the Year for Loma Linda University by the Black Alumni Association in 1997, and one of Loma Linda University's Outstanding Women Alumni in 1998. Dr. Reed believes in "practicing what she preaches." In 1999, she was one of ten finalists for *Heart and Soul* magazine's national fitness competition, and in 2002 placed fourth in a local fitness competition in Orlando.

She has been married for eighteen years to Stanton, and has two lovely daughters, Megan, thirteen, and Melanie, eleven.

DONNA K. WALLACE

Thirteen years of study and teaching on university campuses as well as the founding of two postmodern churches has brought Donna K. Wallace rave reviews from men and women of all ages. A licensed minister of education with a master's degree in Theological Studies, Donna loves speaking, writing, and guiding retreats in the areas of spirituality, intimacy, and identity development.

As a collaborative writer, Donna enjoys the unique synergy that transpires while writing with accomplished speakers, physicians, therapists, and celebrities. She has written over a dozen books, including the international best-seller *What Your Doctor Doesn't Know About Nutritional Medicine May Be Killing You* with Dr. Ray Strand and *The DNA of Relationships for Couples* with Dr. Greg Smalley and Dr. Robert Paul. She and her family live in Bozeman, Montana, where they love the arts, hiking, cycling, and skiing.

FLORIDA
HOSPITAL

About Florida Hospital
AMERICA'S TRUSTED LEADER FOR HEALTH AND HEALING

For nearly one hundred years the mission of Florida Hospital has been to help our patients, guests, and friends achieve whole-person health and healing. With seven hospital campuses and fourteen walk-in medical centers, Florida Hospital cares for nearly one million patients every year.

Over a decade ago Florida Hospital began working with the Disney Corporation to create a groundbreaking facility that would showcase the model of health care for the twenty-first century and stay on the cutting edge of medical technology as it develops. Working with a team of medical experts, industry leaders, and health care futurists, we designed and built a whole-person health hospital named Celebration Health, located in Disney's town of Celebration, Florida. Since opening its doors in 1997, Celebration Health has been awarded the Premier Patient Services Innovator Award as "The Model for Healthcare Delivery in the 21st Century."

When Dr. Lydia Parmele, the first female physician in the state of Florida, and her medical team opened our first health care facility in 1908, their goal was to create a healing environment where they not only treated illness, but also provided the support and education necessary to help patients achieve whole-person health mentally, physically, spiritually, emotionally, and socially.

The lifestyle advocated by our founders remains central to all we do at Florida Hospital. We teach patients how to reduce the risk of disease through healthy lifestyle choices, encouraging the use of natural remedies such as fresh air, sunshine, water, rest, nutrition, exercise, outlook, faith, and interpersonal relationships.

Today, Florida Hospital:

* Ranks number one in the nation for inpatient admissions by the American Hospital Association.
* Is the largest provider of Medicare services in the country.
* Ranks number one in the nation for number of heart procedures performed each year. MSNBC named Florida Hospital "America's Heart Hospital."
* Operates many nationally recognized centers of excellence, including Cardiology, Cancer, Orthopedics, Neurology and Neurosurgery, and Digestive Disorders.
* Is one of the "Top 10 Best Places in the Country to have a Baby," according to *Fit Pregnancy* magazine.

For more information about Florida Hospital and our other whole-person health products, including books, music, videos, conferences, seminars, and other resources, please contact us at:

Florida Hospital Publishing
683 Winyah Drive, Orlando, FL 32803
Phone: 407-303-7711 * Fax: 407-303-1818
E-mail: healthproducts@flhosp.org
www.FloridaHospital.com * www.CREATIONhealth.com

CPSIA information can be obtained
at www.ICGtesting.com
Printed in the USA
BVHW031937280122
627070BV00016B/52/J

9 780446 577625